Robert Muchamore worked as a private investigator before starting to write a story for his nephew, who couldn't find anything to read. Since then, over twelve million copies of his books have been sold worldwide, and he has won numerous awards for his writing, including the Red House Children's Book Award.

Robert lives in London, supports Arsenal football club and loves modern art and watching people fall down holes.

For more information on Robert and his work, visit **www.muchamore.com**, where you can sign up to receive updates on exclusive competitions, giveaways and news.

BY ROBERT MUCHAMORE

The CHERUB series:

1. The Recruit
2. Class A
3. Maximum Security
4. The Killing
5. Divine Madness
6. Man vs Beast
7. The Fall
8. Mad Dogs

Dark Sun

9. The Sleepwalker
10. The General
11. Brigands M.C.
12. Shadow Wave
13. People's Republic
14. Guardian Angel
15. Black Friday
16. Lone Wolf
17. New Guard

The Rock War series:

1. Rock War
2. Boot Camp
3. Gone Wild
4. Crash Landing

The Henderson's Boys series:

Start reading with *The Escape*

THE RECRUIT

Robert Muchamore

HODDER CHILDREN'S BOOKS

First published in Great Britain in 2004 by Hodder Children's Books
This edition published in 2016 by Hodder and Stoughton

51

All characters and events in this publication, other than those clearly in the public domain, are fictitious and any resemblance to real persons, living or dead, is purely coincidental.

A CIP catalogue record for this book is available
from the British Library

ISBN 978 0 340 88153 8

Typeset in Goudy by Avon DataSet Ltd,
Bidford-on-Avon, Warwickshire

Printed and bound in Great Britain by Clays Ltd, St Ives plc

The paper and board used in this book are made from wood
from responsible sources.

Hodder Children's Books
An imprint of Hachette Children's Group
Part of Hodder and Stoughton
Carmelite House
50 Victoria Embankment
London EC4Y 0DZ

An Hachette UK Company
www.hachette.co.uk

www.hachettechildrens.co.uk

WHAT IS CHERUB?

During World War Two, French civilians set up a resistance movement to fight against the German forces occupying their country. Many of their most useful operatives were children and teenagers. Some worked as Scouts and messengers. Others befriended homesick German soldiers, gathering information that enabled the resistance to sabotage German military operations.

A British spy named Charles Henderson worked among these French children for nearly three years. After returning to Britain, he used what he'd learned in France to train twenty British boys for work on undercover operations. The codename for his unit was CHERUB.

Henderson died in 1946, but the organisation he created has thrived. CHERUB now has more than two hundred and fifty agents, all aged seventeen or under. Although there have been many technical advances in intelligence operations since CHERUB was founded, the reason for its existence remains the same: adults never suspect that children are spying on them.

1. SCIENCE

James Choke hated Combined Science. It should have been test tubes, jets of gas and sparks flying all over the place, like he'd imagined when he was still at primary school. What he got was an hour propped on a stool watching Miss Voolt write on a blackboard. You had to write everything down even though the photocopier got invented forty years earlier.

It was last lesson but one, raining outside and turning dark. James was sleepy because the lab was hot and he'd been up late playing Grand Theft Auto the night before.

Samantha Jennings sat next to him. Teachers thought Samantha was fantastic: always volunteering for stuff, neat uniform, glossed nails. She did all her diagrams with three different coloured pens and covered her exercise books in wrapping paper so they looked extra smart. But when the teachers weren't looking Samantha was a total cow. James hated her. She was always winding him up about his mum being fat:

'James' mum is so fat, they have to grease the bath tub or she gets stuck in it.'

Samantha's cronies laughed, same as always.

James' mum *was* huge. She had to order her clothes out of a special catalogue for fat people. It was a nightmare being seen with her. People pointed, stared. Little kids mimicked the way she walked. James loved his mum, but he tried to find excuses when she wanted to go somewhere with him.

'I went for a five-mile jog yesterday,' Samantha said. 'Two laps around James' mum.'

James looked up from his exercise book.

'That's so funny, Samantha. Even funnier than the first three times you said it.'

James was one of the toughest kids in Year Seven. Any boy cussing his mum would get a punch. But what could you do when it was a girl? Next lesson he'd sit as far from Samantha as he could.

'Your mum is so fat–'

James was sick of it. He jumped up. His stool tipped over backwards.

'What is it with you, Samantha?' James shouted.

The lab went quiet. Every eye turned to the action.

'What's the matter, James?' Samantha grinned. 'Can't take a joke?'

'Mr Choke, pick up your seat and get on with your work,' Miss Voolt shouted.

'You say one more word, Samantha, I'll...'

James was never any good at comebacks.

'I'll bloody...'

Samantha giggled. 'What will you do, James? Go home and cuddle big fat Mommy?'

James wanted to see something other than a stupid grin on Samantha's face. He grabbed Samantha off her stool, bundled her up against the wall, then spun her around to face him. He froze in shock. Blood was running down Samantha's face. Her cheek had a long cut where it had caught on a nail sticking out of the wall.

James backed away, scared. Samantha cupped her hands over the blood and started bawling her head off.

'James Choke, you are in extremely serious trouble!' Miss Voolt shouted.

Everyone in James' class was making some sort of noise. James couldn't face up to what he'd done. No one would believe it was an accident. He made a run for the door.

Miss Voolt grabbed James' blazer.

'Where do you think you're going?'

'Get out my way,' James shouted.

He gave Miss Voolt a shove. She toppled backwards, limbs flipping helplessly in the air like a beetle turned upside down.

He slammed the classroom door and ran down the corridor. The school gates were locked, but he escaped over the barrier in the teachers' car park.

*

James stormed away from school, muttering to himself, getting less angry and more scared as it dawned that he was in the deepest trouble of his life.

He was twelve in a few weeks' time. He started wondering if he'd live that long. His mum was going to kill him. He'd definitely get suspended. It was probably bad enough to get expelled.

By the time James got to the little playground near his flats he felt sick. He looked at his watch. If he went home this early his mum would know something was up. He didn't have change for a cup of tea in the chip shop. The only thing to do was go into the playground and shelter from the drizzle in the concrete tunnel.

The tunnel seemed smaller than James remembered. There was graffiti sprayed all over and it smelled like a dog had peed inside. James didn't mind. He felt he deserved to be somewhere cold that smelled of dog. He rubbed his hands to get them warm and remembered when he was little.

His mum was nowhere near as fat in those days. Her face would appear in the end of the tunnel with a daft grin. She'd speak in a deep voice, *I'm coming to eat you up, James*. It was cool, because the tunnel had a killer echo when you were sitting inside. James tried the echo:

'I'm a total idiot.'

The echo agreed with him. He pulled his coat hood up and did the zip to the top so it covered half his face.

*

After half an hour sulking, James knew he had two options: stay in the tunnel for the rest of his life, or go home and get killed.

James stepped into the hallway of his flat and checked the mobile phone on the table under the coat rack:

12 MISSED CALLS
UNIDENTIFIED NUMBER

It looked like school had been trying to get hold of his mum pretty bad, but she hadn't answered. James thanked god, but wondered why she hadn't picked up. Then he noticed Uncle Ron's jacket hanging up.

Uncle Ron had turned up when James was a toddler. It was like having a loud, smelly rug in the flat. Ron smoked, drank and only went out to go to the pub. He got a job once, but it only lasted a fortnight.

James had always thought Ron was an idiot and his mum had eventually agreed and kicked him out. But only after she'd married him and given birth to his daughter. Even now James' mum had a soft spot for Ron. They'd never got divorced. Ron turned up every few weeks, supposedly to see his daughter, Lauren. But mostly he came when Lauren was at school and he was short of a few quid.

James walked into the living room. His mum, Gwen, was spread out on a sofa. Her feet were up on a stool and her left leg was bandaged. Ron was in an armchair, feet on the coffee table, toes poking out of his socks. They were both drunk.

'Mum, you're not supposed to drink with your pills,' James said, so annoyed he forgot his problems.

Ron straightened up and took a drag of his cigarette.

'Hey Jamie boy, Daddy's home,' Ron said, grinning.

James and Ron eyed each other up.

'You're not my father, Ron,' James said.

'No,' Ron replied. 'Your dad legged it the day he saw your ugly face.'

James didn't want to say about school in front of Ron, but the truth was eating at him.

'Mum, something happened at school. It was an accident.'

'Wet your pants again, did you?' Ron giggled.

James didn't want to take the bait.

'Listen, James, me darlin',' Gwen said, slurring her words. 'Whatever trouble you're in this time, we'll talk later. Go and get your sister from school. I've had a few too many drinkies and I'd better not drive.'

'I'm sorry, Mum, it's really serious. I have to tell you…'

'Just get your sister, James,' his mum said sternly. 'My head is pounding.'

'Lauren's big enough to come home on her own,' James said.

'She isn't,' Ron interrupted. 'Do what you're told. He needs my boot up his backside if you ask me.'

'How much money does he want this time?' James asked sarcastically.

Gwen waved her hand in front of her face. She was fed up with both of them.

'Can't you two stay in the same room for two minutes without fighting? James, go to my purse, buy something for tea on the way home. I'm not cooking tonight.'

'But…'

'Get out, James, before I lose my temper.'

James couldn't wait until he was old enough to batter Uncle Ron. His mum was OK when Ron wasn't around.

James found his mum's purse in the kitchen. A tenner was enough for his dinner, but he took two twenties. Ron would steal everything in the purse before he left, so James wouldn't get blamed. It felt nice stuffing forty quid into his school trousers. Gwen never left anything lying around that she didn't expect James or Ron to steal. She kept the big money upstairs in a safe.

2. SISTER

Some kids were happy to have one games console. James Choke had every console, game and accessory going. He had a PC, an MP3 player, Nokia mobile, widescreen TV and DVD recorder in his room. He never looked after any of it. If something broke he got another one. He had eight pairs of Nike trainers. A top-line skateboard. A £600 racing bike. When his bedroom was in a mess it looked like a bomb had gone off in Toys R Us.

James had all this because Gwen Choke was a thief. She ran a shoplifting empire from her armchair while she watched daytime soaps and stuffed chocolates and pizza. She didn't steal, herself. Gwen took orders and passed them down to thieves who worked for her. She covered her tracks, never going near stolen goods herself and switching mobiles every few days so the police couldn't trace her calls.

*

It was the first time James had been back to primary school since his last day as a pupil before the summer holidays. A few mums stood at the gate nattering.

'Where's your mum, James?' someone asked.

'Off her face,' James said sourly.

There was no way James was covering for her after she'd kicked him out of the flat. He saw the other mums exchange glances.

'I want Medal Of Honour for Playstation,' one of them asked. 'Can she get it?'

James shrugged, 'Course, half price, cash only.'

'Will you remember, James?'

'No. Give us a bit of paper with your name and phone number and I'll pass it on.'

The gaggle of mums started jotting things down. Trainers, jewellery, radio-controlled car. James stuffed the papers into his school blazer.

'I need it by Tuesday,' someone said.

James wasn't in the mood.

'If you want to tell my mum something, write it down. I won't remember.'

The kids all started coming out. Nine-year-old Lauren was last out of her class. She had her hands tucked in her bomber jacket and mud on her jeans from playing football with the boys at lunchtime. Lauren had blonde hair, same as James, but she kept asking her mum to let her dye it black.

Lauren was on another planet to most girls her age. She didn't own a single dress or skirt. She'd microwaved her Barbies when she was five and hadn't touched one since. Gwen Choke said if there were two ways of doing something, Lauren would always pick the third one.

'I hate that old bat,' Lauren said, when she got near James.

'Who?' James asked.

'Mrs Reed. She gave us sums. I did them in about two

minutes, and she made me sit still for the rest of the lesson waiting for all the dumb kids to finish. She wouldn't even let me go to the cloakroom and get my book.'

James remembered Mrs Reed had done the same thing when she was his teacher three years earlier. It was like getting punished for being clever.

'Why are you here, anyway?' Lauren asked.

'Mum's drunk.'

'She's not supposed to drink until after the operation.'

'Don't tell me,' James said. 'What can I do about it?'

'How come you got home early enough to pick me up?'

'Got in a fight. They sent me home.'

Lauren shook her head, but she couldn't help smiling.

'Another fight. That's three this term, isn't it?'

James didn't want to talk about it.

'What do you want first?' he asked. 'Good news or bad news?'

Lauren shrugged. 'Just tell us.'

'Your dad's indoors. The good news is Mum gave us money to get take-away. He should be gone by the time we get home.'

*

They ended up in a burger place. James got a double cheeseburger meal. Lauren only wanted onion rings and a Coke. She wasn't hungry, so she got handfuls of little milks and sugar packets and made a mess on the table while James ate. She tipped out loads of sugar, soaked it with milk, then shredded the paper wrappers and stirred it all up.

'What are you doing that for?' James asked.

'As a matter of fact,' Lauren said acidly, 'the entire future of western civilisation depends upon me making a smiley face with this ketchup.'

'You realise some poor sod has to clean all that up?' James said.

'Not my problem,' Lauren shrugged.

James tucked in the last mouthful of his burger and realised he was still starving. Lauren had hardly touched her onion rings.

'You eating those?' James asked.

'Have them if you want. They're stone cold.'

'This is all we've got for dinner. You better eat something.'

'I'm not hungry,' Lauren said. 'I'll make toasted sandwiches later.'

James loved Lauren's toasted sandwiches. They were mad: she got Nutella, honey, icing sugar, golden syrup, chocolate chips. Whatever sweet stuff was going, all poured on thick. The outside was crispy and the hot gloop was about three centimetres deep in the middle. You couldn't eat one without burning your fingers.

'You better clean up afterwards,' James said. 'Mum blew her stack last time you made them.'

*

When James turned into his road it was nearly dark. Two guys came out from behind a hedge. One of them grabbed James and knocked him against a wall, pulling his arm tight behind his back.

'Hello, James,' he said, his mouth up against James' ear. 'We've been waiting for you.'

The other guy grabbed Lauren and stuck his hand over her mouth to stop her screaming.

James' opinion of his own intelligence hit an all-time low. While he'd been worrying about getting in trouble with Mum, school and maybe even with the police, he'd forgotten something: Samantha Jennings had a sixteen-year-old brother.

Greg Jennings hung out with a gang of crazies. They were kings of the estate where James lived: smashing up cars, mugging people, getting into fights. If another kid saw them he'd look down at his shoes, cross his fingers and be happy if all he came away with was a slapped face and his money taxed. A good way to upset the gang was to beat up one of their little sisters.

Greg Jennings grazed James' face along the bricks.

'It's your turn now, James.'

He let go of James' arm. James could feel blood dribbling down his nose and cheek. There was no point struggling: Greg could snap him like a twig.

'Scared?' Greg asked. 'You ought to be.'

James tried to speak, only his voice didn't work and the way he was trembling seemed to answer anyway.

'Got money?' Greg asked.

James took out the rest of the forty pounds.

'Nice one,' Greg said.

'Please don't hurt my sister,' James begged.

'My sister has eight stitches in her face,' Greg said, pulling a knife out of his pocket. 'Lucky I don't go round hurting little girls, or your sister might have ended up with eighty.'

Greg sliced off James' school tie. Then he cut the chest buttons off his shirt and slashed up his trousers.

'This is just the start, James,' Greg said. 'We're gonna be seeing a lot of each other.'

A fist smashed into James' stomach. Ron had hit James a few times, but never that hard. Greg and his henchman walked off. James crumpled up on the ground.

Lauren walked over to James. She didn't have much sympathy for him.

'You got in a row with Samantha Jennings?'

James looked up at his sister. He was in a lot of pain and ashamed of himself.

'She got cut by accident. I only meant to scare her.'

Lauren started walking away.

'Help me up, Lauren. I can't walk.'

'Crawl then.'

Lauren went a few more paces before she realised she couldn't abandon her brother, even if he *was* an idiot. James stumbled towards home with his arm round Lauren's back. It took all her strength to hold him up.

3. WORSE

James stumbled into the hallway, one hand clasped over his stomach. He glanced at the display on his mum's mobile:

48 MISSED CALLS
4 TEXTS

He turned the phone off and stuck his head in the living room. The light was off, TV on. His mum was asleep in her chair and there was no sign of Ron.

'He's gone,' James said.

'Thank god for that,' Lauren said. 'He always kisses me and his breath's revolting.'

Lauren pushed the front door shut and picked a handwritten note off the doormat.

'It's from your school.'

Lauren read aloud, struggling with the messy handwriting:

'Dear Mrs Choke, Please contact either the School Secretary or myself urgently on one of the numbers below, con … Con something?'

'Concerning,' James guessed.

'Concerning James' behaviour at school today,' Lauren continued. 'Michael Rook, Deputy Head Teacher.'

Lauren followed James into the kitchen. James ran a glass of tap water and slumped at the table. Lauren sat opposite and kicked off her trainers.

'Mum will absolutely massacre you,' Lauren grinned. She was looking forward to seeing James suffer.

'Can't you shut up? I'm trying not to think about it.'

*

James locked himself in the bathroom. He was shocked by what the mirror showed him. The left side of his face and the ends of his cropped blond hair were blood red. He emptied his pockets and stuffed his wrecked clothes in a bin-liner. He'd hide them under the other rubbish later so his mum didn't find them.

Ending up in this mess made James start asking questions about himself. He knew he wasn't a very good person. He was always getting in fights. He was clever, but he never did any work so he got bad marks. James remembered all the times his teachers had told him he was wasting his potential and that he'd end up in a bad way. He'd sat through billions of lectures with his brain turned off. Now he was beginning to think they were mostly right and that made him hate them even more.

James unscrewed the cap on a tube of antiseptic, but realised it was pointless without washing off the blood first. The hot shower soothed his face and stomach as a red puddle whirled around his feet.

James wasn't sure if god existed, but he couldn't see how everything just got here without something making it. If there was ever a time to pray this was it. He wondered if you were supposed to pray while naked in the shower, but figured what the hell and pressed his wet hands together.

'Hello, God... I'm not always good. Not ever really. Just help me be good and stuff. Help me be a better person. Cheers... Amen. And please don't let Greg Jennings kill me.'

James looked awkwardly at his hands, not convinced about the power of prayer.

*

After the shower, James put on his favourite clothes: an Arsenal shirt and a pair of tatty Nike tracksuit bottoms. He'd had to hide them from his mum. She chucked out anything that didn't look as if it had been shoplifted the previous week. She never understood that it was cooler if some of your clothes were a bit on the shabby side.

After milk, two of Lauren's toasted sandwiches and half an hour playing GT4 with his duvet over him, James felt a bit better. Except his stomach killed if he moved suddenly and he wasn't looking forward to telling his mum what he'd done when she woke up. Not that she looked like waking up soon. She must have had loads to drink.

James crashed his car into the barrier and six cars whizzed past, leaving him in last place. He hurled the joypad. He always got that corner wrong. The computer-controlled cars went round like they were on rails, which made it seem like the game was rubbing it in. It was boring playing alone, but there was no point asking Lauren. She hated computer games. She only ever wanted to play football or draw.

James grabbed his mobile and called his friend Sam. Sam lived down the balcony and was in James' class.

'Hello, Mr Smith. It's James Choke. Is Sam there?'

Sam picked up the phone in his bedroom, sounding excited.

'Hey there, psycho,' Sam said, laughing. 'You are in *soooo* much trouble.'

That wasn't how James wanted the conversation to start.

'What happened after I left?'

'Man, it was the sickest thing ever. Samantha had blood gushing out of her face. Down her arms, everywhere. They took her in an ambulance. Miss Voolt hurt her back, she was crying and going: *This is the last straw. I'm taking early retirement*. Both the Deputy Heads and the Headmaster came in. The Headmaster saw Miles laughing and gave him a three day suspension.'

James couldn't believe it. 'Three days' suspension for *laughing*?'

'He was livid. You're totally expelled, James.'

'No way.'

'Yes way, psycho. You never even made it to your first half-term. That's got to be the record for getting expelled. Did your mum give you beats?'

'She doesn't know yet. She's asleep.'

Sam burst out laughing again, 'Asleep! Don't you think she might want you to wake her up to tell her you've been expelled?'

'She won't care,' James lied, trying to sound cool. 'So you wanna come over and play Playstation?'

Sam's voice got more serious, 'No, man, I've got homework.'

James laughed. 'You *never* do homework.'

'I started. The folks are pressuring me. Birthday presents hang in the balance.'

James knew Sam was lying but couldn't figure out why. Normally, Sam asked his mum if he could come and she always said yes.

'What? What have I done to upset you?'

'It's not that, James, but...'

'But what, Sam?'

'Isn't it obvious?'

'No.'

'You're a mate, James, but we can't hang out until this dies down.'

'Why the hell not?'

'Because Greg Jennings is going to totally mash you and if I'm seen with you I'll be dead as well.'

'You could help me stand up to him,' James said.

Sam thought this was the funniest thing yet.

'My skinny arse is not gonna make any difference against those guys. I really like you, James. You're a good friend, but at the moment being your friend is a suicide mission.'

'Thanks for your help, Sam.'

'Should have switched your brain on before you decided to stab the hardest kid in school's little sister on a rusty nail.'

'I never meant to hurt her. It was an accident.'

'Ring me back when you get Greg Jennings to believe that.'

'I can't believe you're doing this to me, Sam.'

'You'd do the same if it was me. And you know it.'

'So that's it. I'm a leper.'

'It's a toughie, James. Sorry.'

'Yeah.'

'We can talk on the phone. I still like you.'

'Thanks, Sam.'

'I better go. Bye, James. I'm really sorry.'

'Enjoy your homework.'

James ended the call and wondered about praying again.

*

James watched rubbish TV until he fell asleep. He had a dream where Greg Jennings stood on his guts, and woke with a jolt.

He needed to pee bad. The pain in his guts was fifty times worse than earlier. The first drop of piss hitting the toilet was red. James did a double-take. Bright red. He was peeing blood. After he'd been to the toilet the pain was mostly gone, but he was scared. He had to tell his mum.

The TV in the living room was still turned up loud. James flicked it off.

'Mum,' James said.

James felt weird. His mum was too quiet. He touched her hand. Cold. He put his hand in front of her face. She wasn't breathing. No pulse. Nothing.

*

James hugged Lauren in the back of the ambulance. Their mum's corpse was two feet away with a blanket on top. Lauren's hands clawed into James' back. James was freaking, but he tried to keep a lid on himself to stop Lauren getting worse.

When the ambulance arrived at casualty, James watched his mum get wheeled off on a trolley. He realised this was going to be his final memory of her: a bulging blanket lit by flashing blue bulbs.

James had to step off the ambulance with Lauren holding on. There was no way she was letting go. She'd stopped crying and was panting like an animal.

Lauren walked like a zombie. The driver led them through the waiting room to a cubicle. A doctor was waiting. She knew what had happened.

'I'm Dr May. You must be Lauren and James.'

James rubbed Lauren's shoulder to try and calm her down.

'Lauren, can you let go of your brother so we can talk?'

Lauren acted deaf.

'It's like she's dead,' James said.

'She's in shock. I'll have to give her something to calm down or she'll pass out.'

Dr May picked a syringe off a trolley and pulled up the sleeve of Lauren's T-shirt.

'Hold her still.'

As soon as the needle went in, Lauren went limp. James leaned her down on the bed. Dr May picked up Lauren's legs and covered her with a blanket.

'Thank you,' James said.

'You told that ambulance driver that you had some blood in your urine,' Dr May said.

'Yeah.'

'Did something hit you in the stomach?'

'Some*one*,' James said. 'I got in a fight. Is it bad?

'When you were hit your insides started to bleed. It's the same as a cut on the outside. It should heal itself. Come back here if it hasn't stopped by tomorrow night.'

'So what happens to us now?' James asked.

'There's a social worker coming to see you. She'll contact your relatives.'

'I don't have relatives. My nan died last year and I don't know who my dad is.'

4. CARE

James woke up the next morning in a strange bed with sheets that smelled of disinfectant. He had no idea where he was. The last thing he remembered was a nurse giving him a sleeping pill and walking towards a car with his head weighing a million tons.

He had his clothes on, but his trainers were on the floor. He took his head out of the covers and saw another bed with Lauren poking out of it. She was sleeping with her thumb in her mouth. James hadn't seen her do that since she was little. Whatever dreams Lauren was having, the thumb wasn't a good sign.

He got out of bed. The pill had made him dull, his jaw felt stiff and there was a weird ache in his forehead. The room was bright, even though the curtains were drawn. James slid a door and found the shower and toilet. He was relieved to see that his pee came out the normal colour. James splashed water on his face. He knew he ought to be upset about his mum dying, but he felt dead inside. Everything felt so unreal it was like sitting in an armchair watching himself on television.

James peeked out of the window. Tons of kids were running around. He remembered that one of his mum's favourite threats was to stick him in a home if he didn't behave.

A buzzer sounded when James went out of the room. A care worker came out of an office and offered him her hand. James shook it, a bit stunned by her purple hair and the metalwork hanging off each ear.

'Hello, James, I'm Rachel. Welcome to Nebraska House. How are you?' James shrugged.

'I'm really sorry about what happened to your mum.'

'Thank you, Miss.'

Rachel laughed.

'You're not at school here, James. They call me all sorts of rude things, but never Miss.'

'Sorry.'

'I'll give you the tour, then you can have some breakfast. You hungry?'

'A bit,' James said.

'Listen, James,' Rachel said, as she walked. 'This place is a dump and I know your life seems horrible now, but there are lots of good people here to help you.'

'Right,' James said.

'Our luxury spa,' said Rachel.

She pointed out of the window at a paddling pool filled with rainwater and cigarette ends. James smiled a bit. Rachel seemed nice, even though she probably used the same lines on every freak that ended up here.

'State of the art sports complex. Strictly out of bounds until homework is finished.'

They walked through a room with a dart board and two pool tables. The green felt was stuck down with carpet tape and there was an umbrella stand filled with tipless and split cues.

'All the rooms are upstairs. Boys first floor, girls second. The baths and showers are down here,' Rachel continued. 'We usually have trouble getting you lads into them.'

'My room has a shower in it,' James said.

'That room's the reception for new arrivals. You only get one night in there.'

They reached the dining room. There were a couple of dozen kids, mostly in school uniform. Rachel pointed everything out.

'Cutlery there, hot food at the bar, cereal and fruit juice. Make your own toast if you want it.'

'Cool,' James said.

He didn't feel cool. The room full of strange, noisy kids was intimidating.

'When you've eaten, see me in my office.'

'What about my sister?' James asked.

'If she wakes up I'll bring her to you.'

James got some Frosties and sat on his own. The other kids ignored him. New arrivals were obviously nothing unusual.

*

Rachel was on the phone. Her desk was stacked with papers and folders. A cigarette burned in an ashtray. Rachel put the phone down and took a puff. She saw James glance at the *No Smoking* sign.

'If they sack me they'll be six staff short,' she said. 'Do you want a cigarette?'

James was shocked to be offered a cigarette by an adult.

'I don't smoke.'

'Good,' Rachel said. 'They give you cancer, but we'd rather give them to you than have you stealing them from shops. Shift my junk, make yourself comfortable.'

James moved a pile from the chair with the least stuff on it and sat down.

'How do you feel, James?'

'I think the sleeping pill they gave me is making me groggy.'

'That'll wear off. I really mean how do you feel about what happened to your mum?'

James shrugged, 'Bad, I guess.'

'The important thing is not to keep it to yourself. We'll schedule some time with a counsellor, but you can chat to any of us house parents in the meantime. Even if it's three in the morning.'

'Does anyone know why she died?' James asked.

'As far as I understand, your mum was taking pain killers for an ulcer on her leg.'

'She wasn't supposed to drink,' James said. 'It's something to do with that, isn't it?'

'The pain killers and the alcohol mixed up put your mum into a deep sleep. Her heart stopped beating. If it's any comfort, your mother wouldn't have suffered.'

'What happens to us?' James asked.

'I don't believe you have any relatives.'

'Only my stepdad. I call him Uncle Ron.'

'The police found him last night.'

'They probably had him in a cell,' James said.

Rachel smiled. 'I sensed that the two of you don't get on when I spoke to him last night.'

'You spoke to Ron?'

'Yes ... Do you get on well with Lauren?'

'Mostly,' James said. 'We row ten times a day, but we always have a laugh.'

'Ron was still married to your mum when she died, even though they lived apart. Ron is Lauren's father, so he gets automatic custody of her if he wants it.'

'We can't live with Ron. He's a bum.'

'James, Ron has very strong feelings that Lauren shouldn't be taken into care. He's her father. There's nothing we can do to stop him unless there is a history of abuse. The thing is, James ...'

James fitted the pieces together for himself.

'He doesn't want me, does he?'

'I'm sorry.'

James looked down at the floor, trying not to get upset. Being in care was bad. But Lauren getting stuck with Ron was worse.

Rachel walked around her desk. She put her arm round him. 'I'm so sorry, James.'

James wondered why Ron even wanted Lauren. 'How long can we stay together?'

'Ron said he'd come in later this morning.'

'Can't we stay together for a few days?'

'This might seem hard to understand now, James, but delaying the separation will make things worse. You'll still be able to visit each other.'

'He won't look after her properly. Mum does all the washing and stuff. Lauren's scared of the dark. She can't go to school on her own. Ron won't help her. He's useless.'

'Try not to worry, James. We'll make regular visits to see that Lauren settles into her new home. If she's not properly looked after, something will be done.'

'So what happens to me? Am I stuck here?'

'Until we find you a foster home. That means you go and live with a family that takes in children like you for a few months at a time. There's also a chance that you'll be adopted, which means another couple will look after you permanently, exactly as if they were your real parents.'

'How long does all that take?' James asked.

'We're short of foster families at the moment. A few months at least. Perhaps you should spend some time with your sister before Ron comes.'

James went back to the bedroom. He gently nudged Lauren awake. She came round slowly, sitting up and picking sleep out of the corners of her eyes.

'What's this?' Lauren asked. 'Hospital?'

'Children's home.'

'My head aches,' Lauren said slowly. 'I feel all queasy.'

'You remember last night?'

'I remember you telling me Mum died, and waiting for the ambulance to come. I must have fallen asleep.'

'They had to give you an injection to calm you down. The nurse said you'd feel weird when you woke up.'

'Are we staying here?'

'Ron's coming to pick you up later.'

'Just me?'

'Yeah.'

'I think I'm gonna spew,' Lauren said.

She covered her mouth. James sprang back, not wanting to get sprayed. 'There's a toilet in there,' he said, pointing.

Lauren dashed into the bathroom. James heard her throwing up. She coughed for a bit, then flushed the toilet. It went quiet for a minute. James knocked.

'You OK? Can I come in?'

Lauren didn't answer. James stuck his head round the door. Lauren was crying.

'What's my life gonna be like living with Dad?' she sobbed.

James wrapped his arms round his sister. Her breath smelled like puke, but James didn't care. Lauren had always just been there. James had never realised how much he'd miss her if she was gone.

Lauren calmed down a bit and had a shower. She couldn't face breakfast so they sat in the games room. All the other kids had gone to school.

The time until Uncle Ron arrived was painful. James wanted to say something amazing to cheer her up and make things right. Lauren looked down at the floor, banging her Reeboks on the chair leg.

Ron arrived with an ice cream. Lauren said she didn't want it, but took it anyway. She wasn't in any state to argue. James tried not to cry in front of Ron. Lauren was so choked up she couldn't talk.

'If you want to see Lauren, here's the number,' Ron said.

He handed James a scrap of paper.

'I'm having the flat cleared,' Ron said. 'I spoke to the

social worker outside, they're taking you round later. Any of your crap still there on Friday goes in the rubbish.'

James couldn't believe Ron was acting nasty on a day like this.

'You killed her,' James said. 'You brought all that drink to the flat.'

'I didn't force it down her throat,' Ron said. 'And don't get your hopes up about seeing Lauren very often.'

James felt like he was about to explode. 'When I'm big enough I'll kill you,' he said. 'I swear to god.'

Ron laughed. 'I'm quaking in my boots. Hopefully some of the bigger lads here will knock some manners into you. It's about time somebody did.'

Ron grabbed Lauren's hand and took her away.

5. SAFE

James racked up the pool balls and blasted the white into them. It didn't matter where the balls went. He only wanted a distraction from the awful stuff going around his head. He'd been playing for hours when a jug-eared twenty-something introduced himself.

'Kevin McHugh. Dogsbody, former inmate.' He laughed. 'I mean resident, of course.'

'Hey,' James said, not in the mood for jokes.

'Let's get your stuff.'

They walked outside to a minibus.

'I heard about your mum, James. That's tough.' Kevin craned his neck, looking for a gap to pull out into the traffic.

'Thanks, Kevin. You lived here once?'

'For three years. Dad went down for armed robbery. Mum had a breakdown. I got on all right with all the staff here, so they gave me this job when I turned seventeen.'

'Is it OK?' James asked.

'It's not a bad place. Look after your stuff though, everything gets nicked. First chance you get, buy a decent padlock and stick it on your locker. Sleep with the key tied around your neck. Don't even take it off in the bath. If you've got cash we'll get you a lock on the way back.'

'Is it rough?' James asked.

'You'll be OK. You look like you can stand up for yourself. There's a few hard cases same as anywhere, just don't wind them up is all.'

*

The flat was a tip. A lot of valuable stuff had disappeared. The TV, video and hi-fi were gone from the living room. The telephone was gone in the hall and the microwave from the kitchen.

'What happened?' Kevin asked. 'Was it like this last night?'

'I half-expected this,' James said. 'Ron's been here and stripped the place. I hope he's left my stuff alone.'

James ran upstairs to his room. His TV, video and computer were gone.

'I'll stab him,' he screamed.

James kicked his wardrobe door. At least Ron had left the Playstation 2 and most other stuff. Kevin came in.

'You're not gonna be able to take all this,' Kevin said, looking at the piles of stuff. 'Your mum must have been loaded.'

'We'd better take as much as we can. Ron says the house is being cleared Friday.'

James had a thought. He asked Kevin to start packing his clothes in bin-liners and went to his mum's room. Ron had taken the portable TV and the jewellery box from the dressing table, but that was no biggie because Ron had stolen all the good jewellery years ago.

James opened his mum's wardrobe and looked at her safe.

There were thousands inside. Gwen Choke was a criminal; she couldn't keep money in the bank without people wanting to know where it came from. Judging by the tools on the carpet and the scratches around the safe door, Ron had made a fairly pathetic attempt to get in. He'd be back with better equipment.

James knew he'd never break open the safe. When it was delivered it took three guys to carry it up the stairs. There was no key; you dialled a combination of numbers with the big knob on the front. The only clue James had was that one time he'd walked in and surprised his mum while she was unlocking it. She'd been holding a Danielle Steele novel and it made sense that she would hide the combination inside the kind of book he and Ron wouldn't touch with a ten-foot pole. But what if she'd changed the combination since then? It was James' only chance to beat Ron to the money, so he was at least going to try.

Gwen had a handful of novels on a shelf over her bed. James found the Danielle Steele and flicked through the pages.

'Are you all right in there, James?' Kevin shouted from the other bedroom.

James was so tense he flew about a metre up in the air and dropped the book.

'Fine,' James shouted.

He picked the open book off the floor. There was a set of numbers written in the margin on the page in front of him. The book must have been opened to the same page hundreds of times. It sprung to the right place as soon as he let go. James felt luck was on his side for the first time in days. He scooted across the carpet and dialled in the numbers: 262, 118, 320, 145, 077. He grabbed the handle. Nothing happened. It wasn't going to work. The thought of Uncle Ron getting his hands on the money made James gag.

Then he noticed a sticker under the dial with instructions on how to use the safe. He read the first instruction:

(1) Dial the first number of the combination by turning the dial in an anti-clockwise direction.

James hadn't realised that the direction you turned the dial made any difference. He dialled in the first number and carried on reading:

(2) Dial the subsequent four numbers by turning the dial as follows: clockwise, anti-clockwise, anti-clockwise and clockwise. Failure to observe this procedure will result in non-operation of the mechanism.

He dialled the first four numbers.

'What are you playing at?' Kevin asked.

James spun around. Kevin was standing in the doorway. Luckily the open wardrobe door stopped him seeing the safe. Kevin seemed nice, but James was sure any adult who found out about the safe would make him give the contents either to the police or to Uncle Ron.

'Looking for stuff,' James said, convinced he sounded suspicious.

'Come and help me pack, James. I don't know what you want.'

'I'll be out in a minute,' James said. 'I'm just looking for photo albums.'

'Do you want me to help you look for them?'

'No,' James said, practically squealing.

'We've got fifteen minutes,' Kevin said. 'I've got to do a school run in an hour.'

Kevin finally went back to the other room. James dialled in the fifth number. The safe made a satisfying click. He read the third instruction before he pulled on the handle and couldn't help smiling:

(3) For security purposes, this sticker should be removed once you are familiar with the unit.

James swung the heavy door open. The inside of the safe was surprisingly small because the metal lining was so thick. There were four tall piles of cash inside and a tiny envelope. James took a bin-liner and shoved the money in. He tucked the envelope into his pocket.

James imagined Ron's face when he walked in and saw the safe open. Then he thought of something even better. He peeled the instruction sticker from the safe door and put it and the Danielle Steele novel inside. As a final touch, to make Ron extra mad, James took a framed picture of himself from his mum's bedside cabinet and stood it inside the safe so it would be the first thing Ron saw when he eventually broke it open. James shut the door, gave the dial a spin and replaced the tools exactly how Ron had left them.

*

James was in a slightly better mood when he walked back to his bedroom holding the cash. The room looked bare. Kevin had bagged up all the clothes and bedding that was usually strewn over the floor.

'I found the photo albums,' James said.

'Good. But I'm afraid you're gonna have to make some sacrifices, James. All you've got in Nebraska House is one wardrobe, a chest of drawers and a locker.'

James started hunting through the toys and junk on the floor. He was surprised how little he cared about most of his stuff. He wanted his Playstation 2, mobile phone and portable CD player, but that was about it. Everything else was toys and stuff that he'd grown out of. The annoying thing was, Ron had taken his TV so he had nothing to use the Playstation on.

Kevin crouched down looking at a Sega Dreamcast and a Nintendo Gamecube.

'Don't you want these?' Kevin asked.

'I only use the Playstation 2,' James said. 'Take them if you want them.'

'I can't take gifts from residents.'

James kicked the consoles into the middle of the floor.

'I don't want my stepdad to get the money from selling them. I'm not taking them with me. If you don't take them, I'll trash 'em.'

Kevin didn't know what to say. James slammed the heel of his trainer into the Sega. Surprisingly little happened, so he picked it up and threw it at the wall. The case smashed. It slid down the wall and dropped behind the bed. Kevin quickly bent down and rescued the Gamecube.

'OK, James, I tell you what. I'll take your Gamecube and the games and in return I'll buy your padlock for you on the drive back. Is that a deal?'

'Fair enough,' James said.

*

When they'd packed up the last few things and carried the bin-liners out to the minibus, James had a quick last look into every room of the flat he'd lived in since he was born. By the time he reached the front door he had tears on his face.

Kevin tapped the horn of the minibus. He'd already started the engine. James ignored him and went back one last time. He couldn't leave the flat without a memento of his mum. He rushed upstairs to her room and looked around.

James remembered that when he was a toddler he used to sit at his mum's dressing table after they'd shared a bath. She'd pull a pyjama top over his head then stand over him and brush his hair. It was before Lauren was born. Just the two of them, feeling tired and smelling of shampoo. James felt warm and sad. He found the battered wooden hairbrush and tucked it into the waistband of his tracksuit bottoms. Once he had the brush it felt easier to leave.

6. HOME

James realised he was stupid. He should have left a bit of cash in the safe. That way Ron would never know he'd been in there. Leaving the photo was a nice gag, but Ron would realise James had taken the money when he saw it. He might try and steal the money back. And if Ron was angry he'd make it ten times harder for James to visit Lauren.

*

Kevin found James a room and showed him the ropes. Like where the washing machines were and where he could get toiletries and stuff, then left him to unpack. The room had a bed, a chest of drawers, a wardrobe with a locker on each side and two writing desks under the window. The kid who lived on the other side had decorated his wall with Korn and Slipknot posters. There was a skateboard on the floor and boarder clothes hung neatly in the wardrobe: baggy cargos, a hooded top and T-shirts with Pornstar and Gravis logos on them. Whoever James' roommate was, he looked pretty cool. The other good thing was that the kid had a portable TV on his desk, meaning they could use the Playstation.

James looked at his watch. He reckoned there was about an hour until his room-mate got out of school. James got the cash out of the bin-liner. It was all £50 and £20 notes, separated into bundles by elastic bands. He counted a couple and realised each bundle was £1,000. There were forty-three bundles.

James thought of a way to hide the money in case Ron came after it. He had a portable cassette radio from the flat. It was wrecked; half the buttons had broken and the tape player didn't rewind. James had only taken it because Ron had stolen the good one with a CD player on it.

James rummaged through his bags of stuff until he found his Swiss army knife. He picked out the screwdriver and undid the back of his cassette player. The inside was all circuit boards and wires. James worked fast, taking the guts out of the player, unscrewing and snapping plastic, leaving only the bits you could see from the front, like the speaker and the slot where the tape went in. He stuffed all but £4,000 of the cash inside the hole, packing the money tight so it didn't rattle. He screwed the back on again and slid the radio cassette into his locker.

James took the four odd £1,000 bundles and hid them in obvious places: the back pocket of a pair of jeans, inside a shoe, inside a book. He peeled a hundred off the last bundle to use as walking-around money and taped the rest to the inside of his locker.

The idea was, if Ron tried to break into James' room he'd find £4,000 easily and never realise there was £39,000 more stuffed inside a cassette radio so crummy looking even Ron wouldn't steal it.

James filled the locker with the rest of his valuables. He banged it shut and put the padlock key on a cord around his neck. He couldn't be bothered unpacking anything else. He threw as many bags as he could in the wardrobe and kicked what was left under his bed.

Then he slumped on his bare mattress, staring at the wall. There were hundreds of pin holes and blobs of blu-tack where previous kids had decorated the walls. He wondered what Lauren was doing.

*

Just after four, James' room-mate, Kyle, came running in. He was a skinny kid, a bit taller than James, wearing school uniform. Kyle slammed the door and tried to get his key in the hole to lock it. James wondered what the hell was going on.

Kyle couldn't lock the door before another kid rammed it. This kid looked older. Same height as Kyle but twice the width. Kyle jumped on to his bed. The big kid bundled Kyle over and pulled him to the floor. He sat astride him and punched him a couple of times in the arm.

'You think you're so smart,' the thug said.

'Take it,' Kyle said.

Kyle took a couple of slaps in the face. The thug slid a diary out of Kyle's blazer and cracked him on top of the head with it.

'Touch my stuff again, doughnut, I'll smash your face in.'

He got off Kyle, kicked him in the thigh and walked out.

James sat up on his bed. Kyle tried to act like it was nothing but couldn't hide the pain as he raised himself on to his bed.

'I'm Kyle,' Kyle said.

'I'm James. How'd you upset him?'

'His diary fell out of his pocket this morning. I found it. Most of it's bogus, but he'd written this poem about a girl.'

James laughed. 'That big moose writes poetry?'

'Yep,' Kyle said. 'I read a couple of lines out in front of his mates. He took it badly.' Kyle was holding his face.

'You OK?' James asked. 'You took some serious beats.'

'I thought he'd grab the diary back, not try and kill me ... One bit of the poem was great. *You give me a buzz that's like a bee. Even when I feel melancholy*. Isn't that cute ... Man, is that what it looks like?'

'What?' James asked.

'That skateboard under your bed must have cost over a hundred quid.'

'You reckon?' James asked. 'I only used it about twice.'

Kyle started laughing. 'That board is a legend, James. Kids die to get their hands on them and you've used it twice. Can I see it?'

James shrugged. 'Whatever.'

Kyle seemed to forget his pain as he reached under James' bed and wheeled out the board. He sat back on his bed twisting it in his hands.

'Nice. Hard wheels, must be fast. Can I try it?' Kyle asked.

'Sure. I never use it. As long as I can use my Playstation 2 on your telly.'

'Playstation 2! We have Playstation 2 in this room? James, you're a little beauty. What games have you got?'

'I don't know. About sixty different ones,' James said.

Kyle rocked back on his bed and started kicking his feet in the air.

'Sixty games! I don't believe you, James. You must be the most spoiled kid in the world and you don't even realise.'

'What?' James asked. 'Don't kids in here have games consoles?'

'We get three pounds a week for pocket money. You see that Gravis shirt on the floor? Twenty-five quid. I had to save up two pounds for twelve weeks to get that. I had to steal my Stussy shorts from a shop at Camden Lock. Would have ended up with a security guard standing on my head if I didn't know a few moves.'

'You want to try the Playstation now?' James asked.

'After my homework,' Kyle said. 'I always do homework first.'

James laid back on his bed, wondering if Kyle was a swot. Someone knocked.

'Yeah?' James said.

It was one of the house parents, a bearded hippie type. He looked at James.

'I've sorted you a place at West Road School. You can start there in the morning. You'll have to come back at lunchtime. The counsellor wants to see you.'

James was miffed. He thought that his mum dying, and getting expelled, would get him off school for at least a couple of weeks.

'OK,' James said. 'Where's West Road?'

'Kyle,' the care worker said, 'can you find James a school uniform and show him to school tomorrow?'

'No worries,' Kyle said.

*

Kyle and James spent the whole evening together. After his homework Kyle took James down to dinner. The food wasn't the best but it was better than James got at home. Afterwards they set up the Playstation. While they played they told stories about stuff, like fights at school and how they ended up here. James was surprised that Kyle was thirteen and already in Year Nine. Kyle said he was good at everything except sports. He had a hard time because the rest of his class were bigger than him. James said the only things he was any good at were sport and maths.

Before they went to bed, Kyle took James to the laundry and found a box of school uniforms. James already had school shirts and trousers, but he needed a blazer with the West Road badge and a school tie. There wasn't much choice and everything was trashed. They found a blazer that fitted James OK and a school tie that was in threads.

*

Kyle fell asleep. James' head was too busy. Tomorrow was going to be the first day of a new routine: eating meals with all the other kids, going to a new school, coming home and spending time with Kyle. It wasn't the end of the world, but he wished Lauren was here.

James remembered the little brown envelope in the safe.

He'd forgotten until now. He scrambled out of bed and slipped his tracksuit bottoms on. He rummaged in the pockets. His heart skipped when he didn't find it straight away. He had to go somewhere light where he could look without anyone seeing. The toilet was the obvious place.

James locked himself in a cubicle and opened the envelope gently so he'd be able to reseal it. There was a key and a business card:

REX DEPOSITARY
Deposit Your Valuables with Total Discretion and Security
Individual Boxes in Eight Different Sizes

James flicked the card over. The address was on the back. It looked like his mum had another hidden stash. He put the key on the cord around his neck.

7. SHRINK

James had always been in mixed schools, but West Road was all boys. The lack of girls gave the place an air of menace. It was noisier and everybody in the corridor pushed harder than at his old school. It felt like something could go off any second.

A Year Seven got a hard shove from a Year Ten and knocked into James. The kid went down and yelped as the Year Ten stamped his hand. The kids were all heading somewhere. James had a map that made no sense whichever way he turned it.

'Nice tie, girlie,' somebody said.

James thought it was aimed at him. The tie was a wreck. He decided to steal one from some weed the first chance he got. The bodies were all disappearing into classrooms and within a couple of minutes James only had a few late arrivals for company.

A couple of nasty looking Year Ten kids blocked James' way. One of them had spiked hair and a Metallica T-shirt under his blazer. Both were wearing menacing-looking steel-toe-capped boots with fat laces dragging behind.

'Where you going, squirt?'

James looked up at them, thinking he was going to die before he even made it to his first class.

'Registration,' he said.

The Metallica kid snatched the map out of James' hand.

'Well, you're not going to make it,' Metallica said.

James braced himself for a boot or fist.

'Try using the side of the map that says main building, not annexe. It's over there.'

Metallica turned the map over and handed it back to James. He pointed at a yellow door up a corridor on the left.

'Thanks,' James said.

He hurried off. Metallica shouted after him: 'Take that tie off.'

James looked down at the tie. He could see it was tatty but why all the fuss?

*

James handed his form teacher a note. All the kids in his new class were staring at him as he looked for a seat. He sat at the end of a row, next to a black kid called Lloyd.

'You one of the little orphans from the council home?' Lloyd asked.

The kids sitting around James laughed. James knew first impressions counted. If he said nothing he'd look soft. His reply had to be sharp, but not so nasty it started a fight.

'How'd you know?' James said. 'I suppose your mum saw me when she cleaned our toilets.'

The group of kids laughed. Lloyd looked angry for a second, then he laughed too. 'Like your tie, sister,' he said.

James had had enough with the tie. He pulled it off and

looked. Then he looked at Lloyd's tie. It wasn't the same colour. Nor was anyone else's.

'What *is* this tie?' James asked.

'The good news, orphan,' Lloyd said, 'is that you have a West Road tie. The bad news is, it's from West Road *Girls* School.'

James laughed with the others. These kids seemed OK. He was angry Kyle had tricked him, though.

*

James left at lunchtime to see the counsellor. Her office was on the second floor of Nebraska. It had spider plants branching off everywhere. The counsellor, Jennifer Mitchum, was a rake, barely taller than James. She had veins poking out of her hands that James didn't want to look at and she sounded really posh.

'Would you feel more comfortable in the chair or on the couch?'

James had seen all the psychiatrist scenes on TV and felt he had to lie on the couch to get the full effect.

'Cool,' he said, settling himself down. 'I could sleep all night on this.'

Jennifer walked slowly around the room, lowering the blinds so it was almost dark. She sat down.

'I want you to be relaxed around me, James. Everything you say stays between us. When you talk, don't try and say the correct thing; say what you really think, and remember I'm here to help you.'

'OK,' James said.

'You said you could fall asleep on the couch. Have you been sleeping properly at night?'

'Not really. I have too much to think about.'

'What do you think about most?'

'I wonder if my little sister is OK.'

'It says in the file you're concerned about Ron's ability to look after Lauren.'

'He's a retard,' James said. 'He couldn't look after a hamster. I don't even understand why he wanted her.'

'Perhaps he loves Lauren, but found it difficult to express that while your mother was alive.'

James laughed. 'That's total rubbish. You'd have to meet him to understand.'

'If you see Lauren regularly that should help both of you feel better.'

'Yeah, but it won't happen.'

'I'll talk to Ron and see if we can set up a schedule of meetings. Perhaps you and Lauren can spend every Saturday together.'

'You can try, but Ron hates my guts. I don't think he'll let me see her.'

'What about your mother? How do you feel about her?'

James shrugged. 'She's gone. What can I do? I wish I'd been better when she was alive.'

'In what way?'

'I was always in trouble. Getting in fights and stuff.'

'What made you get in trouble?'

James had to think hard.

'I don't know. I always do stupid stuff without meaning it. I'm a bad person, I guess.'

'The first question I asked you was what you thought about most. You said you were worried about your sister.

Wouldn't a bad person always think about himself first?'

'I love Lauren … Can I tell you something I did?'

'Of course, James.'

'Last year at school. I got in this row with a teacher, so I stormed out to the toilets. This kid in the year below me was in there. I just laid into him. He didn't say one word. I just started beating him.'

'Did you know that what you were doing was bad at the time you were doing it?'

'Of course I knew beating someone up was bad.'

'So why did you do it?'

'Because …' James couldn't bring himself to be honest.

'When you were hitting that boy, how did you feel?'

James blurted it out, 'It was the best feeling. He was crying his eyes out and I felt fantastic.'

James looked at Jennifer to see if she was shocked, but her face was calm.

'Why do you think you enjoyed it?'

'I told you already. I'm sick in the head. Someone rubs me the wrong way and I go psycho.'

'Try and describe how you felt about the person you were hurting.'

'I owned him. There was nothing he could do, no matter how much I hurt him.'

'You went from a situation with your teacher, where you were powerless and had to do what you were told, into the toilet where you saw someone weaker than yourself and exercised your power over him. That must have been satisfying.'

'You could put it like that,' James said.

'It's a frustrating situation at your age, James. You know what you want but you have to do what you're told. You go to school when you're told, go to bed when you're told, live where you're told. Everything is controlled by other people. It's common for boys your age to enjoy sudden outbursts where they have control over someone else.'

'But I'll end up in loads of trouble if I keep getting in fights,' James said.

'I'll teach you some techniques to manage your anger over the coming weeks. Until then try and remember that you're only eleven years old and nobody expects you to be perfect. Don't think of yourself as being a bad person or that you're sick in the head. In fact, I want to do something we call Positive Reinforcement. I want you to repeat what I just told you.'

'Repeat what?' James asked.

'Say *I'm not a bad person.*'

'I'm not a bad person,' James said.

'Say *I'm not sick in the head.*'

'I'm not sick in the head.' James smiled. 'I feel like an idiot.'

'I don't care if you feel like an idiot, James. Take a deep breath, say the words and think about what they mean.'

James had thought that seeing the counsellor would be a waste of time, but he did feel better.

'I'm a good person and I'm not sick in the head,' he said.

'Excellent, James. I think that would be a positive note on which to end the session. I'll see you again on Monday.'

James slid off the couch.

'Before we finish, there is one detail on the notes from your school that made me curious. What's one hundred and eighty-seven multiplied by sixteen?'

James thought for about three seconds.

'Two thousand, nine hundred and ninety-two.'

'Very impressive,' Jennifer said. 'Where did you learn to do that?'

'I just can,' James shrugged. 'Right from when they first started teaching me numbers. I hate it when people ask me to do it, it makes me feel like a freak.'

'It's a gift,' Jennifer said. 'You should be proud of it.'

*

James went down to his room. He started doing some Geography homework but his heart wasn't in it. He switched on the Playstation. Kyle came in from school.

'How was your first day?' Kyle asked.

'Pretty good, no thanks to you.'

'That was a good gag with the tie,' Kyle said.

James jumped up off his seat and grabbed Kyle by his shirt. Kyle shoved James away, sending him crashing into a desk. He was stronger than James had expected.

'Jesus, James. I thought you were cool.'

'Pretty nice thing to do. First day at a new school and you make me look like a tit.'

Kyle threw his schoolbag down.

'I'm sorry, James. If I knew you were gonna have a tantrum I wouldn't have done it.'

James wanted to start a major row, but Kyle was the only kid in Nebraska he could even put a name to. He didn't want to fall out with him.

'Just stay out of my face,' James said.

James sat on his bed sulking while Kyle did his homework. After a bit he got fed up and went for a walk. He saw the kid in the Metallica T-shirt he'd met at school. He was in a corner with a gang who all looked pretty rough. James walked over to them.

'Thanks for helping earlier,' James said.

Metallica looked him over. 'No worries, man. Name's Rob. This is the gang. Vince, Big Paul and Little Paul.'

'I'm James.'

There was an awkward silence.

'You want something else, squirt?' Big Paul asked.

'No,' James said.

'Piss off then.'

James felt his face turn red. He started to walk away but Rob called him back.

'Hey, James, we're going out tonight. Wanna come?'

'Cool,' James said.

*

After dinner James went back to his room to change out of school uniform. Kyle had finished his homework and was lying on his bed reading a skateboarding magazine.

'You want to play Playstation?' Kyle asked. 'I'm sorry about earlier, James. It was mean to trick you on your first day.'

'You play it,' James said. 'I'm going out.'

'Who with?'

'Some guy called Rob.'

'You mean Robert Vaughn? The guy who wears a heavy metal shirt under his blazer?'

'Yeah, him and some mates.'

'Seriously,' Kyle said, 'don't hang out with those guys. They're mental. They go out stealing cars and shoplifting and stuff.'

'I'm not sitting in here watching you doing your homework every night. Get a life, man.'

James put his trainers on and walked to the door. Kyle looked offended. 'Hey, I warned you, James. Don't whinge to me when you land up in deep shit.'

'Use the Playstation whenever you want,' James said.

*

James sat on a brick wall at the back of an industrial estate. The gang were all older. Rob and Big Paul were fifteen. Vince was fourteen. He was the meanest looking, with bleached hair and a busted-up nose. Little Paul was twelve, Vince's younger brother.

They passed cigarettes around. James told them he didn't smoke. This didn't look cool but he thought it was better than pretending he smoked and coughing his guts up.

'I'm bored,' Little Paul said. 'Let's do something.'

They walked to a car park full of Fiesta vans and climbed through a gap in the fence. Vince and Rob walked along the row of vans trying the back doors to see if any were unlocked.

'Bingo,' Rob said.

A door swung open in his hand. Rob leaned in and took out a bag of tools. He put the bag down and unzipped it.

'Feel like causing damage, James?' Rob asked.

James reached in the bag and pulled out a hammer. The others all grabbed something.

James was nervous, but it was cool walking down the street in a gang carrying hammers and wrenches. A woman nearly got herself run over crossing the street to avoid them. James didn't know what they were looking for. Vince stopped when they found a flash Mercedes. The two Pauls walked into the road.

'Go,' Rob shouted.

Rob smashed his hammer through the back window of the Merc. The alarm started screeching. The others all joined in. James hesitated, then took out a side window, knocked off the wing mirror and made two big dents in the door with his hammer. In twenty seconds every panel was dented, the lights and windows all smashed. Vince led off, running up the road and taking a couple more car windows out along the way.

They ran on to a council estate, down a narrow alley and into a concrete square surrounded by flats. James was out of breath but fear kept him moving. A few more turns, over a fence and they were in a playing field. James' trainers slid in the mud. They all stopped, plumes of breath rising into the freezing air. James started laughing, even though he had a stitch burning down his side. Rob put his hand on James' shoulder.

'You're OK, James,' Rob said.

'That was *so* cool.' James laughed. The mix of fear, tiredness and excitement made his head spin. He couldn't believe what they'd just done.

8. BIRTHDAY

James felt like he was floating through his life. Every day was the same. Get up, go to school, come back, play football or hang out with Rob Vaughn and his gang. James never got into bed before midnight: he knew if he was exhausted he wouldn't lie awake feeling miserable about Lauren and his mum.

The only time he'd seen Lauren in the three weeks since his mum died had been at the funeral. The telephone number on the bit of paper Ron had given him didn't work. Ron had told Jennifer Mitchum that James was a bad influence. He didn't want him near his daughter.

*

'You stink,' Kyle said.

James sat on the edge of his bed rubbing his eyes. He didn't need to get dressed because all he'd done the night before was kick off his trainers and climb into bed wearing his football shirt and tracksuit bottoms.

'You've had the same socks on for days,' Kyle said.

'You're not my mum, Kyle.'

'Your mum never had to sleep in a room that stinks of your BO.'

James looked down at the blackened bottoms of his socks. They reeked, but he'd got used to the smell.

'I'll have a shower,' James said.

Kyle tossed a packet of Twix bars on to James' bed.

'Happy twelfth birthday,' Kyle said. 'Should have got you deodorant.'

James was pleased Kyle had remembered. It wasn't much of a gift, but five Twix was quite expensive for someone on three quid a week.

'You'd better clean yourself up, anyway. You've got to go to the police station today.'

James looked at Kyle. His hair was gelled down and his school uniform was immaculate, with the shirt tucked in and the tie done at the proper length, instead of ten centimetres long like most kids did it. James looked at the black under his nails, ran his hand through his gluey tangle of hair and couldn't help laughing about the mess his life was in.

*

Rachel was in a mood. Her car was overheating, the traffic was awful and there was no space in the police station car park.

'I can't park, you'll have to go in by yourself. Have you got the bus fare to come back?'

'Yeah,' James said.

He got out of the car and walked up the steps of the police station. He'd dressed in chinos and his best fleece, even combed his hair back after the shower. Everyone said getting a police caution was no big deal, but it didn't feel that way as James walked up to the desk and said his name.

'Sit,' the policewoman said, pointing at a row of chairs.

James waited for an hour. People came in and filled forms, mostly reporting stolen cars or mobiles.

'James Choke.'

James stood up. A fit-looking cop reached out and gave him a crunching handshake.

'I'm Sergeant Peter Davies, juvenile liaison officer.'

They went upstairs to an interview room. The sergeant got an inkpad and a piece of card out of a filing cabinet.

'Relax your hand, James. Let me do all the work.'

He dabbed the tips of James' fingers in the ink, then rolled each tip firmly against the card. James wished they'd given him a copy because the fingerprints would look cool pinned on his bedroom wall.

'OK, James, this is the caution. Any questions?'

James shrugged. Sergeant Davies began reading from a piece of paper:

'The Metropolitan Police have received information that on October 9th, while attending Holloway Dale School, you seriously assaulted one of your classmates, Samantha Jennings. During the assault Miss Jennings received a severe cut to her cheek, resulting in the need for eight stitches. During the same incident you also assaulted the class teacher Cassandra Voolt, who received injuries to her back.

'As this is the first criminal charge you have faced, the Metropolitan Police have decided to give you a formal caution if you admit to what you have done. Do you admit to the offences detailed above?'

'Yes,' James said.

'If you are found guilty of another criminal act before you reach the age of eighteen years, details of this offence will be given to the Magistrate or Judge and it is likely to increase the severity of the sentence you receive.'

Sergeant Davies put the piece of paper down and tried to sound friendly. 'You look like a decent kid, James.'

'I never meant to cut her face. I just wanted to make her shut up.'

'James, don't kid yourself into thinking it's not your fault Samantha got hurt. You can never predict what will happen in a fight. If you're stupid enough to start one, you're to blame for what happens whether you meant it or not.'

James nodded. 'That's true I suppose.'

'I don't want to see you here again, James. Will I?'

'I hope not,' James said.

'You don't sound sure. Do you know what sentence you would have got for what you did if you were an adult?'

'No,' James said.

'A young girl with stitches in her face, you'd be looking at two years in prison. That's not funny, is it?'

'No,' James said.

*

James was pleased the caution was out the way. Everyone was right; it was no worse than getting told off at school. He'd taken some money out of his locker and thought he'd buy himself a birthday present. He got a new game for the Playstation and a Nike tracksuit. Then he stuffed himself at the buffet in Pizza Hut. He made sure he didn't get back to Nebraska House until it was too late to go to afternoon lessons.

*

James put his new game on and lost track of time. Kyle came in and sat on the edge of his bed, the same as he did every day. Kyle felt something under the covers. He pulled them back and found James' Arsenal shirt.

'Why's your stinking football shirt in my bed?'

James knew he'd be furious. Kyle was a total girl when it came to cleanliness. When Kyle moved the shirt a new CD Walkman slid out on to the bed.

'James man, did you steal it?'

'I knew you'd say that,' James replied. 'Receipt's in the box.'

'This is mine?' Kyle asked.

'You've been whining about your old one since I got here.'

'Where'd you get the money, James?'

James liked Kyle, but he didn't trust him enough to say about the cash in his locker.

'Tied an old lady to a tree, beat her mercilessly and stole her pension,' James said.

'Yeah right, James. Seriously, where did you get sixty quid?'

'Do you want it? Or do you want to ask me stupid questions about it?' James said.

'This is sweet. I hope you didn't get yourself in any trouble. When I get my pocket money on Friday I'll buy you that deodorant you need.'

'Thanks, I think,' James said.

'So you want to do something tonight for your birthday? We could go to the cinema or something?'

'No,' James said. 'I said I'd go out with Rob and the gang tonight.'

'I wish you'd stop hanging around with those freaks.'

James sounded annoyed, 'You give me the same lecture every time.'

*

It was freezing cold sitting on the wall at the back of the industrial estate. After the first night all they'd done was hang around smoking. Big Paul had punched a public schoolboy's tooth out and taken his mobile and wallet, but James hadn't been with them.

The gang congratulated James on his first criminal offence. Vince said he'd been arrested fifteen times. He had half a dozen court cases coming up and was facing a year in a young offenders' prison.

'I don't care,' Vince said. 'Brother's in young offenders. Dad's in prison. Granddad's in prison.'

'Nice family,' James said.

Rob and Big Paul laughed. The look James got from Vince was scary.

'You say anything about my family again, James, you're dead.'

'Sorry,' James said. 'I was out of order.'

'Kiss the floor,' Vince said.

'What?' James asked. 'Come on, I said sorry.'

'He said sorry,' Rob said. 'It was only a joke.'

'Kiss the floor, James,' Vince repeated. 'I'm not saying it a third time.'

Fighting Vince would be suicide. James slid off the wall. He was worried Vince would jump on his back or kick him in the head when he crouched down. But what choice was there? James put his palms on the pavement and kissed the cold stone. He wiped his lips on his sleeve and stood up, hoping Vince was satisfied.

'You know what keeps out the cold?' Rob said. 'Beer.'

'Nobody will serve us round here,' Little Paul said. 'Got no cash either.'

'That off-licence up the road keeps the trays of twenty-four cans stacked up in the middle of the shop,' Rob said. 'You could run in, grab one and be halfway up the street before the tub of lard got out from behind the counter.'

'Who's gonna do it?' Little Paul asked.

'The birthday boy,' Vince said, laughing.

James realised he should have taken a beating; at least that way Vince would still respect him. Showing weakness to a guy like Vince was inviting him to tear you apart.

'Come on, man. I just got a caution this morning,' James said.

'I've never seen you do anything,' Vince said. 'If you want to hang out with us, you'd better be prepared for some action.'

'Fine, I'll go home. This is boring anyway,' James said.

Vince grabbed James and shoved him into the wall.

'You'll do it,' Vince said.

'Leave him, Vince,' Rob said.

Vince let go. James gave Rob a nod of thanks.

'You better do it though,' Rob said. 'I don't like being called boring.'

James wished he'd listened to Kyle.

'OK,' he said, now he had no choice. 'I can handle it.'

The gang walked to the off-licence. Big Paul gripped James' shoulder, making sure he didn't run.

'Be really quick,' Rob said. 'In and out, they'll never get you.'

James walked inside the shop, nervous as hell. The warm air was beautiful. He rubbed his freezing hands together and looked for courage.

'Can I help you, son?' the guy behind the counter asked.

James had no reason to be in an off-licence. The clerk knew something was up. James made a quick grab at the cans of beer. They were heavy and his frozen fingers didn't have much grip.

'Put those down, you little . . .'

James spun around and tore towards the door. He crashed into the glass. Vince and Big Paul were holding the door shut from outside.

'Let me out,' James shouted, hammering the glass.

The assistant lumbered around the counter.

'Please, Vince,' James begged.

Vince gave James an evil smile and flicked him off. James knew he was done for.

Little Paul was jumping for joy. 'You're busted, you're busted.'

The clerk grabbed James' hands and dragged him backwards. Vince and Big Paul let go of the door and walked off casually.

'Nice night in the cells, faggot,' Vince shouted.

James stopped wriggling. There was no point, the clerk was five times his size. He dragged James behind the counter and shoved him into a chair. Then he called the police.

*

They'd taken James' shoes and everything out of his pockets. He'd been sitting here three hours. Back to the wall, arms wrapped round his knees. James had expected the hard rubber mattress and graffiti but he'd never realised how bad a cell smelled. It was a mixture of disinfectant and everything nasty a body could pump out.

Sergeant Davies came in. James had hoped it wouldn't be him. He looked up nervously, expecting an explosion of rage, but the sergeant seemed to find it funny.

'Hello, James. Did you have a problem grasping the meaning of our little chat this morning? Fancied a few beers to celebrate getting off easy?'

The sergeant took James to an interrogation room. Rachel was there, she looked angry. The sergeant was still smiling as he put a cassette into a recorder and spoke his and James' names into the microphone.

'James,' the sergeant asked, 'bearing in mind that the off-licence you were arrested in has three video cameras inside, do you admit trying to steal twenty-four cans of beer?'

'Yes,' James said.

'On the video you can make out a couple of monkeys holding the door and not letting you out of the shop. Would you care to tell me who they were?'

'No idea,' James said. He knew he'd be dead if he grassed on four of the hardest kids in Nebraska House.

'Why not tell me, James? You wouldn't be here if it wasn't for them.'

'Never seen them before in my life,' James insisted.

'They looked like Vincent St John and Paul Puffin to me. Do those names ring a bell?'

'Never heard of them.'

'OK, James. I'm ending the interview.'

Sergeant Davies turned off the cassette recorder.

'Play with fire and you get burned, James. Hanging out with those two is more like playing with dynamite.'

'I messed up,' James said. 'Whatever punishment I get I deserve it.'

'Don't worry about this one, James. You'll go to juvenile court. The magistrate will probably give you a twenty quid fine. It's the bigger picture you want to look at.'

'What do you mean?' James asked.

'I've seen hundreds of kids like you, James. They all start where you are now. Cheeky little kids. They get a bit older. Spottier and hairier. Always in trouble, but still nothing serious. Then they do something really stupid. Stab someone, get caught selling drugs, armed robbery, something like that. Half the time they're crying. Or so shocked they can hardly speak. They're sixteen or seventeen and looking at seven years banged up. You might get off easy at your age, but if you don't start making better choices you'll be spending most of your life in a cell.'

9. STRANGE

This room was flashier than the one at Nebraska House. It was a single for starters. TV, kettle, telephone and miniature fridge. It was like the hotel when his mum took him and Lauren to Disney World. James didn't have a clue where he was or how he'd got here. The last thing he remembered was Jennifer Mitchum asking him up to her office after he got back to Nebraska House.

James burrowed around under the duvet and realised he was naked. That was freaky. He sat up and looked out of the window. The room was up high overlooking an athletics track. There were kids in running spikes doing stretches. Some others were getting tennis coaching on clay courts off to the side. This was clearly a children's home, and miles nicer than Nebraska House.

There was a set of clean clothes on the floor: white socks and boxers, pressed orange T-shirt, green military-style trousers with zipped pockets and a pair of boots. James picked the boots up and inspected them: rubbery smell and shiny black soles. They were new.

The military-style kit made James wonder if this was where

kids ended up if they kept getting in trouble. He put on the underwear and studied the logo embroidered on the T-shirt. It was a winged baby sitting on a ball. On looking closer the ball was a globe and you could see the outlines of Europe and the Americas. Underneath was a set of initials: *CHERUB*. James spun the initials in his head, but they didn't make any sense.

Out in the corridor the kids had the same boots and trousers as James, but their T-shirts were either black or grey, all with the CHERUB logo on them.

James spoke to a boy coming towards him.

'I don't know what to do,' James said.

'Can't talk to orange,' the boy said, without stopping.

James looked both ways. It was a row of doors in either direction. There were a couple of teenage girls down one end. Even they were wearing boots and green trousers.

'Hey,' James said. 'Can you tell me where to go?'

'Can't talk to orange,' one girl said.

The other one smiled, saying, 'Can't talk,' but she pointed towards a lift and then made a downward motion with her hand.

'Cheers,' James said.

James waited for the lift. There were a few others inside including an adult who wore the regulation trousers and boots but with a white CHERUB T-shirt. James spoke to him.

'Can't talk to orange,' the adult said before raising one finger.

Up to now James had assumed this was a prank being played on the new kid, but an adult joining in was weird.

James realised the finger was telling him to get out at the first floor. It was a reception area. He could see out the main entrance into plush gardens where a fountain spouted water five metres into the air. The sculpture in the centre was the winged baby sitting on a globe, like on the T-shirts. James stepped up to an elderly lady behind a desk.

'Please don't say *Can't talk to orange*, I just–'

He didn't get to finish.

'Good morning, James. Doctor McAfferty would like to see you in his office.'

She led James down a short corridor and knocked on a door.

'Enter,' a soft Scottish accent said from inside.

James stepped into an office with full height windows and a crackling fireplace. The walls were lined with leather-bound books. Doctor McAfferty stood up from behind his desk and crushed James' hand as he shook it.

'Welcome to CHERUB campus, James. I'm Doctor Terrence McAfferty, the Chairman. Everybody calls me Mac. Have a seat.'

James pulled out a chair from under Mac's desk.

'Not there, by the fire,' Mac said. 'We need to talk.'

The pair settled into armchairs in front of the fireplace. James half expected Mac to put a blanket over his lap and start toasting something on a long fork.

'I know this sounds dumb,' James said. 'But I can't remember how I got here.'

Mac smiled. 'The person who brought you here popped a needle in your arm to help you sleep. It was quite mild. No ill effects, I hope?'

James shrugged. 'I feel fine. But why make me go to sleep?'

'I'll explain about CHERUB first. You can ask questions afterwards. OK?'

'I guess.'

'So what are your first impressions of us?'

'I think some children's homes are much better funded than others,' James said. 'This place is awesome.'

Doctor McAfferty roared with laughter. 'I'm glad you like it. We have two hundred and eighty pupils. Four swimming pools, six indoor tennis courts, an all-weather football field, a gymnasium and a shooting range, to name but a few. We have a school on-site. Classes have ten pupils or fewer. Everyone learns at least two foreign languages. We have a higher proportion of students going on to top universities than any of the leading public schools. How would you feel about living here?'

James shrugged. 'It's beautiful, all the gardens and that. I'm not exactly brilliant at school though.'

'What is the square root of four hundred and forty-one?'

James thought for a few seconds.

'Twenty-one.'

'I know some very smart people who wouldn't be able to pull off that little party trick,' Mac smiled. 'Myself included.'

'I'm good at maths,' James smiled, embarrassed. 'But I never get good marks in my other lessons.'

'Is that because you're not clever or because you don't work hard?'

'I always get bored and end up messing around.'

'James, we have a couple of criteria for new residents here. The first is passing our entrance exam. The second, slightly more unusual requirement, is that you agree to be an agent for British Intelligence.'

'You what?' James asked, thinking he hadn't heard right.

'A spy, James. CHERUB is part of the British Intelligence Service.'

'But why do you want children to be spies?'

'Because children can do things adults cannot. Criminals use children all the time. I'll use a house burglar as an example:

'Imagine a grown man knocking on an old lady's door in the middle of the night. Most people would be suspicious. If he asked to come in the lady would say no. If the man said he was sick she'd probably call an ambulance for him, but she still wouldn't let him in the door.

'Now imagine the same lady comes to her door and there's a young boy crying on the doorstep. *My daddy's car crashed up the street. He's not moving. Please help me.* The lady opens the door instantly. The boy's dad jumps out of hiding, clobbers the old dear over the head and legs it with all the cash under the bed. People are always less suspicious of youngsters. Criminals have used this for years. At CHERUB, we turn the tables and use children to help catch them.'

'Why pick me?'

'Because you're intelligent, physically fit and you have an appetite for trouble.'

'Isn't that bad?' James asked.

'We need kids who have a thirst for a bit of excitement. The things that get you in to trouble in the outside world are the sort of qualities we look for here.'

'Sounds pretty cool,' James said. 'Is it dangerous?'

'Most missions are fairly safe. CHERUB has been in operation for over fifty years. In that time four youngsters have been killed, a few others badly injured. It's about the same as the number of children who would have died in road accidents in a typical inner city school, but it's still four more than we would have liked. I've been Chairman for ten years. Luckily, all we've had in that time is one bad case of malaria and someone getting shot in the leg.

'We never send you on a mission that could be done by an adult. All missions go to an ethics committee for approval. Everything is explained to you, and you have an absolute right to refuse to do a mission or to give it up at any point.'

'What's to stop me telling about you if I decide not to come here?' James asked.

Mac sat back in his chair and looked slightly uncomfortable.

'Nothing stays secret for ever, James, but what would you say?'

'What do you mean?'

'Imagine you've found the telephone number of a national newspaper. You're speaking to the news desk. What do you say?'

'Um ... There's this place where kids are spies and I've been there.'

'Where is it?'

'I don't know ... That's why you drugged me up, isn't it? So I didn't know where I was.'

Mac nodded. 'Exactly, James. Next question from the news desk: Did you bring anything back as evidence?'

'Well ...'

'We search you before you leave, James.'

'No then, I guess.'

'Do you know anyone connected with this organisation?'

'No.'

'Do you have any evidence at all?'

'No.'

'Do you think the newspaper would print your story, James?'

'No.'

'If you told your closest friend what has happened this morning, would he believe you?'

'OK, I get the point. Nobody will believe a word I say so I might as well shut my trap.'

Mac smiled.

'James, I couldn't have put it better. Do you have any more questions?'

'I was wondering what CHERUB stood for?'

'Interesting one, that. Our first chairman made up the initials. He had a batch of stationery printed. Unfortunately he had a stormy relationship with his wife. She shot him before he told anyone what the initials meant. It was wartime, and you couldn't waste six thousand sheets of headed notepaper, so CHERUB stuck. If you ever think of anything the initials might stand for, please tell me. It gets quite embarrassing sometimes.'

'I'm not sure I believe you,' James said.

'Maybe you shouldn't,' Mac said. 'But why would I lie?'

'Perhaps knowing the initials would give me a clue about where this place is, or somebody's name or something.'

'And you're trying to convince me you wouldn't make a good spy.'

James couldn't help smiling.

'Anyway, James, you can take the entrance exam if you wish. If you do well enough I'll offer you a place and you can go back to Nebraska House for a couple of days to make up your mind. The exam is split into five parts and will last the rest of the day. Are you up for it?'

'I guess,' James said.

10. TESTS

Mac drove James across the CHERUB campus in a golf buggy. They stopped outside a traditional Japanese-style building with a single span roof made of giant sequoia logs. The surrounding area had a combed gravel garden and a pond stuffed with orange fish.

'This building is new,' Mac said. 'One of our pupils uncovered a fraud involving fake medicine. She saved hundreds of lives and billions of yen for a Japanese drug company. The Japanese thanked us by paying for the new dojo.'

'What's a dojo?' James asked.

'A training hall for martial arts. It's a Japanese word.'

James and Mac stepped inside. Thirty kids wearing white pyjamas tied with black or brown belts were sparring, twisting one another into painful positions, or getting flipped over and springing effortlessly back up. A stern Japanese lady paced among them, stopping occasionally to scream criticism in a mix of Japanese and English that James couldn't understand.

Mac led James to a smaller room. Its floor was covered

with springy blue matting. A wiry kid was standing at the back doing stretches. He was about four inches shorter than James, in a karate suit with a black belt.

'Take your shoes and socks off, James,' Mac said. 'Have you done martial arts before?'

'I went a couple of times when I was eight,' James said. 'I got bored. It was nothing like what's going on out there. Everyone was rubbish.'

'This is Bruce,' Mac said. 'He's going to spar with you.'

Bruce walked over, bowed and shook James' hand. James felt confident as he squashed Bruce's bony little fingers. Bruce might know a few fancy moves but James reckoned his size and weight advantage would counter them.

'Rules,' Mac said. 'The first to win five submissions is the winner. An opponent can submit by speaking or by tapping his hand on the mat. Either opponent can withdraw from the bout at any time. You can do anything to get a submission except hitting the testicles or eye gouging. Do you both understand?'

Both boys nodded. Mac handed James a gum shield.

'Stand two metres apart and prepare for the first bout.'

The boys walked to the centre of the mat.

'I'll bust your nose,' Bruce said.

James smiled. 'You can try, shorty.'

'Fight,' Mac said.

Bruce moved so fast James didn't see the palm of his hand until it had smashed into his nose. A fine mist of blood sprayed as James stumbled backwards. Bruce swept James' feet away, tipping him on to the mat. Bruce turned James on to his chest and twisted his wrist into a painful lock. He used his other hand to smear James' face in the blood dripping from his nose.

James yelled through his gum shield, 'I submit.'

Bruce got off. James couldn't believe Bruce had half killed him in about five seconds. He wiped his bloody face on the arm of his T-shirt.

'Ready?' Mac asked.

James' nose was clogged with blood. He gasped for air.

'Hang on, Mac,' Bruce said. 'What hand does he write with?'

James was grateful for a few seconds' rest but wondered why Bruce had asked such a weird question.

'What hand do you write with, James?' Mac asked.

'My left,' James said.

'OK, fight.'

There was no way Bruce was getting the early hit in this time. James lunged forward. Trouble was, Bruce had gone by the time James got there. James felt himself being lifted from behind. Bruce threw James on to his back then sat astride him with his thighs crushing the wind out of him. James tried to escape but he couldn't even breathe. Bruce grabbed James' right hand and twisted his thumb until it made a loud crack.

James cried out. Bruce clenched his fist and spat out his gum shield. 'I'm gonna smash the nose again if you don't submit.'

The hand looked a lot scarier than when James had shaken it a couple of minutes earlier.

'I submit,' James said.

James held his thumb as he stumbled to his feet. A drip of

blood from his nose ran over his top lip into his mouth. The mat was covered in red smudges.

'You want to carry on?' Mac asked.

James nodded. They squared up for a third time. James knew he had no chance with blood running down his face and his right hand so painful he couldn't even move it. But he had so much anger he was determined to get one good punch in, even if it got him killed.

'Please give up,' Bruce said. 'I don't want to hurt you badly.'

James charged forward without waiting for the start signal. He missed again. Bruce's heel hit James in the stomach. James doubled over. All he could see was green and yellow blurs. Still standing, James felt his arm being twisted.

'I'm breaking your arm this time,' Bruce said. 'I don't want to.'

James knew he couldn't take a broken arm.

'I give up,' he shouted. 'I withdraw.'

Bruce stepped back and held his hand out for James to shake it. 'Good fight, James,' he said, smiling.

James limply shook Bruce's hand. 'I think you broke my thumb,' he said.

'It's only dislocated. Show me.'

James held out his hand.

'This is going to hurt,' Bruce said.

He pressed James' thumb at the joint. The pain made James buckle at the knees as the bone crunched back into place.

Bruce laughed. 'You think that's painful, one time someone broke my leg in nine places.'

James sank to the floor. The pain in his nose felt like his head was splitting in two between his eyes. It was only pride that stopped him crying.

'So,' Mac said. 'Ready for the next test?'

*

James realised now why Bruce had asked which hand he wrote with. His right hand was painful beyond use. James sat in a hall surrounded by wooden desks. He was the only one taking the test. He had bits of bloody tissue stuffed up each nostril and his clothes were a mess.

'Simple intelligence test, James,' Mac explained. 'Mixture of verbal and mathematical skills. You have forty-five minutes, starting now.'

The questions got harder as the paper went on. Normally it wouldn't have been bad but James hurt in about five different places, his nose was still bleeding and every time he shut his eyes he felt like he was drifting backwards. He still had three pages left when time ran out.

*

James' nose had finally stopped bleeding and he could move his right hand again, but he still wasn't happy. He didn't think he'd done well on the first two tests.

The crowded canteen was weird. Everybody stopped talking when James got near them. He got *Can't talk to orange* three times before somebody pointed out cutlery. James took a block of lasagne with garlic bread and a fancy looking orange mousse with chocolate shreds on top. When he got to the table he realised he hadn't eaten since the previous night and was starving. It was loads better than the frozen stuff at Nebraska House.

*

'Do you like eating chicken?' Mac asked.

'Sure,' James said.

They were sitting in a tiny office with a desk between them. The only thing on the desk was a metal cage with a live chicken in it.

'Would you like to eat this chicken?'

'It's alive.'

'I can see that, James. Would you like to kill it?'

'No way.'

'Why not?'

'It's cruel.'

'James, are you saying you want to become a vegetarian?'

'No.'

'If you think it's cruel to a kill the chicken, why are you happy to eat it?'

'I don't know,' James said. 'I'm twelve years old, I eat what gets stuck in front of me.'

'James, I want you to kill the chicken.'

'This is a dumb test. What does this prove?' James asked.

'I'm not discussing what the tests are for until they're all over. Kill the chicken. If you don't, somebody else has to. Why should they do it instead of you?'

'They get paid,' James said.

Mac took his wallet out of his jacket and put a five-pound note on top of the cage.

'Now you're getting paid, James. Kill the chicken.'

'I…'

James couldn't think of any more arguments and felt that

at least if he killed the chicken he would have passed one test.

'OK. How do I kill it?'

Mac handed James a biro.

'Stab the chicken with the tip of the pen just below the head. A good stab should sever the main artery down the neck and cut through the windpipe to stop the bird breathing. It should be dead in about thirty seconds.'

'This is sick,' James said.

'Point the chicken's bum away from yourself. The shock makes it empty its bowels quite violently.'

James picked up the pen and reached into the cage.

*

James stopped worrying about the warm chicken blood and crap on his clothes as soon as he saw the wooden obstacle. It started with a long climb up a rope ladder. Then you slid across a pole, up another ladder and over narrow planks with jumps between them. James couldn't see where you went from there because the obstacle disappeared behind trees. All he could tell was that it got even higher and there were no safety nets.

Mac introduced James to his guides, a couple of fit-looking sixteen-year-olds in navy CHERUB T-shirts called Paul and Arif. They clambered up the ladder, the two older boys sandwiching James.

'Never look down,' Arif said. 'That's the trick.'

James slid across the pole going hand over hand, fighting the pain in his right thumb. The first jump between planks was only about a metre. James went over after a bit of encouragement. They climbed another ladder and walked along more planks. This set were twenty metres above ground. James placed his feet carefully, keeping his eyes straight ahead. The wood creaked in the breeze.

There was a one and a half metre gap between the next set of planks. Not a difficult jump at ground level but between two wet planks twenty metres up, James was ruffled. Arif took a little run up and hopped over easily.

'It's simple, James,' Arif said. 'Come on, this is the last bit.'

A bird squawked. James' eyes followed it down. Now he saw how high he was and started to panic. The clouds moving made him feel like he was falling.

'I can't stand it up here,' James said. 'I'm gonna puke.'

Paul grabbed his hand.

'I can't do it,' James said.

'Of course you can,' Paul said. 'If it was on the ground you wouldn't break your stride.'

'But it's not on the bloody ground!' James shouted.

James wondered why he was standing twenty metres up, with a headache, an aching thumb, plus dried blood and chicken crap all over him. He thought about how rubbish Nebraska House was and what Sergeant Davies had said about his knack of getting in trouble landing him in prison. The jump was worth the risk. It could change his whole life.

He took a run up. The plank shuddered as he landed. Arif steadied him. They walked to a balcony with a hand rail on either side.

'Brilliant,' Arif said. 'Now there's only one more bit to go.'

'What?' James said. 'You just said that was the last bit. Now we just go down the ladder.'

James looked. There were two hooks for attaching a rope ladder. But the ladder wasn't there.

'We've got to go all the way back?' James asked.

'No,' Arif said. 'We've got to jump.'

James couldn't believe it.

'It's easy, James. Push off as you jump and you'll hit the crash mat at the bottom.'

James looked at the muddy blue square on the ground below.

'What about all the branches in the way?' James asked.

'They're only thin ones,' Arif said. 'Sting like hell if you hit them though.'

Arif dived first.

'Clear,' a miniature Arif shouted from the bottom.

James stood on the end of the plank. Paul shoved him before he could decide for himself. The flight down was amazing. The branches were so close they blurred. He hit the crash mat with a dull thump. The only damage was a cut on his arm where a branch had whipped him.

*

James could only swim a couple of strokes before he got scared. He'd had no dad to take him swimming. His mum had avoided the pool because she was fat and everyone laughed at her in a swimming costume. The only time James had been swimming was with his school. Two kids James bullied on dry land had pulled him out of his depth and abandoned him. He'd got dragged out and the instructor had had to pump water out of his lungs. After that James refused to get changed and spent swimming lessons reading a magazine in the changing rooms.

James stood at the edge of the pool, fully dressed.

'Dive in, get the brick out of the bottom and swim to the other end,' Mac said.

James thought about giving it a go. He looked at the shimmering brick and imagined his mouth filled with chlorinated water. He backed away from the pool, queasy with fear.

'I can't do this one,' James said. 'I can't even swim one width.'

*

James was back where he'd started, in front of the fire in Doctor McAfferty's office.

'So, after the tests, should we offer you a place here?' Mac asked.

'Probably not, I guess,' James said.

'You did well on the first test.'

'But I didn't get a single hit in,' James said.

'Bruce is a superb martial artist. You would have passed the test if you'd won, of course, but that was unlikely. You retired when you knew you couldn't win and Bruce threatened you with a serious injury. That was important. There's nothing heroic about getting seriously injured in the name of pride. Best of all, you didn't ask to recover before you did the next test and you didn't complain once about your injuries. That shows you have strength of character and a genuine desire to be a part of CHERUB.'

'Bruce was toying with me, there was no point carrying on,' James said.

'That's right, James. In a real fight Bruce could have used

a choke-hold that would have left you unconscious or dead if he'd wanted to.

'You also scored decently on the intelligence test. Exceptional on mathematical questions, about average on the verbal. How do you think you did on the third test?'

'I killed the chicken,' James said.

'But does that mean you passed the test?'

'I thought you asked me to kill it.'

'The chicken is a test of your moral courage. You pass well if you grab the chicken and kill it straight away, or if you say you're opposed to killing and eating animals and refuse to kill it. I thought you performed poorly. You clearly didn't want to kill the chicken but you allowed me to bully you into doing it. I'm giving you a low pass because you eventually reached a decision and carried it through. You would have failed if you'd dithered or got upset.'

James was pleased he'd passed the first three tests.

'The fourth test was excellent. You were timid in places but you got your courage together and made it through the obstacle. Then the final test.'

'I must have failed that,' James said.

'We knew you couldn't swim. If you'd battled through and rescued the brick, we would have given you top marks. If you'd jumped in and had to be rescued, that would have shown poor judgement and you would have failed. But you decided the task was beyond your abilities and didn't attempt it. That's what we hoped you would do.

'To conclude, James, you've done good. I'm happy to offer you a place at CHERUB. You'll be driven back to Nebraska House and I'll expect your final decision within two days.'

11. GO

James was shut in the back of a van for the first part of the drive back to Nebraska House. Even though he was knackered and the driver wasn't allowed to talk, he couldn't sleep. After a couple of hours the driver stopped at motorway services. They both drank nasty tea and used the toilet. James was allowed in the cab for the rest of the journey. He read the first road sign he saw; they were near Birmingham, heading towards London. It wasn't much of a clue about where CHERUB was. James reckoned they'd already gone more than a hundred kilometres.

It was three in the morning when James arrived back at Nebraska. The entrance was locked. James rang the doorbell and waited ages. A house parent shone a torch in James' face before unbolting the door.

'Where on earth have you been?'

It hadn't occurred to James that CHERUB had taken him without telling anyone. He scrambled for an excuse.

'I went for a walk,' James said.

'For *twenty-six hours*?'

'Well...'

'Get to bed, James. We'll deal with you in the morning.'

Nebraska looked even dingier after CHERUB. James crept into his room, but Kyle woke up anyway.

'Hey, Einstein,' Kyle said. 'Where've you been?'

'Go back to sleep,' James said.

'I heard about your adventure in the off-licence. Ten out of ten for being a dumbass.'

James gave his nose a blast of some pain relief spray CHERUB had given him and started undressing.

'Can't say you didn't warn me,' James said.

'Vince is crapping himself,' Kyle said. 'He reckons you grassed him up and they've moved you to another home for protection.'

'I never grassed,' James said. 'I've got to get him back though.'

'Don't mess, James. He'll cut you up if you give him an excuse.'

*

Rachel shook James awake.

'What are you still doing here, James? It's ten-thirty. You should be in school.'

James sat up and rubbed his face. His nose was tender. At least the headache was gone.

'I didn't get in until gone three this morning.'

'Bit young to be out clubbing, aren't you?'

'I just um...'

James still couldn't think of a decent excuse for turning up at 3 a.m.

'I want you in school uniform and out of the door in twenty minutes.'

'I'm tired.'

'Whose fault is that?'

'I'm sick,' James said, pointing at his nose.

'Fighting, I suppose?'

'No.'

'How then?'

'I think I must have slept in a funny position.'

Rachel started laughing.

'James, I've heard some excuses in my time, but a swollen nose and a black eye from sleeping in a funny position is the worst ever.'

'I've got a black eye?'

'A shiner.'

James explored the tender area under his eye with his fingers. He'd always wanted a black eye, they looked cool.

'Can I see the nurse?' James asked hopefully.

'We don't have a nurse here. There's one at West Road School, though.'

'Please let me off school, Rachel. I'm dying.'

'You've been here for three weeks, James. You've been cautioned by the police, arrested for stealing beer, we've had a complaint from school about your behaviour in class and now you disappear for a day and a half. We're pretty lax here, but we have to draw a line somewhere. Get your uniform on. If you want to complain, go and see the superintendent.'

*

James was putting his schoolbooks in his backpack when Jennifer Mitchum came in.

'Aren't you too tired for school, James?'

'Rachel's making me go.'

Jennifer locked the door and sat on Kyle's bed.

'Those tests are exhausting, aren't they?'

'What?'

'I know where you were, James. I was one of the people who recommended you.'

'The last thing I remember is being in your office upstairs. Was it you that gave me the injection to make me sleep?'

Jennifer smiled. 'Guilty as charged ... So have you thought about joining CHERUB?'

'It's so much better than here. I can't see any reason not to go.'

'It is a fantastic opportunity. I thoroughly enjoyed my time there.'

'You were in CHERUB?' James asked.

'Back in the Stone Age. My mother and father died in a gas explosion. I was recruited from a children's home, just like you.'

'You went spying and everything?'

'Twenty-four missions. Enough to earn my black shirt.'

'What's that?' James asked.

'Did you notice everyone at CHERUB was wearing different colour T-shirts?'

'Yeah. Nobody would talk to me because I was wearing orange.'

'An orange shirt is for guests. You need clearance from Mac to talk to a guest. The red shirt is for younger kids being educated on the CHERUB campus. When they reach ten years old they can do basic training and become agents if they choose to. The pale blue shirt is for trainees. When you qualify you get the grey shirt. After that, you can *go dark*, which means you get awarded the navy T-shirt after an outstanding performance on a mission or missions. The real high flyers get awarded the black shirt, which is for outstanding performance over a large number of missions.'

'How many?'

'It could be three or four really outstanding missions, it might take ten. The Chairman decides. The last shirt is the white one, that's for staff and old girls like me.'

'So you still work for CHERUB?' James asked.

'No, I work for Camden Council, but when I see someone like you I make a recommendation. I'd like to give one warning before you decide, though.'

'What?'

'Life on the campus will be hard to begin with. You have to learn a lot of skills and CHERUB needs you to learn them before you're too old to use them. Everyone will seem better than you at everything. How do you think you'll cope with that?'

'I want to try,' James said. 'When I got arrested the other night the policeman said kids like me get out of their depth and end up in prison. It freaked me out when he said it because that's *exactly* what always happens. I never try to get in trouble, but somehow I always do.'

'So would you like longer to think, or shall I ring CHERUB and tell them you're coming?'

'I've got nothing to think about,' James said.

*

James was being picked up at three, leaving tons of time to get packed. He felt a bit sorry for Kyle. He was a nice kid who deserved more from life than a crummy room at Nebraska

House and three quid a week pocket money. James peeled two £50 notes out of his wad and stuck them under Kyle's bedcovers. He scribbled a quick note.

Kyle,
You've been a mate. Moving to another home.
James.

Kyle came in the door. James panicked; he was crap at making excuses.

'What time's our pick-up?' Kyle asked.

'What?' James asked.

'You heard. When's the bus to CHERUB?'

'They recruited you as well?'

'When I was eight.'

'I don't understand,' James said.

Kyle started pulling everything out of his wardrobe.

'Four months ago I was on a mission for CHERUB in the Caribbean. I put something I shouldn't have been touching back in the wrong place. The bad guys noticed, got suspicious and disappeared. Nobody knows where. Two years' work for a dozen MI5* agents down the toilet. All thanks to me.'

'What's that got to do with you living here?' James asked.

'I wasn't exactly the golden boy when I got back to CHERUB, so they sent me on a recruitment mission.'

'Here?'

'Bingo, James. Stuck in this dump trying to find another kid to join CHERUB. Jennifer thought you looked the type

---

*MI5 is the adult branch of British Intelligence.

when she saw your school record. She made sure you got this room so I could evaluate you.'

'So what you told me about your parents and stuff was lies?'

Kyle smiled. 'Hundred per cent fiction, sorry . . . You wanted to get Vince back. Did you have a plan?'

'You said stay away from him.'

'I hate him,' Kyle said. 'He was in a foster home and picked a fight with a seven-year-old. Threw him off a roof and broke his back. The kid's in a wheelchair for the rest of his life.'

'Jesus.'

'You know where they keep the spare sand for the kiddies' pit?' Kyle asked.

'Under the stairs.'

'Get two bags. I'll meet you outside Vince's room.'

'It'll be locked,' James said.

'I can deal with that.'

James struggled upstairs with the sand. Kyle had picked Vince's lock and was already in his room.

'I thought *you* were a slob until I saw this,' Kyle said.

Vince and his little brother Paul weren't big on housekeeping. There were dirty clothes, magazines and CDs everywhere.

'It's a normal boys' bedroom,' James said.

'It's not going to be for long. Start tipping the sand everywhere, I'll find some liquid.'

James put sand in the beds, drawers and desks. Kyle smuggled catering size bottles of Pepsi out of the kitchen. They shook each bottle up so it exploded when the lid came off. When they finished everything was soaked in gritty brown sludge.

James laughed. 'I'd love to see his face.'

'We'll be long gone. Want to see what's in his locker?'

Kyle pulled a metal object out of his pocket.

'What's that?' James asked.

'It's a lock gun. Does most locks. You'll learn to use it in basic training.'

'Cool,' James said.

Kyle slid the gun into Vince's padlock and wriggled it until the metal door sprung open.

'Girlie mags,' Kyle said.

Kyle tipped the magazines on to the floor.

'Hang on.'

'What?' James asked.

'Look at these.'

There was a row of savage-looking knives in the bottom of the locker.

'I'll be confiscating these,' Kyle said. 'Get me something to wrap them in.'

'Everything's soaked.'

'I don't care,' Kyle said. 'I can hardly walk down the corridor with that lot in my hand.'

James found a sweatshirt under Paul's bed that only had a bit of sand on it. Kyle bundled up the knives.

'OK, James, how long to pick-up?'

'Twenty minutes.'

'Twenty minutes too long,' Kyle said. 'I hate this dump.'

12. NAME

James sat in Meryl Spencer's office wearing CHERUB uniform with the pale blue trainee T-shirt. Meryl was James' handler at CHERUB. She'd won a sprint medal for Kenya at the Atlanta Olympics and taught athletics on campus. Her legs looked like they could break rocks.

Meryl held James' safety deposit key in the air over the desk between them.

'Not many kids come in with one of these,' Meryl said.

'I got it when my mum died,' James said. 'I don't know what's inside the box.'

'I see,' Meryl said suspiciously. 'We'll keep the key safe for you. What about the cash Kyle found in your room?'

James was prepared for questions about his cash. He'd realised Kyle had been through all his stuff when he saw him crack Vince's locker.

'It was my mum's,' James said.

'How much is there?' Meryl asked.

'There was four thousand. But I've spent a couple of hundred.'

'Just four thousand?'

Meryl reached into her desk drawer and pulled out a green circuit board and a tangle of electrical wires. James recognised them from when he'd ripped them out of his cassette player.

'Oh,' James said. 'You know about that?'

Meryl nodded.

'Kyle found the insides of the tape player in the bin the day he met you. He found the hidden cash and we worked out that it was from your mother's safe. You even left some lying around in obvious places to deceive Ron if he came after it. Everyone here was impressed when they realised what you'd done. It's one of the reasons you were invited to join CHERUB.'

'I can't believe you found all that out about me,' James said.

Meryl burst out laughing.

'James, we struggle to find stuff out about the international drug smuggling cartels and terrorist groups. Twelve-year-old boys are less tricky.'

James smiled uneasily. 'Sorry I lied. I should have realised.'

'You see that track outside my window?' Meryl asked.

'Yeah,' James said.

'Next time you lie to me, you'll be running laps around it until you're dizzy. Play it straight with me, OK?'

James nodded.

'So what happens to my money? Will you hand it in to the police?'

'Lord no,' Meryl said. 'The last thing we want is the police asking questions about you. Mac and I discussed it before you arrived. I think you'll find we've come up with a reasonable solution.'

Meryl got two little red books out of her desk.

'Savings accounts,' she explained. 'Half for you. Half for your sister when she turns eighteen. You can withdraw thirty pounds a month if you want to, plus a hundred on your birthday and at Christmas. Does that sound fair?'

James nodded.

'What's your sister's name?'

'Lauren Zoe Onions.'

'And your name?'

'James Robert Choke.'

'No, your new name,' Meryl said.

'What new name?' James asked.

'Didn't Mac ask you to think about a new name?'

'No.'

'You can keep your first name if you want, but you have to take a new surname.'

'Anything I like?'

'Within reason, James. Nothing too unusual and it has to match your ethnicity.'

'What's ethnicity?' James asked.

'Your racial origin. It means you can't call yourself James Patel or James Bin Laden.'

'Can I think about it for a while?'

'Sorry, James. There are forms to fill out. I need a name.'

James thought having a new name was cool, but his mind was blank.

'Well, who's your favourite pop star? Or your favourite footballer?' Meryl asked.

'Avril Lavigne is OK.'

'James Lavigne then.'

'No, I've got it,' James said. 'Tony Adams, the old Arsenal player. I want to be James Adams.'

'OK. James Adams it is. Do you want to keep Robert as a middle name?'

'Yeah. But can I be James Robert Tony Adams?'

'Tony is an abbreviation of Anthony. How about James Robert Anthony Adams?'

'Sure,' James said.

James Robert Anthony Adams thought his new name sounded classy.

'I'll get Kyle to show you your room. Basic training starts in three weeks if you pass your medical and learn to swim.'

'Learn to swim?' James said.

'You can't start basic training until you can swim fifty metres. I've put you down for two lessons a day.'

*

Kyle took James upstairs to the living quarters.

'Bruce Norris said he wants to see you.'

Kyle knocked on a door.

'It's open,' Bruce shouted from inside.

James followed Kyle into Bruce's room. One wall had shelves stacked with trophies. The other was a mass of gory martial arts posters.

'Mental posters,' James said.

'Thanks,' Bruce said, getting off his bed and putting out his hand for James to shake.

'I wanted to make sure you're not holding a grudge against me after the test.'

'No worries,' James said.

'You want a drink or something?' Bruce asked, pointing towards his fridge.

'He's not seen his own room yet,' Kyle said.

'Is he on this floor?' Bruce asked.

'Yes,' Kyle said. 'Across from me.'

'Cool,' Bruce said. 'I'll see you at dinner.'

James and Kyle went outside.

'He's a bit scary,' James said. 'It's weird being in a room with someone who could kill you with their bare hands.'

'Most kids here could kill you in two seconds flat, me included. Bruce is hilarious. He acts all macho, but he's a total baby sometimes. After he finished basic training and got his grey shirt he heard all the little red shirt kids were going on an Easter egg hunt. They wouldn't let him go so he burst into tears. He laid in his room and cried for like, three hours. And you'll never guess what else.'

'What?'

'He sleeps with teddy.'

'No way.'

'I swear to god, James. Bruce forgot to push his door shut one night and everyone saw it. Little blue bear in the bed with him.'

Kyle stopped at a room with a key in the door.

'There you go.' Kyle said. 'Home.'

James' stuff was in bags on the floor. Everything in the room looked new. A decent sized TV and VCR. A computer, kettle, microwave and mini fridge. The double bed had a thick duvet and a pile of pressed CHERUB uniform on top of it.

'I'll leave you to turn it into a tip,' Kyle said. 'I'll call you when it's time for dinner.'

James swished open his curtains and saw kids playing football on Astroturf. All ages, boys and girls. Nobody was taking it seriously. Little kids got carried on bigger kids' shoulders.

James fancied joining in, but he was more interested in his new room. There was a telephone beside the bed. He picked up, wondering who he could call, but he got a recorded message: *Dial out privileges are currently suspended.*

The computer looked new and had a flat LCD monitor and Internet access. James realised the best thing of all: for the first time in his life he had his own bathroom. There was a thick towelling dressing gown hanging on the door, piles of different size towels and flannels. The bath was big enough for James to lie flat in. For some reason, he decided to stand in it fully clothed and try out the shower, soaking himself.

He stepped out of the tub and looked at all the unopened bottles and packets: soap, shampoo, electric toothbrush, deodorant, even a box of chocolate bath bombs.

James laid on his bed and sank into his duvet. He rocked the mattress gently, smiling uncontrollably to himself. It was hard to imagine the room being any cooler.

*

Dinner should have been good. The food was top: choice of steak, fish, Chinese or Indian and wicked desserts. James sat with Bruce and Kyle and a whole group of other kids. They all seemed nice and James thought the girls looked cute in their CHERUB uniforms. The downer was, as soon as they saw James' pale blue trainee shirt everyone started telling horror stories about basic training: being cold and muddy, not getting enough to eat, smashed bones, stitched up cuts, being forced to exercise until you either puked or fainted. It sounded bad.

*

James stood in the food store. There were snacks and soft drinks piled on the shelves.

'Take whatever you want for your fridge.' Kyle said. 'It's all free.'

James looked miserably at the goodies and didn't say anything.

'They shitted you up, didn't they?' Kyle said.

James nodded. 'Is it as bad as they all said?'

'I can't sugar-coat it,' Kyle said. 'Basic training is the worst hundred days of your life. That's the point. Once you've been through it you're not scared of much else … At least it doesn't start for three weeks.'

James walked to his room. A timetable had been slid under the door while he was at dinner. Tomorrow he had a medical, a dentist appointment and two swimming lessons.

13. NEEDLE

His alarm went off at 6 a.m. James noticed that a set of swimming shorts and a map had been put on his desk while he was asleep. Nobody else was about this early. James walked to the canteen where a couple of teachers were eating breakfast. He found a newspaper and looked through the sport pages while eating cereal. The map was easy to follow, but James hesitated when he read the sign on the pool door: *Learning Pool. Children Under Ten Only*.

James stuck his head round the door. The pool was empty, except for a girl of about fifteen who was swimming laps. When she saw James she swam to the side and propped her elbows on the edge.

'Are you James?' she asked.

'Yeah.'

'I'm Amy Collins. I'll be teaching you how to swim. Go in the back and get changed.'

James undressed. He noticed Amy's black CHERUB T-shirt on the bench and her bra and knickers on a hook. James had worried his instructor would be some tough guy shouting and bawling at him. Seeing Amy's undies made James realise that making a fool of himself in front of a girl was even worse. He stepped out of the changing room and stood by the steps at the shallow end of the pool.

'Come up this end,' Amy shouted.

James walked along the twenty-five metre pool, nervously reading the depth markings. The deep end levelled off at three and a half metres.

'Stand with your toes curled over the edge,' Amy said.

James shuffled up to the edge. The bottom looked a long way off and the chlorine smelled like the time he nearly drowned.

'Take a deep breath. Jump in and hold the air until you come back up to the surface.'

'Won't I sink?' James asked.

'People float in water, James. Especially if their lungs are full of air.'

James crouched down to jump. He could almost feel the water blocking his mouth.

'I can't,' James said.

'I'm right here to catch you. Don't be scared.'

James didn't want to look soft in front of a girl. He raised his courage and leapt in. The quiet when his head went under was eerie. James' feet touched the bottom of the pool and he pushed himself upwards. As his face broke the surface he let out a gasp and thrashed his arms. He couldn't see Amy. He felt the same terror as when his classmates had nearly drowned him.

Amy grabbed James and with a few powerful kicks she

pushed him to the edge of the pool. James clambered out and doubled over, coughing.

'Well done, James. You've learned the most important lesson: you float back to the surface when you jump in the water.'

'You said you'd catch me,' James said.

He tried to sound angry, but he let out a big sob in the middle of the sentence.

'Why are you upset? You did really well.'

'I'm never gonna learn to swim,' James said. 'I know it's stupid, but I'm scared of water. My nine-year-old sister can swim, but I'm too scared.'

'Calm down, James. It's my fault. I wouldn't have asked you to do that if I'd known you were so frightened.'

Amy took James back to the shallow end. They sat with their feet dangling in the water while Amy tried to calm James down.

'You must think I'm a wimp,' James said.

'Everyone is scared of something,' Amy said. 'I've taught loads of kids to swim. You may take longer to learn than someone more confident, but we'll get through it.'

'I should have stayed where I was,' James said. 'I'm not good enough for a place like this.'

Amy put her arm around James. James was uncomfortable at first. He felt too old for a cuddle, but Amy was nice.

*

'Get down off the treadmill,' the doctor said. His German accent made him sound like an extra from a World War Two film.

James wore shorts and trainers. Sweat dripped out of his

hair and streaked down his face. A nurse started peeling off the sticky patches on his chest. They were all wired up to a machine. The doctor touched the machine and a half-metre long strip of paper shot out. He stared at the paper and shook his head.

'Do you watch a lot of TV, James?'

'I suppose,' James said.

'You just ran one kilometre and you're exhausted. Do you play any sport?'

'Not much,' James said.

The doctor pinched a roll of fat on James' stomach.

'Look at that flab. You're like a middle-aged man.'

The doctor untucked his shirt and slapped a six-pack stomach.

'Like steel,' he said. 'And I'm sixty years old.'

James had never thought of himself as fat before. But now that he looked, he *was* a bit soggy around the middle.

'When does your basic training start?' the doctor asked.

'Three weeks. If I learn to swim.'

'You can't swim either? Pathetic! No need to swim in front of the television, I suppose, James? I'll send you down to the athletics department. Get you to do some running. No puddings, no chocolates. The good news is, apart from too much puppy fat, you seem fine. Now, injections.'

The nurse pulled a plastic tray with hundreds of syringes lined up on it out of a fridge.

'What are all these?' James asked, alarmed.

'CHERUB can send you anywhere in the world at a moment's notice. You have to be vaccinated. Influenza, Cholera, Typhoid, Hepatitis A, Hepatitis C, Rubella,

Yellow Fever, Lassa Fever, Tetanus, Japanese Encephalitis, Tuberculosis, Meningitis.'

'I'm having all those now?' James asked.

'No, that would overload your immune system and make you sick. Only seven injections today. Then five in two days' time and another four in a week.'

'I've got to have sixteen injections?'

'Twenty-three actually. You'll need some booster jabs in six months.'

Before James could comprehend the full horror of this, the nurse wiped his arm with a sterile swab. The doctor tore the packaging off a syringe and jabbed it into James' arm. It didn't hurt.

'Influenza,' the doctor said. 'Thought I'd start you off with an easy one. This next one goes into the muscle and you may feel a teensy little pinch.'

The doctor pulled the cap off a five-centimetre needle.

'OOOOOOOOO WWWWWWWWW.'

*

James was sitting in the changing room in his swimming shorts waiting for his afternoon lesson. Amy rushed in. She threw a bag of school books on the floor and started unlacing her boots.

'Sorry I'm late, James. Got talking and lost track of time. How's your day been?'

'Awful,' James said.

'What's wrong with your voice?'

'Four fillings at the dentist. I still can't feel my tongue.'

'Does it hurt?' Amy asked, stepping out of her trousers.

'Not as bad as my arse where the doctor stuck two needles

in it. Plus he says I'm fat and unfit. I've got to run fifteen laps five times a week and I'm not allowed to eat desserts.'

Amy smiled. 'Not a good day, then.'

14. SWEAT

Fifteen laps of a 400-metre track is six kilometres. James had no time limit; he could walk it in about an hour but that was boring. He wanted to go fast. The first day he raced off and died after three laps. He staggered the rest of the way with his legs aching and it took nearly an hour and a quarter. Next morning James' ankles were puffed up and even walking was agony.

Meryl Spencer showed James warm-up and cool-down stretches and told him only to run every third lap, then gradually to move up; running a lap and a half out of every three, then two out of three, and so on until he could run the six kilometres without a rest.

The third day it rained so hard James could hardly see through the wet hair stuck to his face. Meryl and the other athletics coach hid in the dry. James figured nobody was watching and after thirteen laps went into the changing room where the other drowned-rat kids were diving under the shower.

'Was that fifteen laps?' Meryl asked.

James knew he was busted just from her voice.

'Come on, it's belting down, Miss.'

'You cheat, James, you start again. Fifteen laps. Get going.'

'What?'

'You heard me, James. One smart word and I'll make it thirty laps.'

By the end, James' lungs felt like they were going to explode. Kyle and Bruce thought it was superb when James told them what had happened. Amy said it was good to learn early that discipline at CHERUB was stricter than James was used to.

*

A fortnight later James was getting fitter. He could run two laps out of every three fast and jog the other one. It was Friday, lap fifteen. The pulse in his neck felt like it was about to burst. His body was begging him to quit, but James wanted to do his laps in under half an hour for the first time and he wasn't giving in so close to the end.

James overtook a set of identical twins on the final bend and sprinted to the line. He glanced at his stopwatch: 29:47. Twenty seconds inside his previous best. As James looked at the watch he put a foot down awkwardly and overbalanced. The track slashed the skin off his knee, ripped his T-shirt and grazed his shoulder. The pain from the cuts wasn't as bad as the pain in his lungs, but James didn't care because he'd broken half an hour.

James clamped his hand over his knee. The twins stopped to help.

'You OK?' one of them asked.

'Fine,' James lied.

James hadn't seen them before. He noticed they were wearing pale blue shirts.

'You two starting basic training week after next?'

'Yeah. We arrived last night. I'm Callum, this is Connor. You want us to help you back to the changing room?'

'I'll manage,' James said.

*

'It's my birthday today,' Amy said.

They were in the pool together. James' cuts were stinging from the chlorine.

'How old?' James asked.

'Sixteen.'

'I would have got you a card or something,' James said. 'You never said.'

'I'm having a little gathering. Just a few friends in my room this evening. Want to come?'

'Sure,' James said.

James was more excited about going to Amy's party than he would admit. He liked her a lot. She was funny and beautiful. He was sure Amy liked him, but like a little brother not a mate.

'You have to do something first though.'

'How far?' James asked.

'From the steps in the middle of the pool on that side, to the opposite corner.'

'That's almost a length.'

'Almost. You can do it, James. Your stroke is getting stronger. Basic training starts in nine days and if you don't make it, it's three months until the next course starts.'

'I'll have three months to learn to swim. That's not bad.'

They'll put you in a red T-shirt,' Amy said.

'I'm twelve. Red is for little kids.'

'No, James. Red shirts are for kids who are not qualified for training. Mostly that's because they're too young. But in your case it will be because you can't swim.'

'I'll be two years older than anyone else in a red shirt. I'll be slaughtered.'

'James, I'm not trying to pressure you, but if you have to spend three months in a red shirt, your life won't be a lot of fun.'

'You *are* trying to pressure me,' James said.

'On the bright side, James, red shirt kids are allowed to keep a gerbil or a hamster in their rooms.'

'Well funny, Amy.' James laughed, but he knew this was serious. Kyle, Bruce and everyone else would wet themselves laughing if they put him in a red T-shirt. James started walking through the water towards the steps, determined to swim further than before.

He managed. Amy gave him a hug.

'You'll be OK, James.'

James wasn't so confident.

*

Amy's door was wedged open and you could hear her stereo as you stepped out of the lift. The room was crammed with people and more lined the corridor outside. Everyone was dressed in normal clothes. After two weeks on campus seeing people in olive trousers and boots, James had almost forgotten skirts existed.

Amy had on bright pink lipstick that matched her mini skirt. James felt self-conscious because everyone was older and he didn't know anyone. Amy spun around when she saw James. She had a cigarette in one hand and a can of beer in the other. She gave James a kiss on the cheek, leaving a blur of lipstick.

'Hey James,' Amy said. 'I don't think I'll be in any state for a swimming lesson tomorrow morning.'

'Is this the kid who can't swim?' a guy sitting on the floor asked loudly.

Everyone heard. James thought people were looking at him thinking he was a wimp.

'You want a beer, kid?' a guy sitting by Amy's fridge asked.

James didn't know what to say. If he said yes everyone might laugh because they thought he was too young. If he said no he'd look soft. James picked yes. Nobody laughed at him. James caught the can and pulled the tab. Amy grabbed it out of his hand.

'Don't give him beer, Charles. He's only twelve.'

'Come on, Amy,' Charles said. 'Let's get the little kid drunk. It's always a laugh.'

Amy smiled and handed James the can.

'One can, James,' Amy said. 'No more. And don't tell anyone we let you have it.'

*

Once James had sneaked two of Uncle Ron's beers and got a bit drunk, but this was way beyond that. Amy's girlfriends all loved James. They kept giving him more beer. James blushed when one of them kissed him. So they all kissed him until his face was a mass of lipstick smears. As they got drunker one of the girls decided it would be funny to give him a love bite. They tickled James until he gave in. He knew he wasn't much more than their drunken pet, but it was fun being the centre of attention.

Some of the kids on Amy's floor complained about the racket, so the party had to move outside. It was midnight now and pitch dark. James followed the noise from Amy's portable CD player.

'Wait for me,' James shouted. 'Busting to piss.'

James wandered into a bunch of trees. Suddenly there wasn't any ground under his trainers. His heart shot into his mouth as he lost his balance. He slid two metres down an embankment and crashed into a muddy ditch.

James dragged himself up, spitting nasty tasting water out of his mouth. His sweatshirt was ripped. He shouted for help, but the others couldn't hear over Amy's music. By the time James scrambled back up the embankment there was no sign of anyone.

Campus was bigger than James realised. He got totally lost trying to find the main building. He felt sick from all the beer and started to panic. When he finally sighted the changing room at the edge of the athletics track he was thrilled.

James peered in the window. The lights were off. He tried the door, it wasn't locked. James crept in. The heating was off but it was still warmer than outside. James rubbed his hands together to try and get some feeling back. He found a bank of switches and flipped on the light in the boys' changing room. He left the others off. Any light shining through the frosted windows might have caught someone's attention.

James looked at himself now he could see and was gutted. He'd put his best clothes on for the party. An almost new pair of Nike Air trainers and some Diesel jeans. The bottom of the jeans had mud soaked through them and the trainers were a wet mess, coated with mud. James knew the route back to his room from here, but there could be awkward questions if he got seen like this. He had to tidy himself up.

James kicked his trainers off to avoid marking the floor. He went into the boys' changing room. Fear of getting caught had sobered him up a bit. The changing room was a mess. There was sweat in the air and quite a few bits of clothing tossed about. James found a grey CHERUB T-shirt scrunched up under a bench. It smelled nasty, but it was less suspicious than walking into the main building in a torn sweatshirt. James pulled it on. There were no clean tracksuit bottoms to replace the muddy jeans, so James pushed his jeans down his waist and turned the bottoms up so the muddiest area looked smaller. All he needed now was some trainers that wouldn't spread mud everywhere. There were a few running spikes laying around, but they'd be no good indoors.

James stepped across the hallway into the girls' changing room. He hadn't been in here before, of course. The difference from the boys' room was amazing. It smelled fresh. There was a counter stocked up with toiletries and perfumes. Best of all, there were two pairs of trainers on top of the lockers. One pair was James' size but pink. The other pair was smaller, but James could easily hobble a couple of hundred metres through the main building in them. He squeezed them on.

He caught himself in the mirror and realised his face was filthy. He wished Kyle could see all the lipstick marks. James damped a towel, scrubbed his face and hands, gave the smelly T-shirt a blast with deodorant and gargled mouthwash to mask the smell of beer.

He did a final inspection: not bad. If anyone asked why he was out so late, James decided to say he couldn't sleep, went for a walk and got lost. The only thing that might be tricky was explaining why he was wearing the wrong colour T-shirt.

James stepped into the corridor. A hand clamped his ankle. James shot about a metre in the air with fright.

'Caught you in the girls' changing room, pervert.'

James didn't recognise the voice. Torch beams lit up his face. Amy and the girl who'd given him the love bite burst out laughing. They had changed out of party clothes into uniform.

'Why are you hanging around the girls' changing room, James?' Amy asked.

James panicked. It was so embarrassing.

'I couldn't go back in the main building all muddy, so I came in here to clean up.'

'We're pulling your leg,' Amy said. 'I saw the light was on. We've been watching you for about five minutes. When I realised you didn't make it back we came out looking.'

James smiled with relief. 'I really thought you were going to tell everyone I was a pervert.'

'We still might,' the love bite girl giggled.

'Next time you say only have one drink, Amy, I will. I swear.'

'What makes you think I'll invite you next time? I know a back way into the main building. Let's not hang around here.'

'You saved my life, Amy. Thanks.'

Amy laughed. 'If you turned up drunk after half the school saw you at my party I'd be in as much trouble as you.'

15. TOWN

James swore he'd never drink again. It was a rough night. Throwing up, head floating, dry mouth and a throat like sandpaper. Lucky it was only three steps to the bathroom. It was 3 a.m. before James settled into an uneasy sleep. He kept jerking awake from weird dreams where everything was spinning.

'James,' Kyle shouted.

It was 7 a.m., Saturday morning.

'Wake up, man.'

James sat up in bed rubbing his eyes.

'You got drunk, didn't you?' Kyle said.

'Ugh.'

'This room stinks of beer.'

'I feel like I'm dying,' James groaned. 'How did you get in here?'

'Picked the lock. I did knock first but you didn't answer.'

'Can't you leave me to die?'

'James, shut up and listen. There's a mission in London tonight. Nine of us are spending the day up there hanging out. You're not supposed to come, but it's all been thrown together at the last minute and it's a Dennis King production so we can smuggle you on to the train.'

'What's a Dennis King production?'

'He's one of the mission controllers,' Kyle explained. 'He's a sweet old guy, but he's a bit doddery and he'll never notice an extra kid tagging along.'

'I've got a hangover,' James said. 'And I'm sick of always getting in trouble.'

'Don't you want to visit your sister then?'

'How will we do that?' James asked, excitedly kicking off his duvet and swinging out of bed. 'Ron won't let me in the flat.'

'If Lauren's home, we'll find a way. I wanted to help you visit her when we were at Nebraska House, but I couldn't without breaking my cover. This is your only chance. Once you start basic training, you're cut off from everything for three months.'

'When are we leaving?' James asked.

'Twenty minutes. Have a quick shower, put on civilian clothes and get your butt downstairs.'

*

It was weird being back. London seemed dirty and noisy, even though James had lived here until a few weeks before. The kids all split up when they arrived at King's Cross station. A bunch of girls were going shopping in Oxford Street. Most boys in the group were going to Namco Station, a big amusement arcade opposite Big Ben. They all had to meet outside Edgware Underground at 6 p.m. for the mission. Bruce wanted to go to Namco, but decided to stay with Kyle and James once he heard what they were doing.

'You'll get bored,' Kyle said. 'We're just going to James' old neighbourhood to visit his little sister.'

'You might need me for protection,' Bruce said.

Kyle laughed. 'Protection from what, Bruce? Come if you want. Just don't whine all day if you get bored.'

Bruce had never been on the Underground before. He looked at the map and counted how many stops like a five-year-old. Ron lived behind Kentish Town station, a couple of streets from the estate where James used to live with his mum.

'What do we do?' James asked when they reached the flat.

'Ring the doorbell,' Bruce said.

'Ron won't let me in, dummy,' James said. 'I wouldn't need you guys if I could just ring the doorbell and get in.'

'Oh,' Bruce said. 'I could kick the door down.'

'Like his stepdad isn't going to notice somebody kicking his front door down,' Kyle said sarcastically. 'What's your sister likely to be doing if she's inside?'

'Either drawing in her room or watching TV,' James said.

'And Ron?'

'He'll have been out drinking last night. Probably won't be out of bed for another hour.'

Kyle stuck his lock gun in the keyhole. He turned the lock but the door wouldn't budge.

'Bolt on the inside,' Kyle explained.

'Ring the doorbell,' Bruce said again.

'We can't. I just told you,' James said.

'You and Kyle hide. I'll ring the doorbell,' Bruce said. 'You said your stepdad is probably asleep, so I bet your sister answers. If she answers I'll say what's going on. If Ron answers I'll tell him I've made a mistake.'

Kyle and James walked away. Bruce rang the bell. A few seconds later Lauren's eyes appeared in the letterbox.

'How many packets do you want?' Lauren asked.

'I'm a friend of your brother James. Is your dad awake?'

'You don't want cigarettes?' Lauren asked.

Bruce waved for James to come to the door. James crouched at the letterbox.

'Let us in,' James said.

'James,' Lauren grinned. 'You better not let Dad see you. Every time I mention your name he looks like his head's gonna explode.'

Lauren undid a bolt on the bottom of the door.

'Is Ron asleep?' James asked.

'Won't get up until the horse-racing starts,' Lauren said, opening the door.

'Hide us in your room,' James said.

Lauren led the boys into her bedroom. The room was divided by a curved wall built out of thousands of cigarette cartons.

'What's all this?' James asked. 'You started smoking?'

'Dad buys them cheap in France,' Lauren said. 'He smuggles them in and sells them. He's making loads of money.'

Bruce studied the wall of cartons. 'Did you build this?'

'Yeah,' Lauren said. 'I was bored so I started messing about with the cartons.'

Bruce laughed. 'It's brilliant.'

'She always messes with stuff,' James said. 'When she had chicken pox she got every CD and video case in our flat and used it to make a pyramid.'

Lauren sat down on her bed.

'So what are you up to?' James asked.

'I go round with the kids down the balcony a lot. Ron gives their mum money and she gets me from school and makes my dinner.'

'So you're doing OK?'

'Could be worse,' Lauren said. 'You been in any more trouble?'

'No,' James said.

Kyle and Bruce both grinned.

'Pants on fire,' Kyle muttered under his breath.

'So you want to go out or something?' James asked. 'Can you sneak out?'

'Easy,' Lauren said. 'Dad doesn't like me waking him up. I'll do a note to say I'm round a mate's house.'

*

James took Lauren shopping and got her some jeans she wanted in Gap Kids. They ate pizza and went ten pin bowling. James and Lauren versus Bruce and Kyle. It started getting dark, but they still had an hour to kill before they headed up to Edgware for the mission.

They ended up in the little swing park near James' flat. James hadn't been back there since he'd hidden in the tunnel the afternoon before his mum died. Kyle and Bruce mucked about trying to make each other dizzy on a roundabout. Lauren and James sat next to each other on the swings, swaying gently and dragging their trainers in the gravel. They both felt a bit sad, knowing that their day together was running out.

'Mum used to take us here when we were little,' James said.

Lauren nodded, 'She was good fun when she wasn't in a mood.'

'Remember when you used to climb up the slide, but you could never work out how to sit your bum down and push yourself off the top. I always had to climb up and rescue you.'

'No,' Lauren said. 'How old was I?'

'Only two or three,' James said. 'You know, I can't come back to London till after Christmas?'

'Oh,' Lauren said.

They tried not to make eye contact in case they made each other upset.

'That doesn't get you out of buying me a present,' Lauren said.

James smiled. 'Are you getting me one?'

'You can have a box of cigarettes if you want.'

'Well, well, well,' someone said. 'Haven't seen you round here much lately, James. Been hiding from me?'

It was Greg Jennings and two of his mates.

'I've been looking everywhere for you,' Greg said. 'I knew you couldn't hide that nasty little face for ever.'

The three boys squared up to James, all of them about twice his size. Greg put the toe of his trainer on the swing between James' legs.

'My sister has a scar on her face thanks to you. The only thing that cheered her up was finding out that your pig mother dropped dead.'

'Leave her out of this,' James said angrily, bunching up his fist.

'Oh no,' Greg said, putting on a high pitched voice. 'The little faggot's gonna hit me. I'm so scared!'

A small rock bounced off Greg's head.

'Hey turd,' Bruce shouted. 'Why don't you pick on someone your own size, like me.'

Greg turned round and couldn't believe such a skinny little kid was being so brave.

'Get out of here,' Greg said, pointing at Bruce. 'Unless you want your legs smashed.'

Bruce tossed another rock at Greg's head. James laughed. Greg gave James a slap then spoke to his two sidekicks.

'Snap that little idiot in half.'

James knew Bruce was a good fighter, but he was only eleven and the two guys sizing up to him were massive. Kyle was nowhere to be seen.

Bruce backed into the roundabout, holding his hands out meekly, acting scared. He grabbed the rails on the roundabout and sprung his whole body behind a two footed kick. One of the thugs crumpled up. Kyle jumped out from behind the roundabout and barged the thug over, then smashed him with an elbow that burst his nose and left him unconscious.

Meanwhile, Bruce had taken on the other one. The kid plucked Bruce off the ground. Bruce kicked him in the balls then put a sharp pinch on his neck. He'd been trained to target the main vein running up the side of the neck. It caused an instant build-up of blood in the thug's head. He passed out and hit the ground like a falling tree, with Bruce holding on. Bruce clambered out from under his victim and ran towards Greg Jennings.

Greg still had his trainer pressed in James' crotch. There was a weird look on Greg's face; like his brain wasn't believing what his eyes were seeing. Greg reached inside his coat. James realised he was going for a knife. He dived backwards off the swing and grabbed Lauren.

Greg pulled the knife. Bruce faced him off.

'I'll stick that knife in you if you don't put it down,' Bruce said.

Greg lunged forward with the blade. Bruce stepped backwards. Greg lunged again, Bruce sidestepped. Bruce reached into his pocket and pulled out a coin. The next time Greg moved, Bruce threw the coin in Greg's face. Greg didn't know what was coming towards him and blocked the coin with his free hand. Bruce used the distraction to grab Greg's wrist, twist his thumb into a lock and slide out the knife. Now they were back facing each other, only Bruce was holding the knife.

'I'll stick this knife in you if you don't start running,' Bruce said.

Greg was too proud to run, but he walked off fast. Lauren ran over to Bruce.

'That was like something out of Jackie Chan,' she said. 'You're the best fighter ever.'

'I like to think so,' Bruce said casually, tucking his coin back in his pocket. 'At least for my age.'

James was amazed. First Kyle had set the whole day up for him. Now Bruce had saved him from a beating.

'You guys are great,' James said. 'I owe both of you.'

'I'll settle for cash,' Kyle said, looking at the dirt on his trousers. 'These are Billabong trousers. Sixty quid they cost and they're filthy.'

'You know what I really want?' Bruce said. 'Some business

cards with *Bruce Norris Kicked Your Arse* printed on them. I can stick them in people's mouths when I knock them unconscious, just in case they don't remember me when they come round.'

'Bruce, what you *need*,' Kyle said, 'is some serious time with a psychiatrist.'

*

The kids were gathered in a quiet corner of the car park outside Edgware station. Dennis King passed out copies of the mission briefing.

'You all know the deal,' he said. 'Read the mission and sign your name at the bottom if you want to come along.'

'Don't sign it, James,' Kyle whispered. 'Remember you're not supposed to be here.'

CLASSIFIED MISSION BRIEFING

TARGET:

Bishops Avenue, London. Home of Solomon Gold, owner of Armaments Exchange plc. Gold is suspected of illegally selling American-made tank-buster missiles to terrorist groups in Palestine and Angola.

OBJECTIVES:

Solomon Gold has gone away for the weekend. His home is protected by a two man security post. Gas will be released inside the post. The gas will make the guards sleep for about three hours. This task will be undertaken by an M15 agent, posing as the security guard's supervisor.

Mr Gold is highly suspicious. The area around his house is monitored by thirty-six video cameras. Adult intruders will be suspected of being M15 agents or undercover police. A decision has been taken to use CHERUB operatives, who must behave like vandals to minimise suspicion.

CHERUB operatives will enter the house through the main gate. Three operatives will search the office on the first floor for documents and make copies using handheld photocopiers. Six operatives will be issued with spray paint, bats and hammers. Their objective is to damage fixtures and fittings, creating the impression that the only intention was mindless vandalism.

Afterwards all CHERUB operatives should leave the scene and meet at an agreed point two kilometres from the break-in.

Local police have no knowledge of this operation. If an operative is arrested, they should give false identification details and await release.

Bishops Avenue was locally known as Millionaires Row, though billionaires was more like it. The houses were all massive. Most were set back behind six-metre-high walls. Video cameras stared in every direction.

A bus dropped the ten kids a few streets away. Solomon Gold's house was fifteen minutes' walk. James, Bruce and Kyle were at the back of the group, walking fast. It was dark and raining hard.

'You excited?' Kyle asked.

'Nervous,' James said. 'It said in the briefing about getting arrested. If I get arrested they'll know I'm on the mission.'

'Try not to get arrested, then,' Kyle said. 'Bruce will look after you.'

'What about you?' James asked.

'I'm upstairs photocopying documents.'

'Boring,' Bruce said. 'We get to smash stuff up. It's gonna rock.'

Ever since the fight Bruce had been in the best mood.

'I thought missions would be all sneaking around and stuff,' James said. 'Not bursting in the front door and trashing the joint.'

'What?' Kyle said. 'A bunch of twelve-year-olds creeping around in balaclavas and gloves, disabling burglar alarms and cutting holes in windows? Can you think of anything more likely to attract attention? The first thing you'll learn in basic training is that a CHERUB always has to act like a normal kid.'

Bruce laughed. 'CHERUB has a fifty-year tradition of mayhem and destruction.'

'I never realised,' James said. 'Cool.'

The girl leading them stopped by an open metal gate. She was called Jennie. Fifteen years old, she was mission leader.

'Everyone inside,' Jennie said.

James stepped through the gate last. He noticed the security guards asleep in their glass booth. A couple of kids were already in there grabbing the house keys.

'We've got twenty minutes,' Jennie whispered. 'Keep the noise down and pull the curtains or blinds before you turn any lights on. The only exit is back the way we came, so if the police turn up we're all spending the night in a cell.'

It was a hundred metres along a path lined with sculpted hedges to the house. The hallway was huge. Kyle took a mini photocopier out of his backpack and ran upstairs to find the office. James and Bruce found the kitchen. Bruce opened the fridge, which was empty except for a packet of cream cakes and some milk.

'Thank you,' Bruce said, stuffing a whole cake in his gob and glugging the milk. 'I'm starving.'

James had popped the top off his aerosol paint and started spraying ARSENAL in metre-high letters on the kitchen units. Bruce found the crockery cupboard and tipped it all on to the floor. James stomped the few plates and cups that weren't already broken. A girl came in.

'Bruce, James, come and help us out.'

They ran after the girl to the swimming pool. A few plastic chairs had already been thrown in. Two kids were trying to move a grand piano.

'Come on, help us.'

Five kids, including Bruce and James, lined up behind the piano and pushed it into the pool. A great wave of water sprayed up. The piano hit the bottom of the pool, making a crack in the tiles, before floating back to the surface. Bruce leapt on to the floating piano, pulled down the front of his tracksuit bottoms and started pissing in the pool. Before he finished, a huge air bubble burst out from under the piano lid and capsized it. Bruce fell in and swam to the side. James and the others were cracking up.

They all ran to the living room. James tucked some DVDs in his jacket, then picked up a little coffee table and used it to destroy the plasma TV hanging on the wall. The room stank from all the aerosol paint that was being sprayed. James was smashing ornaments and really getting into the swing of mindless destruction when a deafening alarm sounded and the room started filling with purple smoke.

Jennie was shouting from the hallway, 'Everybody get the hell out of here.'

'Stay with me, James,' Bruce shouted.

They ran through the hallway. Jennie counted them out of the main gate. 'Run away,' she shouted. 'Split up.'

James and Bruce sprinted up Bishops Avenue. Two police vans were heading towards them.

'Walk,' Bruce said. 'It looks less suspicious.'

The vans sped past. James' skin and clothes were stained purple from the smoke.

'What's this stuff?' James asked.

'Never seen it before. Probably harmless. Food dye or something,' Bruce said. 'Whoever did the security survey on that house messed up big time.'

'There's none on you,' James said.

'I suppose it didn't stick to me because I'm still wet from the pool.'

'What about Kyle? Did you see him?'

'He was upstairs. He wouldn't have got out before us. Probably been nabbed. Better start running again. Those cops saw us, it won't take them long to work out what's going on and come back for us.'

16. PENALTY

'This is beyond stupid ... This is beyond a shambles. And you three ... I'm lost for words ... You're the biggest idiots of the lot, aren't you?'

Mac was pacing up and down his office. Not happy. Kyle, Bruce and James kept sinking lower in their chairs.

Kyle had a black eye and his arm in a sling. He'd punched a policewoman trying to escape. Her three colleagues got revenge when he was handcuffed in the back of the police van.

'We never messed up the security survey,' Kyle blurted. 'That was MI5's fault.'

'The security survey was fine,' Mac said. 'The alarm was deactivated. Unfortunately some idiots cracked the bottom of the swimming pool with a grand piano and the leaking water caused the security system to short circuit. That's what set off the alarm and smoke.'

James and Bruce sank lower still.

'So, your punishments. What's it to be? Kyle, you messed up in the Caribbean. You messed up at Nebraska House, now you mess up here,' Mac said.

'You told me I did a good job when I got back from Nebraska House,' Kyle whined.

'When you first got back, Kyle. Then two days later I hear from Jennifer Mitchum that the social workers want you punished. Something about filling someone's room up with sand and spraying Coke everywhere?'

'Oh, that,' Kyle said. 'The guy was a dick.'

'You and James were supposed to disappear *quietly*. No questions asked. I don't like answering questions about where you've gone. I'm sending you on another recruitment mission, Kyle.'

'No,' Kyle said.

'A delightful children's home in a run-down area of Glasgow. I understand kids with English accents are particularly unpopular there.'

'I won't do it,' Kyle said.

'Do it, or I'll put you in a foster home.'

Kyle looked shocked.

'You can't kick me out,' he said.

'I can and I will, Kyle. Pack your stuff and get on the train to Glasgow tomorrow morning or you're out of CHERUB for good. So, Bruce.'

Bruce sat up in his chair.

'Why did you go along with Kyle's idea to take James on the mission?'

'Because I'm a total idiot,' Bruce said.

Mac laughed. 'Good answer. You spend a lot of time in the dojo, don't you?'

'Yeah,' Bruce said.

'For the next three months you're suspended from

missions. I want you in the dojo at the end of every day. Wash the floors, polish the mirrors, tidy the changing rooms and load all the towels and stinking kit into the washing machines. Then in the morning, unload all the kit, put it in the driers and fold it ready for use. Should take three hours a day if you work fast.'

'Fine,' Bruce said.

But he didn't look fine.

'Now, James.'

James was nervous. He didn't know where to look.

'You're new here. Keen to make friends. Two qualified agents put you up to something. Basic training starts in a few days and should straighten you out. You get away with this one. But next time I'll come down like a hammer. Understood?'

'Yes, Mac.'

'I'm Mac on a good day, James. Today you call me Doctor McAfferty or Doctor. Got that?'

'Yes, Doctor.'

James couldn't stop a little smile. Then he saw how upset Kyle and Bruce looked and straightened his face.

'Bruce, Kyle, you can go,' Mac said.

They walked out.

'I understand you went to London to see your sister,' Mac said.

'Yes,' James said. 'I know I shouldn't have. But I wanted to see her before Christmas.'

'I wasn't aware you had difficulty getting access. I'll try and sort something out.'

'My stepdad doesn't want me near her.'

'I can be very persuasive,' Mac said. 'I can't make any promises, but I'll do my best.'

'Thanks,' James said. 'I know it's not my place, but I think you're being too hard on Kyle. He only wanted to help me see Lauren.'

'He's nearly fourteen. Kyle should be in a navy shirt doing the most difficult missions; instead he keeps making silly errors of judgement. If you'd come and asked me, I would have let you go and see your sister. You could have waited at the station while the others went on the mission. Have you swum your fifty metres yet?'

'No,' James said.

'Only five days to go, James. I won't be happy if you fail.'

17. WATER

Amy and James walked towards another swimming lesson.

'I spoke to the head swimming instructor,' Amy said. 'He suggested we try something different. It's a bit drastic, but there are only two days left. Your stroke is good enough to swim fifty metres. What's holding you back is your fear of the water.'

They reached the learners' pool. James stopped.

'We're not going in there this morning.' Amy led James to another set of doors. There was a red warning notice: *Danger. Diving Pool: No Admittance Without A Qualified Diving Instructor.*

James stepped through the doors. The pool was fifty metres long. At one end diving suits and oxygen tanks hung from hooks. The water was clear, cleaned with salt instead of chlorine. James read the depth markings: six metres at the shallow end, fifteen metres at the deep end.

'No way am I swimming in that,' James said, scared out of his mind.

'I'm sorry, James,' Amy said. 'There's no more time for the gentle approach.'

Paul and Arif were walking towards James wearing

swimming shorts and bright red T-shirts with *Dive Instructor* printed on them. James had seen Paul and Arif around, but hadn't spoken to them since they'd helped him through the obstacle course.

'Come here, James,' Paul shouted. 'Now.'

James started walking. He looked back at Amy. She looked worried. Paul and Arif walked James to the deep end of the pool.

'These are the rules,' Arif explained. 'You either dive in or we throw you in. If you swim fifty metres that's the end. If you climb out before you swim fifty metres, you get a one-minute rest before you jump back in or we throw you back in. After thirty minutes you get a ten-minute rest, then we go for another thirty minutes. If you still don't swim fifty metres we'll do more lessons with the same rules. Don't try to run off, don't fight, don't cry. We're bigger and stronger than you. It won't get you anywhere and it will make you tired. Do you understand?'

'I can't do this,' James said.

'You haven't got a choice.'

They were at the end of the pool.

'Dive in,' Arif ordered.

James stood at the edge and hesitated. Arif and Paul each took an arm and a leg and flung him into the water. It was freezing. Salt burned James' eyes. James tipped his body forward to start swimming. His head went under and he breathed a mouthful of salty water. He started panicking. The side of the pool was only a few metres away. He struggled to the side, pulled himself up and took a long gasp of air.

'One minute,' Arif said, looking at his diver's watch.

James could hardly see.

'Please don't make me.'

'Thirty seconds,' Arif said.

'Please, I can't do this,' James begged.

Paul took James by the arm and marched him to the end of the pool.

'If you dive in you get an easier start than if we throw you,' Paul said.

'Time,' Arif said.

James tried not to think about the fifteen metres of freezing water below him. If he could just get his stroke going and not drink any water it wouldn't be so bad. James managed to swim ten metres, but the salt was blinding him and he had to give up.

By the fourth attempt James was used to the salt and cold. He made it nearly halfway along the pool, as far as he'd ever gone without stopping.

'Brilliant,' Amy shouted. 'You can do this, James.'

James was tired but Arif and Paul showed no mercy, giving him one minute and making him dive back in. James only got a few metres before his aching arms got the better of him.

'Not good enough,' Arif said. 'You don't deserve a rest.'

James could hardly hear above his pounding heart and gasps for air. They marched him up the pool and James jumped rather than suffer the humiliation of being thrown. He was so tired he'd forgotten to be scared. He swam a few metres, but his stroke was weak and he swallowed some water. Paul had to lift him out of the pool. James started coughing up water and snot on the poolside. Arif found a cloth and threw it at James.

'Wipe it up, fast.'

James meekly bent over and wiped the tiles. He was in a state, but he didn't want Paul and Arif to see. Paul grabbed him to march him back to the top of the pool. He broke free and swung a wild punch.

'Leave me alone,' James shouted.

Paul grabbed his arm and twisted it tight behind his back. James sobbed in pain.

'You think you can beat us up, James?' Paul asked. 'I'm twenty kilos heavier than you and I've got black belts in judo and karate. The only way you can beat us is to swim that pool.'

Paul let go of James' arm and shoved him into the water.

'Twenty metres this time, James,' Paul shouted. 'You want to punch me? Twenty metres or you're eating my fist.'

James started to swim. He was shattered, but he was scared of what Paul would do when he got out of the pool. James managed twenty metres and a couple more. He swam back to the side. Paul reached to lift James out of the water. James grasped his hand nervously.

'Not bad,' Paul said. 'That's thirty minutes. You've got a ten-minute rest.'

James slumped at the side of the pool. Amy rushed up and handed him a carton of orange juice. Arif and Paul sat down a few metres away.

'You OK?' Amy asked.

'Never better,' James muttered, gulping back a sob.

'Don't cry, James,' Amy said. 'This is tough, but so are you.'

'I'm not crying,' James lied. 'It's the salt in the water.'

James sucked his juice and worked something out. If he was able to swim fifty metres, his best chance would be when he was refreshed after the break. If he couldn't do it straight away, he was in for another half hour of humiliation. The prospect of being dragged about and forced back in the water seemed worse than drowning. If he passed out, so what? Anything was better than more of this.

'Time,' Arif said.

James walked to the end of the pool. It sounded fine in his head, but the pool still looked terrifying when his toes were curled over the edge. He started swimming strongly. He got some water in his mouth and spat it out. For the first time ever it didn't freak him out. Twenty-five metres. It didn't feel too bad. It was a personal best anyway.

James managed another ten metres. His pace was slowing. It was hard to keep his head up long enough to breathe. By forty metres his shoulders were agony. Amy was screaming her head off, James couldn't understand a word. The more effort he put in, the slower he seemed to get.

'Nearly there, James,' Amy screamed. 'Come on.'

The last few metres was just mad thrashing about. He'd lost his breathing pattern, swallowed gallons and was holding his breath. But he made it. James lifted his face out of the water and took in the most beautiful air of his life.

Amy lifted him out and gave him a hug. She was crying, which made James start crying again. He walked over to Paul and Arif.

'I can't believe I'm saying this,' James said, 'but thank you.'

'Your fear of us has to be greater than your fear of the water,' Paul said. 'It's not fun, but it works.'

18. BASIC

James was due at the basic training compound at 5 a.m. He set an alarm and left it on his bedside table. Worrying about training kept him awake for ages. When he woke it was light. It's never light at 5 a.m. in November. This was bad.

The alarm clock was gone. Not set wrong. Not tipped on the floor and the battery dropped out. Someone had crept in while he was asleep and taken it. Kyle warned him they'd play tricks, but James hadn't expected them to start before he'd even arrived.

Clothes and a backpack had been dumped on the floor. There were two differences from standard CHERUB kit. The T-shirt and trousers had white number sevens on them. Second, instead of being fabric-conditioned and pressed, everything was wrecked. Big stains, rips in the trousers. The underwear was disgusting and the boots had done hard time on somebody else's feet. James moved the backpack. There was tons of equipment in it. He probably should have got up early and looked at everything.

James had to wear the wrecked T-shirt and trousers because they had numbers. But he had his own pristine underwear, and boots that were broken in and only smelled of his own feet. Would he get punished for not wearing the clothes on the floor? Or would he get laughed at for being the only one dumb enough to put on second-hand underwear? The state of the boxer shorts made his mind up. He was wearing his own stuff.

There was no time for teeth, comb, or shower. He ran out with the backpack. The lift took ages, like it always does when you're in a rush. There were two older kids in the lift. They knew where James was going from the numbers on his uniform.

One of the kids looked at his watch.

'You starting basic training this morning?' the kid asked.

'Yeah,' James said.

'It's half past seven,' the kid said.

'I know,' James said. 'I'm late.'

The kids burst out laughing.

'You're not late. You're dead.'

'So dead,' the other kid said, shaking his head.

*

The training building was a concrete box in the middle of a huge muddy enclosure, with no windows and no heating. Five-metre-high fences separated it from the rest of campus. Just the look of the place scared James.

He ran inside, puffed from running. The room had ten rusty beds with wretched looking mattresses. Three girls and four boys were in front of the beds, crouching on the balls of their feet with hands on heads. After about ten minutes in that position the bottom of your legs goes dead. Six of the seven had been that way for two and a half hours, waiting for James. The odd one out had done an hour.

The head instructor, Mr Large, and his two assistants stood up and walked towards James. Large's white CHERUB T-shirt was the biggest size you could get, but it still looked like all the muscles inside wanted to burst out. He had buzz cut hair and a bushy moustache.

James flinched when Large reached out and delicately shook his hand.

'Good morning, James,' Large said in a soft voice. 'Smashing of you to pop in. Nice breakfast, was it? Put your feet up, did you? Good read of the papers? No need to worry, James. I didn't want to start without you, so I made all your new friends wait in a highly uncomfortable position until you arrived. Should I let them stand up now?'

'Yes,' James said weakly.

'OK, kiddies,' Large said. 'Up you get. James, why don't you shake all of their hands as a little thank you for waiting.'

The kids stood up, groaning in agony and trying to wriggle cramp out of the backs of their legs. James went along the line, shaking everyone's hand and getting killer looks.

'Stand at bed seven, James,' Large said. 'Nice clean boots, I see.'

Large lifted up the leg of James' trousers and peered at his sock. Large's wrist was bigger than James' neck.

'Clean socks too,' Large noted. 'Anyone else wearing their own boots and clean socks?'

James was relieved that a few hands went up.

'Very sensible,' Large said. 'Sorry about putting those filthy rags and boots out. Must have been some kind of terrible mix-up. Still, you've only got to wear them for a hundred days.'

James smiled and got daggers from the red-headed girl standing on his right in filthy boots.

'Now, before I make my welcome speech,' Large continued, 'let me introduce my two wonderful friends who'll be helping to look after the eight of you. Mr Speaks and Miss Smoke.'

If you wanted two people to make your life a misery, Speaks and Smoke looked ideal. They were both in their twenties and almost as muscular as Mr Large. Speaks was black, shaved bald, sunglasses. Total hard case. Smoke had blue eyes, long blonde hair and was about as feminine as a dustcart.

'Miss Smoke,' Large said, 'would you kindly fetch me a bucket. And James, would you be sweet enough to stand on one leg.'

James stood on one leg, trying to keep his balance. Smoke handed Large a metal bucket.

'Hopefully this will teach you to be more punctual from now on.'

Large stuck the bucket over James' head. James' world turned black and the smell of disinfectant blasted his nose. He could hear the other kids laughing. Large pulled a baton out of his belt and rapped it over the top of the bucket. Inside the noise was deafening.

'Can you hear me speak, number seven?' Large asked.

'Yes sir,' James said.

'Good. I wouldn't want you to miss my speech. The rule is, every time your foot touches the floor you get another crack with the baton, like this.'

The baton whacked the bucket again. James was learning that standing on one leg is harder when you're blind.

'So kiddies, you're mine for the next hundred days,' Large said. 'Every day will be equally joyous. There are no holidays. No weekends. You will rise at 0545. Cold shower, get dressed, run the assault course. 0700 breakfast, followed by physical training until school starts at 0900. Lessons include Espionage, Language, Weaponry and Survival Skills. At 1400 you run the assault course again. Lunch at 1500. At 1600 two more hours of physical training. At 1800 you return here.'

James' foot touched the floor. Large smashed the baton into the bucket. The noise inside was incredible.

'Keep that foot up. Where was I? At 1800 you return here. Another shower, warm water if I'm feeling kind. Wash your clothes in the sinks and hang them up so they're dry for morning. Then clean and polish your boots. At 1900 you get your evening meal. 1930 to 2030 homework. Brush your teeth, lights out at 2045. There will also be trips off campus for survival training, the last of which will take us to sunny Malaysia.

'If anyone is accusing me of cruelty, I remind you that the fences that surround us are not to keep you in, but to keep your little chums from slipping in and giving you a helping hand or a tasty snack. You are free to leave the training facility at any time, but if you wish to be a CHERUB agent you will have to resume basic training from day one. If you get an injury that stops you training for more than three days, you start again from day one. James, put your foot down and take off the bucket.'

James lifted the bucket off his head. It took his eyes a few seconds to readjust to the light.

'You were very late this morning, James, weren't you,' Large said.

'Yes sir,' James said.

'Well everyone, because James is still so full after his lie-in and his cooked breakfast, I think you can all skip lunch. Not to worry though. It's only eleven and a half hours until dinner.'

*

The eight kids in training were split into pairs. The first pair, numbers one and two, was Shakeel and Mo. Shakeel was as big as James but only ten years old. Born in Egypt, he'd been at CHERUB for three years and in that time he'd learned a lot that would help in basic training. James realised he was going to be at a big disadvantage to trainees who had spent years in a red shirt.

Mo was another veteran, three days past his tenth birthday. A policeman had found him abandoned at Heathrow Airport when he was four. Mo's parents were never found. Mo always jiggled his bony arms like he was trying to swat flies off himself.

Three and four were Connor and Callum, the twins James had met on the running track a few days earlier. James had had a few conversations with them and they seemed OK.

Five and six were Gabrielle and Nicole. Gabrielle was from the Caribbean; her parents had died a few months earlier in a car wreck. Eleven years old, she looked tough as boots. Nicole was smaller. Twelve, red-haired and overweight.

Number eight, James' partner, was Kerry. She was eleven

years old, small and boyish with a flat face and dark eyes. Her black hair was shaved down to a number one. James had seen her in a red shirt with shoulder length hair a few days earlier. Now she looked totally different. She didn't look as nervous as the others.

*

Large led them out to the assault course at a jog.

'Do exactly what I do,' Kerry said as their feet squished in the mud.

'Who made you boss?' James asked.

'I've been at CHERUB since I was six,' Kerry said. 'I did sixty-four days of this course last year before I broke my kneecap and got chucked off. You've been here what? Two weeks?'

'About three,' James said. 'Why did you cut off your hair?'

'Quicker to wash, quicker to dry, doesn't get in your face all day. If you do things quickly and get a few minutes' extra rest, it makes a difference. I'll do everything I can to make life easy for you, James, if you do one thing for me.'

'What?' James asked.

'Protect my knee,' Kerry said. 'There are titanium pins holding the bits together. When we do karate, please don't kick me on that part of my leg. If we have to run with heavy packs, take some of my weight for me. Will you help me, James, if I help you?'

'Whatever I can do,' James said. 'We're partners anyway. How come they're letting you take this course if your knee isn't better?'

'I lied. I said the pain was gone. All the kids I grew up

with are living in the main building and going on missions. I spend my evenings watching six-year-olds cut up sticky paper. I'm getting through basic this time or I'll die trying.'

*

Kerry knew all the cheats on the assault course. One side of the muddy tunnel was drier than the other. There was a knack to how you caught the rope to swing across the lake. She pointed out one of the hidden video cameras. The instructors dragged you out of bed at 3 a.m. and made you re-run the whole course if they caught you cheating on videotape. Best of all, Kerry knew there was a raised bar under the water, which cut ten metres out of the swim across the lake.

'You swim like a five-year-old,' Kerry said.

After fifty minutes, James was muddy and freezing cold, but they'd finished tons ahead of anyone else. Kerry found a standpipe, turned on the water and pulled off her T-shirt. She started washing out the mud.

'James, always wash out your T-shirt. Use it to wipe yourself off, then wash it again. It will be freezing when you put it back on, but we do the assault course first thing every morning and have to wear the same clothes for the rest of the day. If you leave the mud on it dries out and itches like crazy.'

'What about the trousers?' James asked.

'Won't get time to wash them. But first chance you get, pull off your boots and wring the water out of your socks. You hungry?' Kerry asked.

'I never had breakfast despite what Large said. I'll be starving by this evening.'

Kerry unzipped a pocket on her trousers and pulled out a king-size Mars bar.

'Cool,' James said. 'I'm sorry it's my fault we're not getting any food till this evening.'

Kerry laughed. 'It's not you, James. There's always some excuse why you don't get lunch. Or why everyone has to do an extra run of the assault course. Or why everyone has to drag their beds outside and sleep in the open air with no covers on. They try and find ways to make you hate everyone else. Don't let it get to you, everyone will get their turn.'

Kerry bent the Mars bar in half.

'You want this, James? Make the promise first,' Kerry said.

'I promise I'll help protect your knee,' James said.

'Open wide.'

Kerry crammed half a Mars bar into James' mouth.

Shakeel and Mo were heading across the last obstacle, with Callum and Connor a few metres behind. James could hear Large shouting at Nicole in the distance:

'Move that bum before I stick my boot up it.'

James felt a bit sorry for her; but on the other hand, as long as they were shouting at Nicole, they weren't shouting at him.

*

Everyone had to do physical training in the mud. Crunches, squats, push-ups, star jumps. After an hour James was numb all over from cold and muscle pain. His uniform was a heavy sheet of mud.

Nicole was on the ground, too tired to move. Miss Smoke put her boot on Nicole's head, dunking her face in the mud.

'Get up, tubby,' Smoke screamed.

Nicole got up and stormed towards the gate.

'You can't come back,' Smoke shouted. 'One step outside and that's it.'

Nicole didn't care. She went out the gate. Fifteen minutes later she was back. Bawling her eyes out and begging for another chance.

'Come back in three months, sweetheart,' Large shouted. 'Get rid of that wobbly arse or you'll never make it.'

*

It was a bit of a sensation being down to seven kids on day one. All the trainees talked about it. Nicole seemed soft giving up so early. On the other hand they were all envious, imagining her back in her room watching TV after soaking in the bath.

James had warmed up as much as he could in the shower and now sat at the table with the other six trainees, waiting for dinner. Having Kerry for a partner was great. Especially watching the other kids make all the mistakes Kerry warned him about.

The dinners got wheeled up from the main building in a heated trolley. Smoke handed out the dishes. James ripped off the metal lid. The stir fry rice was a bit dry from being kept warm, but it tasted OK and everyone was starving. Kerry got her plate last. James could tell something was wrong from the noise when it hit the table.

Kerry lifted up the lid. She had no food, just an empty Mars bar wrapper in the middle of her plate. She looked gutted. Large rested his massive hands on Kerry's shoulders.

'Kerry poppet,' Large said, 'you're not the first kid to come back here. You may think you know all the tricks, but so do we.'

Large walked away. Kerry stared at her empty plate. James couldn't let her starve after all the help she'd given him. He made a line down the middle of his plate and gave half to Kerry.

'Thanks, partner,' Kerry said.

19. MERRY

Imagine you are on an early level of a video game. It seems hard. Everything happens too fast, but you eventually make it through. You progress through the game to much higher levels. One day you try the early level again. What was once fast and difficult now appears easy.

This is the principle behind basic training. You will be asked to perform difficult tasks while under physical and mental strain. You will achieve things far beyond what you dreamed possible. When basic training is over, your mind and body will be able to perform at a higher level.

(From the introductory page of the CHERUB Basic Training Manual)

Callum dropped out on day twenty-six. He fractured a wrist on the assault course. The course wasn't that hard, but it was easy to have an accident when you'd already done three hours' physical training and hadn't slept the night before because Large blasted everyone in their beds with a fire hose.

Connor got partnered up with Gabrielle, but he'd never spent more than a few hours without his identical twin before. He was thinking about giving up and restarting with his brother in a few months' time.

The physical training was the hardest thing James had ever done. The first time he threw up from exhaustion he froze in shock. Kerry told him to keep running but James didn't listen. Speaks shoved James in the back, then crushed James' hand under his boot.

'If you stop training, you'd better be dead or unconscious,' Speaks shouted.

That was the closest James had come to quitting.

James was getting used to life in hell. He counted twelve scabs and twenty-six bruises on his body. That didn't include places he couldn't see. He showered twice a day, but he never had time to scrub the filth from difficult spots like nails or ears. His hair felt like straw, and grit sprayed out if he ran his hand through it, even if he'd just washed. If he got a chance for a haircut he was having the lot chopped off.

The worst part about training wasn't exhaustion, it was always being cold. James slept under a wafer-thin blanket in an unheated room. In the morning the floor was like ice on your soles. The instructors forced everyone under a freezing shower. Breakfast was always cereal and cold juice. Clothes never dried, they were damp and stiff as soon as you put them on. Not that it mattered for long. After five minutes on the assault course you were drenched in icy water and mud that crept down your trousers and kept you soggy for the rest of the day.

The trainees only felt tiny hints of warmth and each was bliss. Hot drinks at lunchtime, the warm evening shower and meal. If you were lucky you got an injury serious enough for a visit to the medical centre but not so bad you were thrown off the course. Then you got to wait for the nurse in a room kept at 22°C with a coffee machine and chocolate digestives, which you could dunk in your coffee and eat soggy and warm. Shakeel and Connor got these golden injuries; James could only dream.

The five hours of lessons sandwiched between physical training were the easiest part of the day. Weaponry was coolest. Shooting was only part of it. James now knew how to strip and clean a gun, how to defuse a bullet so it doesn't go off, how to put a gun back together wrong so it jams. Even how to take a bullet apart so that it explodes inside the chamber and blows away the finger on the trigger. They were starting knives in the next lesson.

Espionage was all about gadgets. Electronic listening devices, computer hacking, lock picking, cameras, photocopiers. Nothing as fancy as you see in the movies. Mrs Flagg, the ex-KGB espionage teacher, always stood in the unheated classroom wearing fur-lined boots, a fur coat, hat and scarf while the trainees shivered in damp T-shirts. Occasionally she would bang her gloved hands together and moan about the cold not doing her varicose veins any good.

The best espionage lessons were about explosives. They were taught by Mr Large. He dropped his usual psycho persona and took childlike pleasure in showing off the finer details of dynamite sticks and plastic explosive putty. He blew stuff up at every opportunity, even sticking a directional charge on James' head. The charge leapt up and blew a golf ball sized hole in the ceiling.

'Of course, little James would have been killed if I had

placed the charge upside down. Or if the charge had misfired.'

James hoped he was joking, but judging by the size of the hole in the ceiling, he wasn't.

Survival Skills was taught by the three instructors and took place outdoors. It was interesting, building shelters, learning what parts of animals and plants were safe to eat. The best lessons were on fire-building and cooking because you got a chance to get warm and eat extra food, even if it was squirrel or pigeon.

There were two lessons James hated. The first was Language. Kids like Kerry who had been at CHERUB for a few years already had good language skills. Kerry was fluent in Spanish and decent at French and Arabic. For basic training everyone started a new language from scratch and had to master a thousand word vocabulary by the end of the course. CHERUB picked a language from a country that matched your ethnicity. Mo and Shakeel got Arabic, Kerry got Japanese, Gabrielle got Swahili, James and Connor got Russian. The languages were extra hard because none of them use a Latin alphabet, so you had to learn to read and pronounce weird-looking letters before you could try saying the words.

For two hours each day James and Connor sat next to each other while the Russian teacher barked orders and insults. He smacked pens out of their hands, whacked them with his wooden ruler and showered them in spit as he spoke. By the end of a lesson Mr Grwgoski left the two boys with sore hands and blurred minds. James wasn't sure he was learning anything except that learning Russian made his head hurt. On his exit, Grwgoski often shouted to one of the instructors that James and Connor were bad pupils and deserved to be punished. This usually cost the pair an hour of precious sleep while they were made to stand in the cold wearing shorts. If Large was bored he might give them a good blast with the fire hose too.

The other lesson James hated was Karate.

*

'Day twenty-nine,' Large said.

Large had a green baseball cap on his head. His two sidekicks weren't beside him, for the first time ever. It was 0550. The six remaining trainees stood rigid at the foot of their beds.

'Can anybody tell me what is special about day twenty-nine?'

They all knew the answer. They wondered if it was the answer Large wanted. Your answer to Large's questions could have nasty consequences. Best to cross your fingers and hope somebody else took the bullet.

'Number seven, can you tell me why today is special?'

James cursed his luck.

'It's Christmas Day,' he said.

'That's right, my little pumpkins. Christmas Day. Two thousand and three years since the birth of our Lord, Jesus Christ. What should we do to celebrate, James?'

This was the trickiest kind of question because it didn't have an obvious answer.

'Get the day off,' James said optimistically.

'Well that would be nice,' Large said. 'Miss Smoke and Mr Speaks have the day off. All your teachers have the day off. It's just you six little muffins and my good self. I think we'll have a little celebration of Christmas. Then we'll devote the rest of the day to karate and physical training without any of those pesky lessons that usually get in the way.'

Large pushed a button on his baseball cap. Red lights illuminated in the shape of a Christmas tree and it played a tinny rendition of Jingle Bells.

'That was so beautiful it brought a tear to my eye,' Large said, throwing away the cap. 'Now that celebrations are behind us, shall we get on with the training?'

*

The trainees didn't get to use the springy floors of the dojo. They learned Karate in the fields surrounding the training building, freezing mud smothering bare feet. All the lessons were the same. You learned a move or two, then drilled until it was perfect. Then you drilled on other moves you'd learned before. Each lesson ended with full contact sparring.

James liked the idea he was learning Karate. He'd always wanted to do it but had been too lazy to stick at it. He was doing five lessons a week now which meant he was learning fast, but he couldn't stand being partners with Kerry. She was already a black belt. While James was falling over and getting out of breath, Kerry did every move effortlessly. She helped James and saved him from getting punished by the instructors at least once every lesson, but James hated the smug look on her face when she pointed out his mistakes and she always killed him in the sparring at the end.

You were supposed to anticipate attacks and dodge or block most of them. But Kerry was fast and knew moves James hadn't even tried. He always ended up on the ground in pain, while Kerry hardly took a hit. James was too proud to admit he was getting hurt. Kerry was smaller, younger and a girl. How could he whimper that she was beating him up?

*

Without the usual lessons, Christmas morning turned into six hours of merciless physical training. The trainees could barely walk. Large didn't let them have breakfast. James' vision was blurry from the water running into his eyes, but his hands were so numb from the cold he couldn't do anything to wipe it away. On top of all his usual aches and pains, Kerry gave him a painful kick in the side during sparring.

At 1300 Large walked the six trainees out of the training compound. They buzzed with excitement. They hadn't been out since day one. Maybe they were getting a Christmas treat. But they'd all played enough of Large's mind games not to get their hopes up.

Large told the trainees to stop walking when they were close enough to see through the windows of the dining hall in the main building. The room had a four-metre tree in the centre, decorated with thousands of twinkling lights. The tables had been put together to make four long bars, covered with gold tablecloths. Each place was set with fancy cutlery and crackers. All James could think about was how warm it must be.

'If you quit right now,' Large said, 'you could run up to your room, have a shower and be down in time for Christmas dinner.'

James knew Connor was thinking about quitting and was sure this would push him over the edge. Large made them run on the spot and do squats and star jumps. Inside kids were taking up places at the dinner table. Some waved to the trainees outside. James looked for Kyle, Bruce and Amy, but couldn't see any of them.

'You might as well all give up now,' Large shouted. 'None of you will make it. Go inside. Have a nice dinner. Chat to all your friends. You know you want to ... No? Are you sure, cupcakes? How about thinking the idea over while you do twenty push-ups?'

When they stood up after the push-ups Callum and Bruce were by the windows inside. Callum had a cast over his hand. He opened a window.

'Don't give up, Connor,' Callum shouted. 'The next time I see you, you'd better be wearing a grey T-shirt.'

Connor nodded to his brother, 'I'll do what I can. Happy Christmas.' Bruce shoved Callum away from the window.

'Don't worry about Mr Large,' Bruce shouted. 'He's just a sad old creep who likes pushing little kids around.'

James smiled a bit, but not enough that Large might see it. Large ran up to the window.

'Shut that window, now,' Large shouted.

'OK, saddo,' Bruce said.

Bruce shut the window. When Large turned around his face was burning. 'Right, all of you, run back to the assault course.'

*

Kerry and James led on the assault course. They still managed it a bit faster than the others. Large had gone. Kerry and James reckoned he was sitting in his heated office stuffing

Christmas lunch while watching their suffering on a TV screen.

Near the end of the assault course was a two-hundred-metre stretch where you ran over jagged rocks. As long as you didn't trip it was nothing, but when you were exhausted you made mistakes. Kerry lost her footing. James saw her hand on the rock in front of him and thought about all the times she'd hurt him in Karate class. He felt a surge of anger and crunched his boot over her hand. Kerry screamed out.

'What did you do that for, arse-wipe?'

'It was an accident,' James said.

'I saw you look at my hand. You practically had to turn round to step on it.'

'You're nuts, Kerry.'

Kerry shoved James backwards.

'We're supposed to be a team, James. Why did you hurt me?'

'You always hurt *me* in Karate class,' James screamed back.

'You only get hurt because you suck.'

'You could go easy on me, Kerry. You don't have to batter me every single time.'

'I *do* go easy on you.'

James lifted up his T-shirt to show Kerry a massive bruise across his ribs.

'You call that going easy?'

Kerry launched a kick at James. She always hit him in the ribs, but this was a few centimetres lower, slamming his kidneys. James doubled up in the most unbelievable pain.

'*That's* how I can kick you if I want to,' Kerry shouted. 'If

I go too easy the instructors will know I'm not trying and punish both of us.'

James could see Kerry was right. He'd been a total idiot, but he was past logic. James lunged at Kerry. She stumbled back on the rocks. James started throwing crazy punches. Kerry got him back with a powerful fist on the nose. James felt himself being pulled up.

'Break it up,' Gabrielle shouted.

Connor and Gabrielle struggled to pull James off Kerry.

'Care to tell me what's going on here?' Large said, running towards the scene.

Nobody knew what to say.

'Connor, Gabrielle, scram. Kerry, show me your hand.'

Large looked at the cut.

'Go to the medical centre.'

Large crouched in front of James and looked at his nose.

'You'd better go with her. When you get back you're *both* in a lot of trouble.'

*

James sat in the warm room waiting for the nurse. Hot coffee wrapped in his hand, downing one mushy chocolate digestive after another. Kerry sat opposite doing the same. They wouldn't even look at each other.

20. COLD

'Welcome back, my two little bunny rabbits,' Large said. 'Nice warm afternoon, was it? Lovely choccy biscuits? Nursey made you all better? Well I have another special treat for you two love birds. Take off your boots and everything but your underwear, then go outside and, in the unlikely event you make it through the night, I'll let you come back in the morning. Remember, it's nice and warm in the main building if you want to quit.'

James and Kerry stripped off and stepped into the dark.

'Merry Christmas,' Large shouted after them.

The door shut, closing off the last tiny arc of light. The wind was bitter. Frost burned their feet. Kerry was only a few metres from James, but he could barely see her. James heard her sob.

'I'm sorry, Kerry,' James said. 'This is all my fault.'

Kerry didn't answer.

'Please talk to me, Kerry. I know I was stupid. Seeing everyone sitting in the warm and it being Christmas made me crazy. You know?'

Kerry started crying quite noisily. James touched her shoulder. She backed off.

'Don't touch me, James.'

This was the first thing Kerry had said to James since the fight.

'We can get through this together,' James said. 'I'm so sorry. You want me to beg? I'll go down on the ground and kiss your feet if you just start talking to me.'

'James,' Kerry sobbed, 'we're done for. You can say you're sorry a thousand times, but you've still got us both thrown out.'

'We can get through this, Kerry. Find somewhere warm and go to sleep.'

Kerry laughed a little.

'Find somewhere warm! James, there is *nowhere* warm. There's a big muddy field and an assault course. Nothing else. It's already close to freezing. An hour out here and we'll start getting frostbite in our toes and fingers. It's fourteen hours until morning. If we fall asleep we'll die of cold.'

'You don't deserve this, Kerry. I'll bang on the door and ask to speak to Large. I'll say it's all my fault and that I'll quit if he lets you back inside.'

'He won't bargain with you, James. He'll laugh in your face.'

'We could start a fire,' James said.

'It's raining. It's pitch dark. We'd need something dry to start the fire and somewhere out of the wind to start it. Any suggestions?'

'The bridge over the lake on the assault course,' James said. 'There's a gap under there before the water starts. We could put branches and stuff along the sides to keep out the wind.'

'I suppose,' Kerry said. 'We've got to try. There might be stuff in the rubbish.'

'What?'

'There are two rubbish bins at the back of the building,' Kerry said. 'We could go through them. There might be stuff inside we could use.'

Kerry led James to the back of the training building. They each pulled the lid off a bin. Both were full of rubbish tied up in bags.

'Reeks,' James said.

'I don't care *what* it smells like,' Kerry said. 'Here's what I'm thinking. We take the bins with all the stuff in to the bridge. Then we go through all the bags. Hopefully there's something to start a fire with. The bags will help us keep warm if we wear them.'

It was hard finding the bridge in the moonlight. It was too dark to make out any more than the outline of the ground. There was a risk of hitting something sharp with every step. James and Kerry took a bin each. They weighed a ton. James tried rolling his instead of carrying it, but the bin kept jamming in the mud. Kerry was having an even tougher time because her hand was bandaged. They walked the path at the side of the assault course. James' feet were numb already. He thought about the gruesome photos of black frostbitten toes in the training manual and shuddered.

The wooden bridge spanned twenty metres over the river in the middle of the assault course, and was about two metres wide. When they reached it, Kerry started untying and rummaging around inside the stinking rubbish bags. James clambered into the low space under the bridge.

'It's pretty dry under here,' James said. 'It's concrete, no mud.'

'OK,' Kerry said. 'I'm trying to get stuff to start a fire.'

James ran back and forth, stripping off branches and wedging them against the side of the bridge. Kerry dunked her hand in a bag and hit a mix of food slops and muddy rags used for boot cleaning. She sniffed her hand and couldn't believe she was touching all this nasty stuff. She threw anything that was dry and would burn into an empty bin.

Kerry tore the bags up, covered her feet in the boot-cleaning rags and then wrapped them with plastic. She tore holes in bin bags to make a plastic smock and skirt for herself and James. They looked like muddy scarecrows, but the important thing was it kept out the cold. James finished turning the bridge into a shelter and they clambered under, rubbing their hands together.

'Here,' Kerry said.

She handed James two small boxes. It was too dark to see what they were. James felt the familiar shape of a straw on the side of a carton.

'Breakfast,' James said. 'This was in the rubbish?'

'God must be on our side,' Kerry said. 'Six cartons of orange juice, six mini packets of cereal, all unopened. Large must have thrown them out this morning when he didn't give us breakfast.'

James punched the straw into the orange juice carton and sucked the contents in two long gulps. Then he ripped open the cereal and scoffed dry flakes.

'We've got clothes, food and shelter,' James said. 'We should last until morning.'

'Maybe,' Kerry said. 'I'd be happier if I could get the fire going.'

'There's tons of stuff there that will burn,' James said.

'But the only way I know to start a fire is with two dry pieces of timber. We've got zero.'

They sat there for a few minutes, huddled close, jiggling arms and legs to keep warm.

'I think I know a way to start a fire,' James said. 'You know the security cameras all over the assault course?'

'What about them?' Kerry asked.

'They must be powered by electricity.'

'So what?'

'So if we find one and pull the power cord out the back then we can use it to make a spark.'

'It's pitch dark,' Kerry said.

'I know roughly where a few of the cameras are.'

'James, you're talking about messing with electricity. You could end up getting killed.'

James stood up.

'Where are you going?'

'Have faith, Kerry. I'm going to start a fire.'

'You're a total idiot, James. You'll get zapped.'

James clambered out of the shelter. The foot coverings Kerry made kept his feet warm but slid everywhere. He found the bin Kerry had filled with flammable stuff. He tucked bits of tissue and cardboard inside his plastic suit, then grabbed a dustbin lid and started his search. James found a camera only a few metres from the shelter. The tiny red lamp below the lens made it easier to spot the cameras in the dark than in daylight.

James felt behind the camera and tugged the wires out of the back. One looked like the picture output, so he threw it away. The other wire had a two-pronged rubber plug on the end. James figured this was the power supply. He twisted the plug until it snapped off, leaving two bare wires at the end of the lead.

It had seemed a good idea in theory. But now he was on the spot, with his little store of fuel standing on the dustbin lid, water all around and a live electric cable in his hand, James' confidence plummeted.

He crouched over the bin lid. He split the cable, pulling the two bare ends of wire further apart, then lined them up over a piece of tissue. He slowly moved the two ends closer together. A blue spark lit up James' face. The corner of the tissue ignited. A couple of embers flew off and the fire snuffed out. James' heart stopped. He doubted he'd get another chance because the spark had probably fused the circuit. Then a second burst of flame rose from the centre of the tissue. James dipped a scrap of cardboard in the flame. The fire caught hold.

He had to move back to the bridge before the fuel burned out. His feet slid everywhere and the wind was doing its best to kill the flames.

'Kerry,' James shouted. 'Get some of the fuel.'

Kerry dashed out and put more bits of card on the fire. The metal lid was getting hot in James' hands and the last part of the journey was trickiest, down the muddy river bank and into the shelter. Kerry helped keep the lid steady. James pushed the lid into the shelter, careful not to set light to the branches lining the sides. Kerry got the rest of the fuel and they cuddled up to each other as the shelter filled with flickering orange light. The smoke made their eyes sting, but all they cared about was being warm. Kerry rested her head on James' arm.

'I still can't believe you stomped my hand,' Kerry said, looking at her bandage. 'I thought we were a good team.'

'I know sorry doesn't make it all better, but I really am. If there's anything I can do to make it up, I will. Just name it.'

'You know what,' Kerry said. 'I'll forgive you now. But after training finishes I'll fight you in the dojo. I'll beat you until you scream for mercy. Then I'll beat you some more.'

'Deal,' James said, hoping she was joking. 'It's what I deserve for getting us into this mess.'

*

Mr Speaks stuck his head inside the shelter. It was starting to get light. The fire was burned out. James and Kerry were asleep with their arms around each other.

'Wake up,' Speaks said.

James and Kerry rustled to life in their plastic suits. Kerry had said it was best not to go to sleep; better to stay alert and not get frostbite. But the shelter was warm and they'd both drifted off.

'I love you two with all my heart,' Speaks said.

Speaks reached into his trouser pocket and pulled out a couple of bars of Fruit and Nut. James couldn't understand why Speaks was being nice to them.

'I am so impressed with the way you two got through this. Mr Large was convinced you would quit. He couldn't find you. All the video cameras have stopped working for some reason.'

'What time is it?' Kerry asked, cheeks stuffed with chocolate.

'Six-thirty. You two better run back to the main building and get dressed. Mr Large is going to be furious when he sees you.'

'Doesn't he like us?' James asked. 'I mean, I know he hates everyone, but why is he so keen to get rid of us?'

'You don't understand,' Speaks said. 'We had a bet. Fifty pounds that Mr Large could make a trainee quit on Christmas Day. He thought making Connor watch his brother eat Christmas dinner would work, but Callum told him to stick it out. Then you two started fighting, which gave him the excuse to punish you. He was sure he'd broken you. I can't wait to see the look on his face.'

'After this he's gonna make our lives even more miserable,' Kerry sighed.

21. AIR

The six trainees and three instructors were heading to Malaysia for the final days of basic training. James' only previous flight was an eight-hour holiday trip to Orlando, crammed with hundreds of wriggling kids and bawling parents. This time it was business class.

James' toes couldn't reach the seat in front. The puffy leather chairs had pull-up screens for Nintendo and movies and a button that tipped the seat back so it was like a bed. Before take-off the stewardess came round serving sandwiches and fruit juice. It would have been good any time. After thirteen hard weeks, he was in heaven.

The jumbo finished its climb out of Heathrow and the seatbelt sign beeped out. James slouched with his headphones on, flipping through the different music channels until he came across Elton John's song 'Rocket Man'. His mum had loved Elton. James felt guilty that he'd hardly thought about her since he got to CHERUB.

Kerry's sock flew over the screen between the seats and landed in James' lap. He sat up as Kerry lowered the screen and yanked off his headphones.

'What was that for?' James asked.

'You wanted to know how long the flight was. Turn your TV to channel fifty.'

James flicked his remote. The screen changed to a blue map with London on the left and Kuala Lumpur on the right. Every few seconds the screen switched to a bank of figures, which included distance travelled, air speed, external temperature and time to destination.

'Thirteen hours eight minutes,' James said. 'Cool. I think I could sleep about that long.'

Kerry looked disappointed.

'Don't you want to play Mario Kart?' she asked.

'A couple of games, I guess. I'll sleep after they serve dinner.'

*

The sign over the automatic door of the airport terminal said, *Enjoy Your Stay In Malaysia*. The doors split apart. James slung his backpack over his shoulder and took his first outdoor breath. The screen on the plane said it was 40°C when they landed. James knew that was hot, but the baking air was beyond anything he'd imagined.

'Imagine running in this heat,' Kerry said.

Connor and Gabrielle walked behind.

'I bet we won't need to imagine for long,' Gabrielle said.

Large, wearing shorts and a Hawaiian shirt, wound the group through lanes of jammed traffic to a shuttle van. Speaks peeled notes out of a bundle of currency and handed them to the driver while everyone else climbed in with their luggage.

They pulled into the flow and drove for half an hour

along wide empty roads, heading against the evening rush hour. The trainees watched out of the windows. It could have been a modern city anywhere. Only the wide storm drains and the odd palm tree amongst the concrete told them they were in the tropics.

*

The other trainees had been James' only human contact for three months. They hadn't spoken much. If you got a spare half hour you didn't waste it talking, you used it to sleep. The few conversations they'd had were mostly bitching about training over the dinner table.

The instructors punished everyone for an individual mistake, so the trainees developed a sixth sense for covering each other's weaknesses. James knew before a long swim that Kerry and Shakeel would stick close and grab him if he lost his nerve. Everyone took Kerry's stuff when her knee was painful. Mo was weedy and needed help climbing and lifting. They all needed each other for something.

James wasn't worried about the four-day tropical survival course. He knew it would be tough, but everything had been tough since day one. Training had succeeded: exhaustion and danger didn't scare James any more. He'd been pushed to the limit so often it felt routine. It was something you didn't enjoy but always got through, like a trip to the dentist or a science lesson.

*

The hotel was plush. James and Kerry shared a room with two queen beds and a balcony that overlooked the pool. It was nine at night, but they'd all slept on the plane and felt lively. The instructors were going to the hotel bar and didn't want to be bothered. The trainees were given the run of the hotel and told to order whatever they wanted from room service, but not to stay up late because there was an early start in the morning.

The six kids met by the outdoor pool, the first chance they'd had to relax as a group. It was dark now. There was a breeze but the temperature was still in the thirties. Millions of insects chirped and smacked into the mosquito nets that wrapped the pool area. An attendant in a bow tie handed out robes and cotton slippers.

It was the first time in weeks that James had felt well-fed and relaxed. He also felt awkward. All the others were dive-bombing the pool and swimming confidently. James was ashamed that all he could manage was a clumsy front crawl and sat with his ankles in the water sucking Coke through a straw.

'Come on, James,' Kerry shouted. 'Chill out.'

'I think I'll go back to the room,' James said.

'Misery,' Kerry said.

James walked up to his room. He took a leak, then caught himself in a mirror for the first time since training started. It was weird seeing his own body but not quite recognising it. The belly that rolled over the elastic of his shorts was gone. His chest muscles and biceps were bigger and he thought the razor cut hair and all the scabs and bruises made him look hard. James couldn't help smiling. He was totally in love with himself.

He lay on his bed and watched TV. Only a few channels were in English. He found BBC World and realised half the planet could have been rubbed out in a war for all he knew.

He hadn't seen a newspaper or TV for the three months he'd been isolated in the training compound. It didn't look like much had changed. People still killed each other for no good reason, politicians wore dull suits and gave five-minute answers that had nothing to do with the question. At least they showed Arsenal winning in the sports round-up. After the sports, James flipped through channels and wished he'd stayed downstairs with the others.

Suddenly, the door of the hotel room opened and the light went out.

'Shut your eyes,' Kerry shouted.

'Why?' James asked.

'We've got a surprise.'

James could hear the other trainees outside in the corridor.

'No way, what are you gonna do?'

'If you don't shut your eyes you'll never know.'

It was unlikely to be anything good if they were asking him to shut his eyes, but James didn't want to seem boring.

'OK, they're shut.'

James heard them all file in. Kerry emptied an ice bucket over his chest. The cubes slid inside his robe and down his back. Connor, Mo, Gabrielle and Shakeel followed with more ice buckets. James jumped off his bed and trod on an ice cube.

'Scumbags,' James yelped, shaking the cubes out of his robe and laughing.

The others were cracking up. Kerry put the light back on.

'Thought we'd all order room service in here,' Kerry said. 'If you're not still sulking.'

'Whatever, cool,' James said.

They sat on the balcony talking about training and picking bits of each other's food. Afterwards the four boys decided to impress the girls by standing in line and pissing on to the plants two floors down. Kerry and Gabrielle slipped inside and locked the French windows.

'Let us in,' Connor shouted.

'Tell us how beautiful we are,' Kerry said.

'Ugly pigs,' Shakeel shouted. 'Let us in.'

'Sounds like you're staying out there for a long time,' Kerry said.

James looked down. They were too high to jump. He walked to the glass and spoke.

'I think you're both beautiful.'

'Arse kisser,' Connor said.

James looked at Connor. 'You want to stay out here all night?'

'Very beautiful,' Connor agreed.

'Supermodels,' Mo added.

The girls looked at Shakeel.

'Well?'

Shakeel shrugged, 'You're two radiant beams of golden sunshine. Come on, let us in.'

'Shall we?' Kerry asked Gabrielle, enjoying her sense of power.

Gabrielle put a finger on her mouth and acted puzzled.

'If they kiss the glass to show how much they love us,' she decided.

Kerry laughed. 'You heard her, boys. Nice big smooch on the glass.'

The four boys looked at each other.

'Oh, for god's sake,' Connor muttered.

Connor kissed the glass first. The other three did the same.

Someone knocked at the door. Kerry answered. It was Large and Smoke. Gabrielle unlocked the French doors. The boys rushed inside, hoping they hadn't been spotted peeing on the plants.

Large sounded drunk. 'It's gone eleven. I want you all in bed in five minutes.'

The others filed out. James and Kerry got into bed.

22. BEACH

A military helicopter picked them up from the hotel roof before dawn. The trainees sat on their packs in the dusty cargo area behind the pilots. Their tropical uniform had lightweight trousers, long-sleeved blue tops without numbers or CHERUB logos, and hats with pull-down flaps to protect their necks and ears from the sun.

Large crawled around fitting each trainee with an electronic wristband. The plastic strap locked on so it could only be cut off with a knife.

'Don't remove the bracelet under any circumstances,' Large shouted over the noise of the rotor. 'In an emergency, unscrew the button on the side and press it down firmly. The helicopter is on standby and will reach you within fifteen minutes. If you get bitten by a snake press it right away.

'We'll be at the first drop point soon. Everything you could possibly need is in the backpacks. It's now 1000 hours. Each team has four checkpoints to reach within the next seventy-two hours. If you don't reach all the checkpoints before the target time, you have failed training and you'll have to start again at day one. Remember, this is not a training area. Mistakes down there will not get you punished, but they might get you killed. There are about a thousand things in the jungle that will kill you or make you so sick you'll wish you were dead.'

The helicopter stopped moving about ten metres off the ground. The side door slid open, filling the cargo area with sunlight.

'One and two, get out there,' Large shouted.

Mo and Shakeel dangled their feet over the side of the helicopter. Large threw out their backpacks. James saw the boys disappear, but couldn't see if they'd landed OK because of the dust blown up by the rotor. Large gave the pilot a thumbs-up and the helicopter moved on to the next drop. Kerry looked unhappy. Jumps put a strain on her weak knee. Gabrielle and Connor dropped, then they moved to the final position.

James looked down. There was wet sand covered with a few centimetres of seawater beneath him. He watched his pack splash down, summoned his courage and slid off the platform. They'd been trained how to jump safely. The trick was to collapse on to your side so the impact was absorbed by the whole body. If you landed too straight you risked smashing your hips or ankles. Too flat and your whole body smacked down hard, often breaking an arm or shoulder. James got the landing spot on. He scrambled up, splattered in wet sand but unhurt.

Kerry screamed as she hit the ground. James rushed over.

'You OK?' he asked.

Kerry got up slowly and took a few nervous steps on her weak knee.

'No worse than usual,' she said.

The helicopter flew off. James shielded his eyes from the swirls of sand. They dragged their backpacks out of the wash and up the beach. The sun made the white sand dazzle.

'Let's get into the shade,' James said.

They settled under a palm. James rubbed wet sand off his hands on to his trousers. Kerry found the mission briefing in her pack.

'Oh crap,' Kerry said.

'What?'

Kerry showed James a page of her briefing. It was in Japanese. James quickly found his own copy. His heart sank.

'Great, all in Russian,' James said. 'If I'd known my life would depend on it I probably would have paid more attention in class.'

They realised the two briefings were identical. James could understand half the Russian, Kerry was a bit better with the Japanese. By comparing the two versions and making a few assumptions they worked out almost everything.

There were a couple of sketchy maps, marked with the position of the first checkpoint, but no indication of where they had been dropped, or where they had to go after that. They had to reach the first checkpoint by 1800 and sleep there overnight.

'I suppose there'll be another briefing when we get there,' Kerry said.

James went through his backpack. There was tons more than they could carry. What was worth taking? Some stuff was obvious: machete, compass, plastic pool for collecting rainwater, emergency rations, empty water canteen, first-aid kit and medicine, water purification tablets, sunscreen, mosquito nets, matches, Swiss army knife. A roll of plastic bin-liners weighed next to nothing and had a dozen potential uses. There was also a tent with metal poles.

'Leave it,' Kerry said. 'It weighs a ton and we can make a shelter out of palms.'

They threw out a lot of heavy items: spare boots, umbrellas, cutlery, thick jackets. Some items were bizarre. They couldn't think of any use for a rugby ball or a table tennis bat. The paperback edition of *The Complete Works of Shakespeare* might have helped start a fire, but they decided it was too bulky. The packs were manageable once they were stripped out. James kicked through the stuff in the sand, hoping they hadn't left anything that would turn out useful.

'What now?' James asked.

Kerry held out the map and pointed to a mountain in the distance.

'The checkpoint is on the bank of the river,' Kerry said. 'That mountain over there is marked on the far side of the river so we walk towards it.'

'How far?'

'Impossible to tell. There's no scale on the map. We'd better move fast though, we'll never find the checkpoint once it gets dark.'

The plan was to follow the coastline until they hit the river mouth, then walk upstream to the checkpoint. Walking inland was more direct, but there would be no way to tell which direction to turn when they reached the river.

Walking on the beach was impossible because of the bright sun and heat. Instead they stuck to the jungle a hundred metres or so inland. The trees here formed a shady canopy filled with screeching birds. The only plants beneath the canopy were a few mosses and fungi. Apart from giant tree roots and the odd detour around a fallen trunk, the terrain was level and they made a steady pace.

It was a battle keeping insects off. Kerry had a screaming fit when a ten-centimetre-long millipede tickled up her leg. Its bite swelled into a red lump. Kerry reckoned it hurt worse than a wasp sting. After that they tucked their trousers into their socks.

Once an hour James and Kerry moved on to the beach. Trees nearer the beach were smaller and more spread out. They knocked down coconuts and, once they got the knack of opening them, gorged on the sweet milk. There were fruit trees everywhere, but they only ate fruits they recognised in case any were poisonous. After drinking they would put down their packs, kick off their boots and run fully clothed into the sea.

The biggest risk in the jungle doesn't come from predators but mosquitoes. The tiny flying insects stick their proboscis under the skin to drink your blood. The bite only leaves an itchy red mark, but the microscopic malaria parasites they spread from one victim to the next can make you sick or even kill you. The kids hadn't been given malaria tablets, so all they could do was cover up their skin, try to keep dry and wear insect repellent.

Mosquitoes are attracted to the smell of sweat, so after each dip James and Kerry put on dry clothes. They wrung out the sea-drenched clothes and draped them over their backpacks, knowing the heat would dry them before the next stop. After changing they smeared on mosquito repellent and sunscreen before heading back into the shade under the dense trees.

The coconuts and fruit juice were too rich to keep drinking in large quantities. The fruit acid gave James a sickly burn in the back of his dry mouth. By early afternoon thirst was slowing them down.

Sea water is too salty to drink and all they could find in the jungle were stagnant pools, swarming with mosquitoes and probably contaminated by animal urine. There was no chance of finding a spring unless they diverted towards higher ground inland. They wouldn't get fresh water until it rained. A storm was a certainty. The tropical heat evaporated so much water that by afternoon the skies were bursting with clouds. James and Kerry watched the sky gradually darken. When the first lightning cracked they ran to the nearest stretch of beach, inflated a plastic paddling pool and waited.

The rain was like nothing they'd ever seen. The first spots were the size of ping-pong balls. James tipped his head back to drink. When the sky opened properly it was like being under Large's fire hose. The water blasted holes in the smooth sand. James wrapped one arm over his face and struggled to hold the pool as it filled up.

Kerry sheltered their packs under a tree. They stuck their faces in the pool and gulped. When the shower finished there was enough in the pool to fill both canteens. Rather than risk going thirsty again they tipped the rest into a plastic sack and took it with them.

Once they reached the river mouth the going was easier.

The river was bordered by an unmade path, chewed up with tyre tracks. Kerry counted the bends in the river to find the checkpoint. They arrived an hour inside the deadline, feet killing them after walking for nearly seven hours.

The checkpoint was marked by a flag. A three-metre-long wooden boat with an outboard motor stood at the edge of the river under a tarpaulin. James lifted back the cover and was pleased to discover junk food, cooking pots and cans of fuel inside the hull. Then something moved. At first James thought it was just a trick of the light, but it moved again and hissed. James dropped the tarp and scrambled backwards.

'Snake,' he screamed.

Kerry rushed across from the riverbank.

'What?'

'There's a bloody enormous snake in that boat.'

'Are you sure?' Kerry asked. 'The manual says snakes are very rare out here.'

'The instructors must have put it there,' James said. 'I suppose if we pull off the cover it will slide away.'

'How big did you say it was?' Kerry asked.

'Huge,' James said, making a twenty-centimetre circle with his hands.

'There's no snake in Malaysia that big,' Kerry said, puzzled.

'You're welcome to stick your head in there if you don't believe me.'

'I believe you, James. But I don't think we should let it go, I think it was put there for our dinner.'

'What? That thing could be poisonous. How are we going to kill it?'

'James, were you listening during survival training? The only snakes that size are constrictors: snakes that crush you by wrapping themselves around you. It's not poisonous, but if we let it go what's to stop it coming into our shelter and squishing us in the night?'

'OK,' James said. 'You want snake for dinner. How do you plan to kill it?'

'Pull back the cover, poke it till sticks its head out then hack it off with the machete.'

'Sounds like fun,' James said. 'This is your idea, so I'm poking it and you're doing the hacking.'

'Fine,' Kerry said. 'But if I kill it, *you're* cutting all the guts out and cooking it.'

*

There was loads to do before dark. Kerry made a clearing near the river. James built a fire and butchered the snake, throwing the remains into the river to keep scavengers away.

Kerry put the finishing touches to a shelter made with giant palms as the sky blacked out. She protected the floor with the tarpaulin and lined the inside with mosquito nets.

They ate the snake meat with coconut and instant noodles. James made wire traps baited with leftover meat and pressed them into the river bed by torchlight, hoping they would have fish in them by morning. Well-fed but exhausted, they climbed into the shelter. They tried to translate the briefing while pricking the blisters on their feet with a sterile needle.

Reaching the second checkpoint involved a twenty-five kilometre cruise upstream, navigating a complicated network of channels and tributaries, until they reached a giant lake. The checkpoint was located aboard an abandoned fishing trawler on a mud bank near the far side of the lake. They had to get there by 1400. It would be an early start.

*

The temperature hardly dropped in the night. It was boiling in the shelter, hard to sleep. The wailing birds were harmless, but served as an eerie reminder that civilisation was a long way off. They kept a small fire burning to deter animals and insects.

James was awake to see dawn. Sun burst over the river and in minutes the dry ground was too hot to touch. James checked inside his boots for nasties before slipping them on his painful feet and walking to the river to check the traps. Two of the four traps had caught fish, but one fish had been ripped apart by a predator. James grabbed his catch and held it in the air until it stopped struggling. It was enough to make breakfast for the two of them.

Kerry built up the fire and began purifying river water. She boiled it for ten minutes, then dropped in chlorine tablets. James cooked the fish and picked a heap of mangoes. He saved one each for breakfast and loaded the rest into the boat.

The fish cooked quickly. He sliced one of the mangoes in half and called Kerry. 'Breakfast's ready.'

James couldn't see Kerry either near the camp or at the riverside.

'Kerry?' he called, slightly worried.

He pulled the steaming fish off its skewer and split it on to two plastic plates. Kerry emerged from behind some trees.

'I had to crap,' Kerry said. 'All that fruit I ate yesterday cleaned me right out.'

'Thanks for the detail, Kerry. I'm just about to eat.'

'Something occurred to me,' she said.

'What?'

'Remember we left *The Complete Works of Shakespeare* on the beach?'

'Yeah.'

'I think we were supposed to use it as toilet paper.'

23. CRUISE

James and Kerry stood on either side of the outboard motor with their palms pressed against the back of the boat. It had taken a succession of almighty shoves to nudge the bow over the edge of the riverbank.

'We should have emptied everything out first,' Kerry said, wiping a gallon of sweat off her face.

'Not worth it now,' James puffed. 'I think the next one will do the trick. Ready?'

They pushed the hull past its centre of gravity. It tipped forward and began sliding. A backwash ran up the shallow embankment, the muddy water swirling over the toes of their boots.

Water surged over the bow as the boat punched the water. For a second, they both thought it was going under. When the craft stopped rocking, the rim of the hull was only a couple of centimetres above the waterline. Each swell in the river splashed a drop more water over the side. The river wasn't deep enough to put the boat beyond rescue if it sunk, but the engine and half their equipment would be wrecked, along with any chance they had of making the next checkpoint.

Kerry waded in up to her waist and grabbed a can of fuel out of the boat, being careful not to lean on the hull. James positioned himself nearer to shore, took the can off Kerry and hurled it towards dry ground.

Once they'd pulled out their sodden packs, fresh water and fuel cans, the boat sat higher in the water.

'Phew,' James gasped. 'That was too close.'

'Brilliant time-saving idea,' Kerry said furiously. 'I told you we should have taken the stuff out.'

'You didn't,' James said.

James was nearly right. Leaving the stuff in the boat was his idea, but Kerry's objection had been on the basis that they wouldn't have the strength to push it, not that the extra weight might make the boat sink when it hit the water.

James grabbed a couple of cooking pots from the shore and they bailed out all the water. When the bottom of the boat was dry, they turned to the fuel and equipment scattered along the embankment.

'I suppose it's the same as yesterday,' Kerry said. 'What do we need? What can we leave behind?'

*

It made James queasy when he thought about how close they'd come to failing on the ninety-eighth day out of a hundred. Failing this close to the end of training would completely do your head in. The boat was now trundling upstream, against the current. Their sodden packs and equipment were spread over the deck, drying in the morning sun.

The river varied in size. Some places, shallow water stretched over thirty metres wide. They had to go slowly, with James leaning over the bow, shouting directions so that Kerry didn't ground the hull. When things got desperate, James used a wooden oar to nudge them away from disaster. In the narrow sections, the river was deeper and the currents stronger. Trees and bushes loomed over the water and they had to duck under low branches.

When it was plain sailing, Kerry would open up the throttle and the gentle put-put of the engine turned into a whine, accompanied by thick blue exhaust fumes. She stayed on the wooden bench near the outboard motor, making gentle adjustments to their course and marking off progress on her chart. James' job was more physically demanding; but even though the sun was fierce and working with the oar strained his shoulders, he preferred it to taking responsibility for navigating them safely through the dead ends and tributaries leading towards the lake.

*

It was the hottest part of the day when they broke on to open water. The lake ran further than you could see through the glaring sun. James abandoned his oar and sat on a fuel can in the middle of the boat, occasionally bailing out the water sloshing around the hull.

'Can you see the trawler anywhere?' Kerry asked. 'If I've read the Japanese in my briefing right, it's on a mud bank at the north end of the lake, marked by three red warning buoys.'

James stood up, squinting in a vain attempt to cut out the glare off the water. It was a pity they didn't have sunglasses.

'I can't see squat,' James said. 'We'll just have to keep cruising around the edge until we spot it.'

Kerry looked at her watch.

'We've got two hours until the deadline, but the sooner we get to this checkpoint, the longer we have to reach the next one.'

There was no other traffic on the lake. The fishing wharves, shacks and warehouses along the shoreline were desolate. There were well maintained roads and even a couple of telephone boxes, but no people anywhere. Red warning posts were hammered into the mud every few hundred metres. The writing was in Sarawak, so James couldn't read the words, but the yellow and black stripes and the bolts of lightning sent out a message that was clear in any language: stay the hell out of here.

'This is freaky,' James said. 'What's going on?'

'According to this map, they're building a giant dam upriver,' Kerry said. 'I guess this whole area is going to be flooded. Everyone's had to leave, which makes this the ideal spot for us to train without any locals sticking their noses in.'

James toppled backwards as Kerry put on full rudder and opened up the throttle. For a couple of nervous seconds he thought he was going over the side.

'For god's sake,' James shouted furiously. 'Tell me before you do that next time.'

The boat bounced over tiny waves towards the silhouette Kerry had spotted in the distance. The rusting trawler was about fifteen metres long, leaning on its side in the mud. Another boat, identical to their own, was tied to the metal deck rail.

Kerry bumped the boat into the mud bank. James hopped over the bow and tied it off.

'Anybody in there?' James shouted.

Connor stuck his head through a window.

'What took you two so long?' Connor asked.

The exterior of the boat was crusted in bird crap. They tried not to touch it as they crawled through a lopsided doorway into the bridge. There were masses of holes and hanging wires. Everything of value had been stripped for salvage, including the navigational equipment, the glass in the windows and even the seat cushion off the captain's chair. Connor and Gabrielle looked muddy and tired. They had maps and briefing papers spread out over the floor.

'How long have you been here?' Kerry asked.

'Twenty minutes or so,' Gabrielle said

'Any sign of Shakeel and Mo?'

'They'd been and gone before us,' Gabrielle said. 'They left the envelope from their dossier on the floor. Yours is over there as well.'

Kerry grabbed the padded envelope, tore it open and handed James the half written in Russian.

'So we're running last,' James said.

'We've already worked out most of ours,' Connor said. 'Maybe we can help you two catch up.'

James thought it was a kind offer, but Kerry took it the wrong way.

'We're quite capable of working it out for ourselves,' she said indignantly. 'We've all come from different camps and we're all going to different places. Maybe we had a longer first stint and a shorter second stint. I don't see how anyone could have done the journey much faster than we did.'

'We wasted a good half hour when we nearly sank the boat,' James said.

Connor laughed, 'How did you manage that?'

'It was loaded up when we pushed it off the embankment.'

'God,' Gabrielle gasped. 'You never would have got up the river if you'd flooded the engine.'

'I know you guys are on a different route to the final checkpoint,' Connor said. 'But if your briefing is the same as ours, it tells you to take a different route back towards the sea and get to the third checkpoint, less than fifteen kilometres away, by 2200.'

Kerry had done a quick skim through her briefing and nodded. 'Different route… Fifteen kilometres by 2200 … That's more or less what it says here.'

James broke into a grin. 'Fifteen kilometres in nine hours. That's easy.'

Connor, Gabrielle and Kerry all stared at him like he was a total idiot.

'Oh,' James said, when it clicked into place how dumb he was being. 'There's going to be some kind of catch, isn't there?'

24. FLASH

'We could play I spy,' James grinned, trying to break the tension as they headed downstream.

Kerry didn't appreciate his stab at humour.

'Shut your face, and keep your eyes open.'

'It'd better not be rapids,' James said anxiously. 'I couldn't handle that.'

'For the hundredth time, James, they won't send us down rapids. This is the wrong type of boat, we'd disintegrate in two seconds.'

James could cope with swimming in a pool, or a fairly still section of river, but the idea of a getting thrown into raging water without a life-jacket scared him like mad.

Things were easier for Kerry. She had the map spread over her lap and the boat to steer. All James had was twitchy fingers and a brain packed with unpleasant thoughts about whatever awaited them.

'Maybe nothing will happen,' James said. 'Maybe the trick is to make us think something horrible is going to happen when nothing really is.'

'A few seconds' warning could make all the difference,'

Kerry said sharply. 'Be quiet and concentrate.'

When the skies darkened for the afternoon rains, James stretched the tarp over their stuff and lashed the paddling pool on top, to capture a fresh supply of drinking water. The violent rain made it impossible to navigate safely. As soon as it started, Kerry pulled into the embankment. James tied the boat to a branch and they snuggled under the tarp until it stopped.

Before setting off again, they quickly changed into dry clothes and put on more insect repellent. James' body was a mass of angry red bites.

'This is getting out of hand,' James said. 'Even my bites have got bites on them. Do you think we could get malaria?'

'Maybe,' Kerry shrugged. 'But there's nothing we can do, so what's the point dwelling on it?'

*

An hour after the rain, they spotted a light pulsing in the trees up ahead.

'Did someone just take our photo?' James asked.

Before Kerry could answer, an electronic squeal broke out under the top of the outboard motor. She cut the throttle and reached into her pocket for her utility knife.

'Is that some kind of warning buzzer?' James asked.

Kerry shrugged. 'I'll have a look under the engine cover, but I'm no mechanic.'

She undid two plastic catches with the blade of her knife and lifted off the plastic faring.

'Jesus,' Kerry gasped. 'I think we've got a bomb on board.'

Not quite believing his ears, James scrambled down the boat and looked at the metal cylinder duct-taped to the engine block. James recognised the timing switch from Mr Large's weapons and explosives class. Unlike the ones you see in the movies, it didn't have a clock saying how long you had until the bomb exploded.

A wire ran from the timer and out of the engine, alongside the rubber hose linking the outboard motor to the auxiliary fuel tank. James had noticed the wire before, but he'd never given it a thought.

'Did the flashing light set off the timer?' James asked.

'It must have a photo trigger,' Kerry said. 'Remember when Mr Large showed us how you could set up a motion detector and a photographic flashgun to set off a bomb? It's ideal if you want something to explode when it reaches a certain position.'

'We could die,' James said.

'Don't be dopey,' Kerry said. 'They're not gonna kill us. It's probably just a tiny bit of explosive that will blow a hole somewhere in the...'

The centre of the boat suddenly ruptured upwards. James got the first whiff of burning as the shockwave threw him into the water.

He blacked out for a few seconds. The next thing he knew, he was floating in the river, surrounded by smoke and chunks of wood. His ears were ringing and petrol in the water was stinging his eyes so badly that he couldn't open them.

'Kerry,' James shouted desperately as he thrashed about. 'Please ... Kerry.'

The petrol was burning his throat and he felt like he was choking.

'Kerry, I can't see.'

'Stand up,' she shouted.

James could barely hear her voice over the ringing in his ears. Her hands slid under his armpits.

'Put your feet down.'

James felt a surge of relief as his boot touched the sandy river bottom, just over a metre below the surface.

'I thought I was gonna drown,' James gasped, as Kerry steadied him. 'I thought it was deep.'

Kerry led James by the hand towards a boulder sticking out of the water. His eyes felt like they were on fire. All he could see were blurs of light.

'Sit there a minute,' Kerry said. 'Keep blinking as much as you can.'

'Are your eyes OK?' James asked.

'Fine,' Kerry said. 'I jumped off the back of the boat and swam away from the debris.'

Kerry had spotted her backpack tangled in a bush on the riverbank and waded to its rescue. By the time she got back, the stinging had died down enough for James to keep his eyes open for a couple of seconds at a time.

'Give us some drinking water,' James said.

Kerry looked inside her sodden pack.

'There isn't any,' Kerry said. 'My canteen was out on the deck.'

'How far do you reckon it is to camp?'

'Three kilometres,' Kerry said. 'We'll have to swim it.'

'I've never gone more than a hundred metres,' James said warily.

'I'll make you a float out of the backpack.'

'It's a long way,' James said. 'Couldn't we walk along the bank?'

Kerry pointed at the tangle of branches and leaves hanging over the edge of the river.

'You'll never crawl three kilometres through that lot in a million years.'

'I suppose,' James said.

'You'll swim better without boots. Give them to us and I'll tie them around my waist.'

'Seriously, Kerry, I don't think I'm up to this.'

As James pulled off his soggy boots, Kerry found the roll of plastic bin liners in her pack. She stripped out everything but absolute essentials: knife, map, insect repellent and compass. Then she got one of the bin liners and blew it up until it was big enough to fill the backpack.

'We'll both hold on to the straps and float downstream,' Kerry said. 'Just kick gently, the current will do most of the work for us.'

*

Training was supposed to push you to the limit. They could starve you, humiliate you and work you until you were begging to quit; but at the end of the day, they didn't want to kill you. The route downriver had been carefully selected by the instructors, so that the danger to anyone who could swim was minimal. The water was never more than a few metres deep, the currents were moderate and the banks were rarely more than twenty metres apart.

That still left water snakes and sharks to worry about. The sharks were only little, but they looked perfectly capable of nipping off fingers and toes, and it wasn't a nice feeling when one swam up close, showing off rows of teeth. James panicked a couple of times when he lost sight of Kerry and grazed his thigh on a jagged rock, but they reached the checkpoint as it was turning dark, with three spare hours before the 2200 deadline.

They were desperate for water and James had a couple of leeches stuck on his back, but apart from that, they felt OK as they staggered out of the water. The checkpoint was on an open stretch of land that had been cleared out by a logging company. There was a tin shed that had once served as sleeping quarters to half a dozen loggers. Ever wary of traps, James nervously poked his head inside the metal door and was surprised to find Mr Speaks sitting in a hammock doing a crossword.

'Good trip?' he asked, pushing his ever-present sunglasses down his nose and giving them the once-over.

'Not bad,' Kerry gasped.

Their eyes fixed on a giant bottle of mineral water, glinting on the window ledge.

'Help yourself,' Mr Speaks said. 'There are fresh packs and equipment for both of you, plenty of food in the ice box and there's a tank of rainwater on the roof that links up to the shower head if you want to use that. After that, I suggest you read your briefings and try to grab some sleep before the helicopter picks you up. It's the only rest you'll get in the next thirty-eight hours.'

'Aren't we sleeping here tonight?' James asked.

'If you want to reach the fourth checkpoint, you're not sleeping anywhere, either tonight or tomorrow night. The chopper picks you up here at 2200 and drops you on a footpath 188 kilometres from your final checkpoint. That's the exact distance from London to Birmingham and you've got until 1000 hours on the final day to get there. If you fall asleep, you'll never make it.'

25. JELLY

Going 188 kilometres in thirty-six hours works out at slightly over five kilometres an hour. That's about normal walking pace, but you had to stop to eat and drink, to check you weren't veering off an overgrown footpath in the middle of the night, and when the pain got so bad that you couldn't take another step. It wasn't just James' and Kerry's legs that hurt from the walking, their whole bodies ached with tiredness.

Precautions went out of the window. Sweaty and covered in insect bites, there wasn't time to put on dry clothes or insect repellent. Their canteens were empty. They didn't have time to stop and collect rainwater, so they had to drink water trapped on giant palms and leaves. James and Kerry dumped most stuff and carried one light pack between them, with nothing in it but a torch, compass and maps.

They reached the final checkpoint less than half an hour before the deadline. As they staggered towards a wooden building, Gabrielle and Shakeel ran out and gave them fresh water.

'We were getting worried about you two,' Shakeel said. 'You cut it pretty close.'

The building was locked, but there was a tap on the outside. Kerry filled a rusty bucket, threw half at James and poured the rest over her head.

The trainees were too tired to do anything but crash out on the shady side of the building, waiting for the instructors to turn up.

'I hope we don't get malaria,' James said, scratching the bites on his neck.

'It's not a malaria zone,' Gabrielle said, matter-of-factly.

'What makes you say that?' Kerry asked.

'I knew we were going to the jungle and they didn't give us malaria tablets before we left,' Gabrielle said. 'That made me think. The night we were in the hotel I sweet-talked the guy behind the front desk and he let me use the Internet. No malaria in this part of Malaysia.'

'Smart thinking,' Kerry said. 'You could have told us.'

'I told James in the helicopter before the drop,' Gabrielle said. 'Same time I told Shakeel.'

'You didn't,' James said defensively.

'She told both of us. I saw you nod,' Shakeel said.

'Oh,' James said. 'It was noisy. I thought you were saying good luck, so I nodded.'

Kerry punched James on the arm.

'Dumbo,' Kerry said. 'You know how much time we could have saved not changing clothes so often? And I was worried to death we were going to get sick.'

'I'm sorry,' James said. 'There's no need to start hitting me.'

'Idiot,' Kerry laughed. 'I can't wait to get you in that dojo.'

'What?' James asked.

'Remember our deal after you stomped on my hand? The day after training stops I get to fight you in the dojo.'

'I thought you were joking,' James said.

Kerry shook her head. The others were all laughing.

'She'll mash you,' Connor said. 'Can we watch?'

'Who says you're both gonna make it through training?' Mo asked. 'It's a four-day course and it's only the morning of the fourth day. I bet the instructors will have something else up their sleeves.'

*

The instructors led them inside. The trainees each had a chair with two buckets in front of it. Speaks covered their eyes with a mask. Smoke tied their ankles to the frame of the chair.

'Welcome to the ultimate test,' Large said. 'Before we can make you six tired little bunnies into operatives, we need to be sure you can cope with the worst thing that could ever happen to you. Number eight, what do you think is the worst thing that can happen on a mission?'

'We could be killed,' Kerry said.

'Death would be easy by comparison,' Large said. 'I was thinking about torture. What happens if you're captured on a mission? You know something, and some people will do anything to get that information from you. Don't expect mercy because you're children. They'll still slice your toes off. Rip out your fingernails or teeth. Wire you up and blast those sweet little bodies with a thousand volts of electricity. We hope it never happens to any of you, but we have to know you can take the pain if it does.

'This test will show us if you've got guts. It will last one hour. You each have two buckets in front of you. Miss Smoke is placing a jellyfish in the buckets to your left. Its tentacles have hundreds of microscopic spikes; each one packs a dose of poison. A few minutes after contact your skin will start to burn. Within ten minutes the pain is extreme. A few years ago an operative jumped a fence, misjudged the jump and ended up with a metal railing stuck in her back. Afterwards she said it was less painful than this test.

'The bucket on your right contains an antidote to the poison. Within a few seconds of touching the antidote the pain will begin to decrease. After two minutes the pain will be almost gone.'

James felt his head being grabbed.

'Open wide,' Smoke said.

Smoke shoved a rubber plug into James' mouth. It was held in with an elastic strap that wrapped around the back of his head.

'You are being given mouth guards,' Large continued, 'because it is not unknown for people in extreme pain to bite off their own tongues. You will each place your hands in the bucket, knuckles touching the bottom, for thirty seconds. The jellyfish will grab you. You will feel nothing at first. You will have to tolerate the pain for one hour. Anyone placing their hands in the antidote before one hour has elapsed has failed the entire course. Due to the toxicity of the poison you may not retake the test. Any questions?'

None of the trainees could talk with the plugs in their mouths.

'OK then. Put your hands in the bucket.'

James leant forward, feeling blindly for the bucket. He'd

thought he had the measure of training but this was scary. What if the pain was so bad he couldn't help sticking his hands in the antidote? Ninety-nine days of training for nothing.

The water was tepid. He felt something light and rubbery wrap itself around his wrists.

'Take them out,' Large said. 'If the jellyfish sticks, slide it off gently.'

James lifted his hands and pushed off the gripping tentacles. He sat up straight and waited for the pain to start.

'Two minutes,' Large said. 'It should start hurting soon.'

James' hands started feeling hot. Sweat was running down his forehead, building up along the rim of the eye mask. He didn't wipe it off in case it spread the poison to his face.

'Five minutes,' Large said.

The heat in James' hands was gone. He wondered if he'd imagined it. Kerry sounded like she was struggling with her mouth guard. It looked like the pain had got to her sooner.

'Ten minutes. You all seem to be holding up quite well. But I can see some twisted faces,' Large said.

Kerry shouted out:

'What would be the point of an animal stinging you if it didn't hurt straight away?

Large ran over to Kerry.

'Get that guard back in now.'

James could hear Kerry squealing as they shoved the plug back in her mouth.

'The next person who spits out their guard has to go two hours without touching the antidote,' Large shouted.

Kerry had made James think. There still wasn't any pain

from the jellyfish and what Kerry said made sense. What good would an animal sting do if it only hurt its enemy *after* it had been eaten or attacked?

'Fifteen minutes,' Large said.

'Two hours without the antidote?' Gabrielle shouted. 'Why not make it ten? Tell you what, I'll stick my head in the bucket.'

James couldn't see the commotion, but heard water running and a plastic bucket rolling across the floor.

'This is totally bogus,' Kerry said calmly.

James was sure it was a trick now. He pulled down his eye mask. Kerry had plucked a harmless white squid out of her bucket and was holding it up for inspection. James took off his mouth guard.

'OK people,' Large said. 'Glad you all enjoyed my little joke. Don't forget to untie your ankles before you stand up.'

Kerry was looking at James with a massive grin.

'Were you scared?' James asked.

'I thought it was a trick,' Kerry said. 'Why put the eye masks on us unless it was fake?'

'That never occurred to me,' James said. 'I was too scared to think straight.'

'Look under your seat,' Kerry said.

Something had been put under everyone's chair while they were blindfolded. James undid his ankles and picked up the present. It was grey. He unfurled it and looked at the winged baby sitting on the globe and the letters: CHERUB.

'Beauty,' James shouted.

Kerry was already putting her T-shirt on. James pulled off his blue shirt for the last time. When his smiling head popped through the neck hole, Large was standing in front of him holding out his hand. James shook it.

'Congratulations, James,' Mr Large said. 'You two worked well together.'

It was the first nice thing James had heard him say.

26. BACK

You weren't supposed to wear CHERUB uniform off campus for security reasons, but James wore his grey shirt all the way home hidden under his tracksuit. He woke up on the plane and peeked down his chest to make sure it wasn't a dream. Kerry was asleep in the next seat. James could see the grey tail of her CHERUB shirt hanging out the back of her jeans.

Everyone was in a good mood. Even the instructors, who got a three-week holiday before the next batch started training. Kerry stopped acting tough and surprised James by turning into a normal eleven-year-old girl. She told James she couldn't wait until her nails and hair grew back. She even bought a pen and card in the airport gift shop and got everyone to sign it for the instructors. James told her he thought it was dumb. He remembered that Large had been happy to get them thrown off the course to win a bet. It might be Large's job to make trainees suffer, but he seemed to enjoy it as well.

*

The van from the airport left them at the training building. The new operatives picked a few things up from their lockers and changed out of their casual travel clothes into uniform. James kept one of the filthy blue shirts with the number seven on as a memento. Kerry was holding out a key.

'Help me move my stuff?' Kerry asked.

'Where to?' James asked.

'The main building. Red shirts live in the junior block.'

The instructors wanted them all out of the training area fast so they could get home.

Callum was waiting for his twin outside the training compound. His arm was out of the sling. James felt sorry for Callum having to start training again. James gave him a friendly shove.

'You'll get there,' James said. 'No worries.'

Connor put his arm round his brother.

Kerry was running ahead, excited, 'Come on, James.'

James went after her to the junior block. He hadn't been there before. It was the middle of the morning so everyone was in class. Kerry's room had kiddies' furniture: a plastic desk, bunk beds and a big wooden trunk with *My Toys* painted on the side. The wardrobe had a green teddy on the doors.

'What a divine room,' James said, trying not to laugh.

'Shut your pie hole,' Kerry said, 'and carry.'

She had packed everything before training started.

'You must have been confident,' James said.

'If I failed this time, I was going to leave CHERUB. You don't have to become an agent if you don't want to.'

'Where do you go if you leave?' James asked.

'They send you to a boarding school. In the holidays you stay with a foster family.'

'You really would have left?'

'I promised myself,' Kerry said. 'That's why I got so upset on Christmas Day when you got us in trouble.'

James stayed quiet. He didn't want the conversation straying towards their agreement to fight in the dojo. They packed Kerry's stuff on to one of the electric buggies that staff used around campus.

'Where's your new room?' James asked.

Kerry showed him the number on her key ring.

'Sixth floor,' James said. 'Same as me, we're practically neighbours.'

They walked back to Kerry's old room and did a final check to make sure nothing was left behind. Kerry had tears streaking down her face.

'What?' James asked.

'This has been my room since I was seven,' Kerry sobbed. 'I'll miss it.'

James didn't know where to look.

'Kerry, the rooms in the main building are about fifty times cooler. You've got your own bathroom and computer and everything.'

'I know, but still ...' Kerry sobbed.

'Give over,' James said. 'Can I drive the buggy, I've never done it before?'

*

The buggy was overloaded with Kerry's stuff and felt like it might tip over on a bump. The bell had gone for a lesson change. Kids were going between the buildings. A few of Kerry's friends stopped the buggy and congratulated them on passing basic.

Amy burst out of a door.

'Hey,' she shouted.

James hit the brake.

'Congratulations,' Amy said, leaning into the buggy and hugging both of them.

'You taught James to swim, didn't you, Amy?' Kerry asked.

'Yes,' Amy said.

'What's with all this?' Kerry asked, flapping her arms about in a wobbly front crawl.

'I don't swim like that,' James said peevishly.

Amy and Kerry both laughed.

'I only had three weeks to teach him,' Amy said. 'He's getting more lessons.'

Amy copied Kerry's impression of James' swimming and they both laughed even harder. James would happily have thumped them, only they could both easily batter him.

'Anyway, James,' Amy said. 'I've been looking for you everywhere. I've got something to show you.'

'What?' James sulked.

'James, I'm sorry,' Amy said. 'I'm your teacher so I shouldn't laugh at you. I promise I'll cheer you up if you come with me.'

James climbed out of the buggy.

'Where to?'

'You look really fit, James,' Amy said.

James wasn't sure if she was saying it to make him feel better.

'Are you OK to move that stuff on your own?' Amy asked Kerry.

Kerry nodded. 'Someone will help.'

Amy led James back towards the junior building.

'What is this?' James asked.

'I wasn't sure you'd make it through training first time,' Amy said. 'I'm impressed.'

James smiled. 'Another three or four compliments and I'll forgive you for what you said about my swimming.'

They walked into the education block in the Junior building. It looked like any ordinary primary school, with little kids' paintings on the walls and plasticine models on the window ledges. Amy stopped by a classroom door.

'There,' Amy said.

'What is this?' James said. 'Can't you just tell me?'

Amy pointed at the door. 'Have a look.'

James stuck his face up to the glass. Inside, ten kids sat on the floor chanting phrases in Spanish. The red shirts wore the same uniform as everyone else, only with trainers instead of boots.

'See it?' Amy asked.

'No,' he said impatiently. 'I don't even know what I'm looking for.'

Then it hit James like a bomb.

'Shit,' he said, grinning.

He knocked on the classroom door and walked in.

'Shit,' James said again, loudly, in front of the teacher and all the kids.

The Spanish teacher looked furious.

'My sister,' James said.

He couldn't think of anything else to say and stood with his mouth open.

'Excuse our interruption, Miss,' Amy said calmly. 'This is

Lauren's brother, James. He's just finished basic training and was wondering if you could excuse her.'

The teacher flicked her hand at Lauren. 'Go on, just this once.'

Lauren scrambled up from the carpet and jumped into James' arms. She was heavy. James stumbled back a couple of paces before he got his balance.

'Hola hermano grande,' Lauren said, grinning.

'What?' James asked.

'It's Spanish,' Lauren said. 'It means hello, big brother.'

*

Amy had a lesson to go to. Lauren walked James to her room.

'I can't believe this,' James said, grinning uncontrollably.

The best he'd hoped for was being able to see Lauren a couple of times a month. Having her walking along in front of him in a CHERUB uniform was too much to take in.

Lauren's room was like Kerry's old one, except everything was newer.

'Can't believe this,' James said again, slumping on to a beanbag. 'I just cannot believe this.'

Lauren laughed. 'So you're pleased to see me?'

She got Cokes out of her fridge and threw one at James.

'I mean how ... I mean ...' James giggled. 'Why are you here?'

'Because Ron punched me in the face,' Lauren said.

'He did *what*?' James said, shocked.

'Punched me. I had massive black eyes.'

'That arsehole,' James shouted, kicking out at the wall.

'They never should have let him look after you. I knew something like that would happen.'

Lauren squeezed up next to James on the beanbag.

'I hate Ron's guts,' Lauren said. 'Mrs Reed asked what happened to my eyes when I went to school the next day.'

'You told her the truth?' James asked.

'Yeah. She got the police. They saw all the smuggled cigarettes when they went round to arrest him; so they busted him for that as well.'

James laughed. 'Serves him right.'

'I got taken to Nebraska House,' Lauren said. 'Nobody could find where you'd gone. I got really upset. I thought I was never gonna see you again.'

'So how long did it take them to find me?' James asked.

'I was at Nebraska House three days. Fourth day I woke up here.'

James laughed. 'Freaks you out, doesn't it?'

'They wouldn't let me speak to you. Mac took me to see you though. I watched you and that Chinese girl doing Karate. She was killing you. It was so funny.'

'Did you have to do the tests to get in?'

'No,' Lauren said. 'They're only if you're older and you're going straight into training.'

'That's so jammy,' James said. 'The tests half killed me.'

Lauren whacked him across the arm. 'Leave my hair alone.'

James was winding it around his fingertips. She hated him doing that.

'Sorry,' he said. 'Never even realised I was doing it.'

'I'm on a special programme,' Lauren said. 'Loads of

running, swimming, Karate and stuff, so I'm really fit when I start basic training.'

'You're ten this year, aren't you?' James said.

Lauren nodded. 'September. I'm trying not to think about basic training.'

'But you think it's cool here, don't you?' James asked. 'You're happy?'

'It's superb,' Lauren said. 'There's always loads to do. Did I tell you, they took us skiing? I got this bruise on my arse the size of a CD.'

James laughed. 'I can't imagine you on skis.'

'And you want the best news?'

'What?'

'They found drugs and tons of stolen stuff in Ron's flat. Guess how long they put him in prison for?'

James shrugged. 'Five years?'

Lauren pointed a finger at the ceiling.

James grinned. 'Seven years?'

'Nine,' Lauren said.

James punched the air.

27. ROUTINE

They had a week off after training finished. James went to check out Kerry's room now she'd unpacked. He wasn't happy.

'My new timetable is mental,' James said. 'Six hours of lessons every day. Two hours' homework a night and two hours of lessons on *Saturday* morning. That's forty-four hours a week of schoolwork.'

'So?' Kerry said. What did you do at your old school?'

'Twenty-five hours at school and a few hours' homework, which I never did. There's no way I'm doing all that homework.'

'Better get used to scrubbing floors then,' Kerry said.

'For not doing homework?'

'Yep. Or cleaning out the kitchen, mowing lawns, wiping windows. Repeat offenders get toilets and changing rooms. The reason you do all those lessons is you miss loads when you're on missions and you have to catch up. They're not all lessons anyway, some of them are sport and teaching and stuff.'

'That's the other thing,' James said. 'I've got to teach maths to little kids.'

'All grey and dark shirt kids have to teach. It gives you a sense of responsibility. Amy teaches swimming. Bruce teaches martial arts. I've got to do Spanish with the five- and six-year-olds. I'm really looking forward to it.'

James slumped on Kerry's bed.

'You sound exactly like Meryl Spencer, my handler. I can't believe you're happy about all this work.'

'It's not much more than I had as a red shirt.'

'I wish I'd never come here.'

'Stop being a drama queen,' Kerry said. 'CHERUB gives you a great education and a cool place to live. When you leave here you'll speak two or three languages, have qualifications coming out of your ears, and be set for life. Think where you'd be now if you hadn't come here.'

'OK,' James said. 'My life was down the toilet. But I hate school. It's so boring I want to smash my head up against the wall half the time.'

'You're lazy, James. You want to sit in your room with your stupid Playstation going blip, blip, all day. You said yourself you were gonna end up in prison the way you were carrying on. If you get bored in a classroom, how would you like eighteen hours a day in a cell? And take those filthy boots off my bed before I bust your head open.'

James put his feet down.

'Playstation is not a waste of time,' he said.

'You want the best reason why you should work hard?'

'What?'

'Lauren. She loves you. If you do good, she'll do good. If you muck up and get thrown out, she'll have to make a choice between staying with you and staying at CHERUB.'

'Stop being right,' James said. 'Everyone in this place is clever, level-headed, and I'm always wrong. I hate all of you.'

Kerry started laughing.

'It's not funny,' James said, starting to smile.

Kerry sat beside him on the bed.

'You'll get used to it here, James.'

'You're right about Lauren,' James said. 'I have to think about her.'

Kerry moved a bit closer and rested her head on James' shoulder.

'Beneath that dumb exterior you're a good person,' Kerry said.

'Thanks,' James said. 'So are you.'

James put his arm round Kerry's shoulders. It felt like the natural thing to do, but two seconds after he did it his brain was spinning. What did this mean? Did he want Kerry to be his girlfriend, or was it just that they'd been through so much together in training? He'd showered with her and slept next to her, but until training ended James had barely noticed that Kerry was a girl. Not a dream girl like Amy, but not bad either. He thought about kissing her cheek, but chickened out.

'The room looks nice,' James said, scratching for something to say. 'All your pictures and stuff. I'll have to get some. My walls are white.'

'I was thinking,' Kerry said. 'We should renegotiate our deal.'

James had avoided Kerry for two days, hoping she'd forget.

'How?' he asked.

'Friday night,' Kerry said. 'Take me to the cinema. I pick

the movie. You pay the bus fare, the cinema tickets, hot dogs, popcorn, Pepsi and whatever else I want.'

'That's gonna be easily twenty quid for the two of us,' James said.

'That kid you're friendly with, Bruce.'

'What about him?'

'He broke his leg once,' Kerry said. 'When we were eight.'

'He said it broke in nine places.'

'He exaggerates. I only broke it in seven places.'

'You?' James said.

'Snapped it like a twig. Kicked him in the head for luck.'

'OK,' James said. 'Cinema, my treat.'

*

Kyle arrived back from a mission Friday morning with sunburn and a sack-load of fake designer gear. James followed Kyle into his room. It was freakishly neat. Even inside the wardrobe Kyle's clothes were all in dry cleaner's bags, above a row of boots and trainers with shoe trees in them.

'Philippines,' Kyle said. 'I'm back in Mac's good books.'

'What happened?' James asked.

'Confidential. Here, these were supposed to make you feel better when you got kicked out of training.'

Kyle tossed over a pair of fake Ray Ban sunglasses. James slipped them on and posed in the mirror.

'These are cool, cheers,' James said. 'Everyone thought I'd fail.'

'You would have,' Kyle said. 'If you hadn't got Kerry as a partner, Large would have chewed you up in a week.'

'You know Kerry?' James asked.

'Bruce does. He said you had a chance once he found out Kerry was your partner. She cost me ten quid.'

'You bet against me getting through training?'

'No offence, James, but you're a spoiled brat and a total whiner. I thought I'd make an easy tenner.'

'Thanks,' James said. 'Good to know who your friends are.'

'You want to buy a fake Rolex watch?' Kyle asked. 'Same as the real thing, four quid each.'

*

The whole crowd went to the cinema Friday night. Bruce, Kyle, Kerry, Callum, Connor, James, Lauren and a few other kids. James was happy being part of a big group, all messing about and slagging each other off. The film was a twelve. The rest of them could pass for twelve, but they had to smuggle Lauren through the emergency exit.

James worried about what would happen with him and Kerry, especially with everyone else watching. He sat down. Kerry sat with one of her girlfriends a few seats away. James was relieved, but disappointed as well. The more he thought about it, the more he realised how much he liked her.

*

Four days into his timetable James realised he could live with it. In his old life he'd always got up late, sat in class mucking about all day then come home and either played Playstation, watched TV, or hung out on the estate with his friends. Most of the time he was bored. The routine at CHERUB was hard but it never got dull.

You weren't allowed to slack off in lessons. Every class had ten kids or fewer, which meant as soon as you stopped working the teacher was on your back asking what the problem was. Pupils were picked by ability not age. Some classes, like James' advanced maths group, had kids who were fifteen and sixteen. His Spanish, Russian and self-defence classes were with six- to nine-year-olds.

Punishments were psycho if you got out of line. James swore in history and got a ten-hour shift repainting the lines in the staff car park. Next day his palms and knees were blistered from crawling around on tarmac.

Most days had a PE session. After training, James was really fit. Two hours' running around felt like a warm-up. They started with circuit training inside the gym. The second half was always a game of football or rugby. James liked it best when they played Girls versus Boys, which usually went a bit mad, with insane tackles and punch-ups breaking out everywhere. What the girls lacked in strength they made up for with cunning and gang tactics. Boys always scored most goals, the girls edged the carnage.

After lessons James got an hour's rest before dinner, then it was a scramble to do homework, before rushing off to extra martial arts training. James volunteered because he was ashamed that half the nine-year-olds at CHERUB could beat him in a fight. On the nights he didn't have martial arts he'd go to the junior building and hang out with Lauren.

At the end of each day James was worn out. He'd sit in his bath and watch whatever was on TV through the doorway before drying off and collapsing into bed.

28. DETAIL

It was two months since training. Kerry had done a mission, come back, and gone on another. She was so superior about it, James could have thumped her. Gabrielle was in Jamaica. Connor had disappeared with Shakeel. Bruce was away for days at a time. Kyle went off one morning promising that this mission was going to earn him his navy shirt. James was still at CHERUB and felt like a lemon.

Amy was the only one who hadn't been away. She spent hours on the eighth floor in one of the Mission Preparation rooms. James still got to swim with her four times a week. He was good now. Four hundred metres front crawl, keeping his body under the water and tipping his face to the side to breathe without lifting his head out of the water. He never got scared and Amy said his stroke was almost perfect.

*

James and Amy were putting their uniforms back on. All they'd done was swim lengths together, then sit on the poolside and talk for a bit.

'That was our last lesson,' Amy said.

James had known it was coming for ages, but that didn't

stop him feeling bad. He liked hanging around with Amy. She was funny and always gave good advice on stuff.

'Is your mission starting?' James asked, sitting down to lace up his boots.

'In a couple of weeks,' Amy said. 'I need to devote all my time to it.'

'I'll miss having lessons with you. You're a brilliant teacher.'

'Thanks, James, you're sweet. You should go swimming with Kerry when she gets back. You swim as well as she does now, probably better.'

'She'll be too busy rubbing my nose in it about her mission experience. I saw Meryl Spencer again yesterday, she still says there's no mission for me.'

'I can confess now,' Amy said. 'I had you suspended from mission activity.'

'Because of swimming?' James asked.

Amy went in her swimming bag and got out a plastic card. James had seen people swipe them in the lift to get up to the secure part of the main building where missions were planned.

'This is yours,' Amy said, handing it across.

James broke out smiling. 'I've got a mission with you?'

'Yes,' Amy said. 'I put in some work on this job before you even came here. When you arrived I realised we looked alike. Same colour hair, similar build. I knew you could pass as my little brother. We set you up with Kerry so you had the best chance of passing training. I wasn't happy when I heard you started a fight with her and nearly got thrown out.'

'Don't remind me,' James said. 'I was so dumb.'

'You're lucky Kerry didn't retaliate. All she had to do was flip you up and break your arm and you would have been out of training. Nobody would have blamed her either.'

'I was on top of her,' James said. 'She couldn't get up.'

Amy laughed, 'If you got on top of Kerry it's because she let you. She could squash you like an egg under her boot if she wanted.'

'Is she that good?' James asked.

Amy nodded. 'She must like you a lot to let you off like that.'

*

The eighth floor was exactly like the accommodation floors below: a long corridor with rooms off either side. Entering the Mission Preparation room meant swiping your security card and staring into a red light while the blood vessels in your retina were scanned for identification.

After the hi-tech entry, James expected something flash inside: a map of the world with a bank of computer screens above it or something. It was actually a bit of a dump. Old computers, chairs with sponge bursting out of cushions and metal cabinets covered with stacks of files and papers. The only good feature was the view over campus.

Ewart Asker stuck his hand out for James to shake and introduced himself as the Mission Controller. He was in his twenties, CHERUB uniform, bleached hair with black roots and a stud through his tongue.

'First mission, James,' Ewart said. 'Worried?'

James shrugged. 'Should I be?'

Ewart laughed. 'I'm nervous, James. This baby is complicated. You wouldn't normally get something like this until you'd done a few easy missions, but we needed a twelve-year-old boy who could pass for Amy's brother, and you're the best we've got.

'There's a ton of stuff to learn. I've cut your school schedule back. Amy has written a mission dossier for you. Don't be afraid to ask questions. The mission starts in about ten days.'

James pulled up a chair and opened the briefing:

CLASSIFIED

MISSION BRIEFING FOR JAMES ADAMS
DO NOT REMOVE FROM ROOM 812
DO NOT COPY OR MAKE NOTES

(1) Fort Harmony
In 1612 King James made a fifty square kilometre area near the Welsh village of Craddogh into common land. The charter allowed people to graze animals and build a small shelter on the land. By the 1870s everyone who lived on Craddogh Common had moved to the village to work in the coal mine. Nobody lived on the land for the next ninety-seven years.

In 1950 Craddogh Common was made part of West Monmouthshire National Park. In 1967 a small group of hippies led by a woman called Gladys Dunn settled on Craddogh Common. Gladys named the settlement Fort Harmony. They kept chickens and built wooden shelters, claiming they could do so under the 1612 charter.

At first the National Park tolerated the settlers, but numbers grew, and within three years about 270 hippies lived in a hundred or so ramshackle buildings. The National Park Authority began legal action to evict the hippies. After two years the High Court decided that the king's charter ended when Craddogh Common was made part of the National Park. The court gave the hippies one week to pack up and leave.

The hippies would not go. Police began destroying huts and arresting the hippies in the winter of 1972. The size of the community soon dropped to less than fifty, but this hard core was determined to stay.

(2) The Battle

The Fort Harmony residents fled every day, allowing police to demolish the shelters. They returned and made new shelters every night. The hippies dug underground tunnels. They also dug traps for the police to fall into.

In one incident a series of nets were hidden under leaves. When police moved in to demolish huts, the trap was sprung. Three policemen were left swinging in nets twenty metres above ground. The hippies tied off the nets and ran away. A fire engine came to the rescue, but got bogged down in thick mud. It was seven hours before firemen found a way to cut down the nets without their cargo crashing to earth. Pictures of the policemen in the nets made most newspapers the following day.

Newspaper coverage of the battle attracted dozens of new residents to Fort Harmony.

On 26 August 1973, police launched an all-out effort to destroy Fort Harmony. Three hundred police were drafted from across Britain. Television and newspaper journalists watched. Roads were blocked to stop supporters reaching Fort Harmony. Police destroyed the camp and arrested anyone who resisted. By late morning only twenty hippies remained, all barricaded in underground tunnels. Police decided entering the tunnels was too dangerous and waited for the hippies to come out for food and water.

At 5 p.m. a section of tunnel collapsed under a passing police car. Police rushed to grab a pair of legs sticking out of the earth. Joshua Dunn, aged nine, son of the founder of Fort Harmony, was pulled out of the mud. While two officers held the wriggling boy by his ankles, a third officer hit him over the head with a truncheon. A photographer captured the brutality. Pictures of the boy being stretchered into an ambulance made the television news. This incident caused a surge of public support for the hippies.

The crowd tying to break through blockades and reach Fort Harmony grew to more than a thousand. By midnight the police were exhausted. There were no reinforcements. By 3 a.m. the following morning police lines were broken. At sunrise on 27 August, over 700 supporters were camping in the mud around Fort Harmony. A stream of cars and vans brought wood and supplies to build new shelters. The hippies left the tunnels and began rebuilding their homes.

Next morning the photograph of police beating nine-year-old Joshua Dunn made the front page of every newspaper in Britain. The police announced they would withdraw and destroy the camp at a later date. The police made a plan. A thousand officers would be needed to remove all trace of Fort Harmony while successfully blockading the surrounding countryside. The police and National Park Authority didn't have enough money to pay for such a massive operation, so nothing further was done.

(3) Fort Harmony Today

Thirty years later Fort Harmony still exists. The residents live a harsh life, without running water or electricity in their homes. Camp founder, Gladys Dunn, is now seventy-six. She wrote a bestselling autobiography in 1979. Her three sons – including Joshua, who suffered brain damage from the police assault – still live on site, as do many of her ten grandchildren and twenty-eight great-grandchildren. The camp has about sixty permanent residents. In warmer months Fort Harmony swells to as many as two hundred, mostly students and backpackers who think Gladys Dunn is a hero.

(4) Green Brooke

By 1996 the nearby village of Craddogh was in crisis. The coal mine was closed. Over half the population was unemployed and the village population had fallen from 2,000 residents in 1970 to less than 300. Run-down houses and mountains of black coal waste meant tourists didn't stop at Craddogh on their way to Fort Harmony or the National Parks.

Because of the high local unemployment, the National Park allowed Green Brooke Conference Centre to be built on part of Craddogh Common. Green Brooke opened in 2002. It is enclosed by a five-metre-high fence with video cameras and electrified razor-wire along the top. The Centre hosts conferences and training courses. Facilities include a 765 room hotel, 1200 seat auditorium, gym, spa, and two golf courses. There is parking for 1000 cars and thirty helicopters.

Many residents of Craddogh and Fort Harmony work in Green Brooke as receptionists, cooks and cleaners.

(5) Petrocon 2004

In late 2003 Green Brooke announced the most prestigious event in its brief history. Petrocon takes place in May 2004. It is a secretive three-day meeting of two hundred oil executives and politicians. The media is kept out. Among the guests will be oil ministers from Nigeria and Saudi Arabia and the chief executives of every major oil company. The two most important guests will be the United States Secretary of Energy and the Deputy Prime Minister of Great Britain.

Security will be handled by the Diplomatic Protection Branch of the police, with MI5 and a small unit from CHERUB.

(6) Help Earth

At the end of 2003 a series of bombs were posted to United States Congressmen and members of the British Parliament who support the oil industry. Four workers in the US Congress building suffered injuries. Help Earth claimed responsibility. A month later a French oil company executive working in Venezuela was killed by a car bomb. Help Earth again claimed responsibility.

Shortly before its first attacks, Help Earth sent letters to the editors of several international newspapers, stating its aim to 'Bring an end to the environmental carnage wreaked on our planet by the international oil companies and the politicians who support them.' It then added, 'Help Earth! is the desperate cry of our dying planet. Time is running out. We are prepared to use violent means in the battle to save our environment.'

Peaceful environmental groups are at pains to distance themselves from Help Earth and have helped investigators compile a list of likely terrorist suspects. Despite this, nobody involved with Help Earth has been identified, although several environmental campaigners with a violent history are under suspicion. Four of these suspects are current residents of Fort Harmony.

The limited information on Help Earth suggests an attack on Petrocon 2004 is likely. The size and nature of the attack is unknown. It could range from a small bomb destroying a car or helicopter, to a device capable of killing hundreds.

Any Help Earth members planning terrorist action at Petrocon 2004 will probably attempt to make links with Fort Harmony residents for the following reasons:

a) Many Fort Harmony residents are veteran environmental campaigners.

b) All Fort Harmony residents have a good knowledge of the local area.

c) Many Fort Harmony residents have worked inside Green Brooke and can provide terrorists with information on operations and security.

(7) The Role of CHERUB

MI5 already has informers and undercover agents within the environmental movement. However M15 wants extra agents at Fort Harmony in the build-up to Petrocon 2004.

Any new adult residents arriving at Fort Harmony before Petrocon will be suspected of being undercover police or MI5 operatives. The chances of them getting useful information are small. Therefore it has been decided that two CHERUB operatives posing as relatives of Cathy Dunn, a long-standing member of the Fort Harmony community, will have the best chance of a successful undercover mission. Children will not be suspected of being intelligence agents, and they should mix easily with other members of the community.

29. AUNTIE

James reckoned he now knew more about Fort Harmony than anyone, including the people who lived there. He'd read Gladys Dunn's autobiography and three other books, as well as seeing tons of press cuttings, videos and police files. He'd memorised the names and faces of every current Fort Harmony resident and loads of regular visitors. James also read the criminal records and MI5 files on anyone likely to be involved in the terrorist group Help Earth.

James' undercover name was Ross Leigh. His job was to hang out with kids at Fort Harmony, picking up gossip, sticking his nose where it didn't belong and reporting anything suspicious to CHERUB.

James had a mobile to call Ewart Asker. Ewart was staying at Green Brooke for the duration of the mission. James' other equipment included a digital camera, his lock gun and a can of pepper spray that was only for an emergency.

Amy was his sister, Courtney Leigh. Her job was to befriend Scargill Dunn, the seventeen-year-old grandson of Fort Harmony founder Gladys Dunn. Scargill was a loner who had dropped out of school and washed dishes in the kitchen at Green Brooke.

Scargill's twenty-two-year-old twin brothers, Fire and World, had both served short prison sentences for attacking the chairman of a fast food chain. MI5 believed Fire, World and a couple called Bungle and Eleanor Evans were the residents of Fort Harmony most likely to be part of Help Earth.

*

Cathy Dunn had briefly been married to Fire, World and Scargill's dad, some years before they were born. Since then, Cathy had lived alone at Fort Harmony. Like most residents she grew food and kept a few chickens, but it wasn't enough to survive. She did odd jobs when they cropped up: cleaning, fruit picking. Sometimes Cathy sold information to the police.

There were always a few dodgy people at Fort Harmony. If a drug dealer or a runaway kid turned up, Cathy would walk to Craddogh and call from the village phone box. Half the time the police weren't interested in what Cathy had to tell them. If they were, they only paid ten or twenty quid. Maybe fifty if it was a drug dealer and they caught him with a lot of stuff.

Cathy wasn't comfortable being a snitch, but sometimes it made the difference between having enough to buy a bottle of gas for the heater and freezing in her hut.

After Petrocon was announced the police got more interested in what Cathy had to say. The value of information went up. Cathy got at least thirty pounds every time, and they wanted to know everything that was going on at Fort

Harmony. Who came, who went, if anyone did anything suspicious, if there was an argument. Cathy got a taste for the money. She soon had a roll of notes stashed in a baked bean tin.

MI5 made Cathy an offer: £2,000 to let a couple of undercover agents stay with her at Fort Harmony in the weeks before Petrocon. Cathy didn't like the idea much; she'd lived alone for thirty years. MI5 offered more money until Cathy gave in.

*

James, Amy and Ewart walked into the Bristol Travelhouse. It was a basic hotel attached to a motorway service station. Cathy Dunn was waiting in her room in a cloud of cigarette smoke.

'My name is Ewart, these two are Ross and Courtney.'

Cathy sat up on her bed. She looked half drunk and tons older than in all the pictures James had seen of her.

'Who the hell are you?' Cathy asked.

'We spoke on the phone,' Ewart said. 'You're going to be looking after Ross and Courtney until the conference.'

'You've had me stuck in this hole for three days,' Cathy said. 'Now you turn up with two kids. If this is your idea of a joke, I'm not laughing.'

'You made a deal with us,' Ewart said. 'This is the deal.'

'I agreed to let two undercover agents stay with me. Not look after two kids.'

'Ross and Courtney are agents. Make their breakfast and send them to school for a few weeks, it's not brain surgery.'

'The government uses *children* to do its dirty work?' Cathy asked.

'Yes,' Ewart said.

Cathy laughed. 'That's absolutely appalling. I won't do it.'

'You already took our money,' Ewart said. 'Can you afford to pay us back?'

'I went to Greece, and I spent some money tidying up my hut.'

'Looks like you're stuck with us then.'

'What if I refuse to take them?' Cathy asked 'What if I went to the press and told everyone you're using kids to spy on people?'

'If you go to the press, they'll just think you're some flaky old hippy,' Ewart said. 'Nobody will believe a word out of your hole. Even if you get someone to believe you, you signed the Official Secrets Act before you took the money. You'd be looking at ten years in prison for releasing classified information.'

Cathy looked upset. 'I've always helped the police, now you treat me like dirt.'

Ewart grabbed Cathy's jumper. He lifted her up and knocked her against the wall.

'You don't break deals with us,' Ewart shouted. 'There's six months' work gone into this operation. You're getting eight grand to look after these kids for a few weeks. If that's being treated like dirt, you can treat me like dirt whenever you like.'

James was shocked seeing Ewart flip out. Until now the mission had felt like part of a competition to do better than Kyle, Bruce and Kerry. Now it felt real. People could get blown apart by bombs or end up in prison for the rest of their lives. James suddenly didn't feel up to the job. He was a twelve-year-old kid who should be going to school and messing around with his mates.

Amy noticed the scared look on James' face. She put a hand on his shoulder.

'Stand outside if you want to,' Amy whispered.

'I'm fine,' James lied.

Amy gave Ewart a shove.

'Calm down. Leave her alone,' Amy said.

Ewart backed off, giving Amy a filthy look. Cathy sat on the bed. Amy passed Cathy a cigarette. Amy had to light it because Cathy's hands were shaking.

'Sorry about Ewart,' Amy said. 'Bit of a short fuse. You OK?'

Cathy nodded.

'Listen Cathy,' Amy said gently. 'We get up, go to school, hang out at Fort Harmony. Then we go away again. It's the easiest money you'll ever make.'

Cathy shook her head, 'It's all a bit of a shock, that's all.'

Amy smiled, 'It always is. Nobody gets told we're kids until the last minute.'

'How can I explain that I've got you two living with me?' Cathy asked, taking a deep puff on her cigarette.

'Niece and nephew,' Amy said. 'Remember your sister?'

'I haven't seen her in twenty years,' Cathy said. 'She wrote a few times.'

'Remember what your sister called her kids?' Ewart asked, voice back to normal.

Cathy worked it out.

'Ross and Courtney,' she said.

We tracked down your sister,' Ewart said. 'She lives in Scotland. Still married. The real Ross and Courtney are fine. But here's your story:

'A week ago, you got a letter. Your sister is going through a nasty divorce. You rushed to London to meet her. She couldn't cope with her kids, especially Ross who's been expelled from school. You got on well with the kids, so you offered to look after them at Fort Harmony until your sister gets her life back on track.'

Ewart handed Cathy a set of car keys.

'Land Cruiser,' Ewart said. 'Big four wheel drive. It's a couple of years old. Worth about ten grand. Tell everyone it's your sister's car. If you look after the kids and the mission works out, we won't be asking for it back.'

*

The four of them made their way down to the hotel lobby.

'You better go in the toilet with me,' Ewart said. 'It's a long drive down to Wales.'

'I just went,' James said.

Ewart gave James a look. James realised Ewart wanted to speak to him. The toilet was deserted.

'You OK, James?' Ewart said, unzipping his jeans. 'You looked a bit off-colour when I grabbed Cathy.'

'Why'd you go psycho with her?'

Ewart smiled. 'Ever heard of good cop bad cop?'

'They do it on TV,' James said. 'Is that what you and Amy just did?'

'If Cathy's not sure whose side she's on, you and Amy wouldn't be safe. Once I realised Cathy was getting stroppy, I had to be the bad cop and scare her. Amy's job was to be the good cop. Amy defended Cathy when I threatened her, then calmed her down.'

James smiled. 'So Cathy's afraid of what might happen if she doesn't do what we want her to do, but at the same time she thinks Amy is her friend.'

'Exactly, James.'

'You could have told me when you arranged to do it.'

'We didn't arrange it. Amy knew what to do when I started getting rough with Cathy. Amy's brilliant at picking up stuff like that.'

'What if Cathy caused any more problems? Would you really hurt her?'

'Only if the mission depended on it and I had no other choice. Sometimes we have to do bad things to make missions work. Remember when you sneaked to London before training?'

'Sure,' James said. 'Smashing up that big house.'

'The security guards on the gate got gassed by MI5. What do you think happened to them after they woke up?'

'How should I know?'

'They got sacked for sleeping at work. They won't get another security job with that on their records.'

'So what happened to them?'

'We ruined their lives,' Ewart said. 'Hopefully they got jobs doing something different.'

'We didn't help them or nothing?'

'No. We couldn't without risking the secrecy of the mission.'

'That's terrible,' James said. 'How can we do that to people?'

'We were trying to get info about a man selling weapons

to terrorists. The weapons could kill hundreds of people, so we decided it was OK if two people lost their jobs.'

'And it's the same with scaring Cathy,' James said. 'People could get killed.'

'Like they say, James: you can't make an omelette without breaking eggs.'

*

Cathy enjoyed driving James and Amy in the Land Cruiser; blasting down the M4, testing all the buttons and gadgets. Amy was up front. James laid flat across the back seat. Cathy and Amy chatted like old pals.

When they stopped for petrol Cathy bought a Jefferson Airplane CD with some housekeeping money Ewart had given her. She put it on full blast. Amy and Cathy puffed one cigarette after another. James stuck his coat over his head to escape the noise and smoke.

James sat up when they got off the motorway. He was impressed with the green fields and hills with sheep dotted over them. They stopped in Craddogh for cigarettes and groceries and reached Fort Harmony soon after 3 p.m. Half a dozen grimy kids ran towards the four wheel drive as it climbed uphill to Cathy's hut. James knew the name and age of every kid.

Cathy's ex-husband, Michael Dunn, and his brother, Joshua, walked towards the car. Michael thumped the bonnet.

'Nice wheels, Cathy,' Michael said. 'You win the lottery or something?'

James got out. His trainer was swallowed by mud. The camp looked a mess, flaking paint and windows stuck up with tape. James decided he was going to hate living here.

Amy squelched to the back of the car and grabbed two pairs of wellies.

'My niece and nephew,' Cathy said.

James sat in the car and pulled on his wellies. Joshua Dunn held out a gloved hand. James shook it.

'Come soup,' Joshua stuttered.

Amy and Cathy were heading towards a big hut. James and Joshua followed. About fifteen people were inside. Chickens and a huge pot of vegetable soup cooked over an open fire.

'Vegetarian?' Joshua asked.

James shook his head.

Joshua fetched James a bowl of soup and some chicken. There were cushions and beanbags along the walls, but the kids all sat cross-legged near the fire. James sat with them. He ate a couple of spoonfuls of soup. It tasted pretty good. Then he looked at his hands. They were filthy, but the other kids, who were all ten times dirtier, scoffed the chicken with bare fingers.

A hand rested on James' shoulder. It was Gladys Dunn.

'A bit of dirt won't harm you, boy,' she laughed.

Gladys looked her seventy-six years, but the outdoor lifestyle kept her lean and she moved well for her age.

A five-year-old girl sitting beside James ran her tongue up her filthy palm and held it out for James to see. James grabbed a bit of chicken and stuffed it in his mouth. The girl smiled.

*

A group led by Michael Dunn built an extension on Cathy's hut for James and Amy to sleep in. It was impressive watching the community work as a team.

First they laid out paving slabs to raise the floor off the ground. The floor was chipboard wrapped in plastic. The framework was timber. Michael Dunn had obviously built loads of huts. He sawed each piece without measuring and never made a mistake. Others took the wood as soon as it was cut and knew where each piece fitted.

Thick corner posts were bashed into the ground. Trusses were nailed between them. Hardboard was nailed to either side of the frame, with shredded paper packed in the cavity as insulation. A hole was made in one side and a recycled window was fixed in. When it got dark Cathy turned on the Land Cruiser headlamps. Once the roof was on two boys were lifted up. They crawled around nailing down a layer of waterproof felt. Inside James helped seal the gap between the floor and the walls with grey putty.

After it was finished Amy got a rug from the Land Cruiser and set out sleeping bags and pillows. Cathy found a small paraffin heater. Michael Dunn said he would paint the outside in the morning. Finally, James and Amy were left alone.

30. CAMP

The new shelter was quite cosy once you got used to the wind blasting the outside. James' sleeping bag rested on a foam camping mattress. He couldn't get comfortable. Amy snored. James shouted at her twice. The third time, Amy said she'd punch him if he woke her up again. James stuck a pillow over his head.

*

James woke at 3 a.m., busting for a pee. He was used to walking two steps to his bathroom at CHERUB. It was tougher here. He couldn't find his torch, so he had to put on jeans in the dark, then make his way blindly through the main part of the hut, stepping around Cathy who was sprawled over a futon. James felt for the door, where all the wellies were lined up. He wasn't sure which pair was his, so he stuck on the first pair he found and stepped into the blackness.

There were portable toilets on site, but James couldn't find them in the dark so he wandered into the nearest group of trees. He wiped mud off his hands on to his trousers, undid his jeans, and started to piss. Something shrieked and brushed against his leg. James jolted. He was peeing on one of the chickens that roamed around camp.

He turned away, but that was into the wind, so his urine got blown all over his jeans. James stumbled back, tripped over the hysterical chicken and hit the mud. There was no way to get clean. He wondered why this type of thing never happened to spies in films.

*

Amy was up, and she'd slept fine. She stuck her foot over James' face to wake him up.

'Shower day, Ross,' Amy said.

James burst into life.

'Get that stink off my face,' James said, pushing Amy's foot away. 'Who's Ross?'

'You are, stupid,' Amy whispered.

'Sorry,' James gasped, realising where he was. 'I *must* remember that.'

'There's a rota for hot water,' Amy said. 'You get one shower a week. Friday is boys.'

'One shower a week?' James said. 'With all this mud.'

'How do you think I feel? I've got to wait four days and I don't exactly smell great now.'

Cathy showed him where the wash hut was. It was narrow, with a reservoir of rainwater on the roof. Every morning a gas boiler heated enough water to run the showers for ten minutes. If you missed out, you stank for another week. James dashed to the shower hut and stripped. There were eight boys under the water, sharing bars of soggy white soap and messing about. Mums stood outside, telling the little ones to get a move on. The water was barely warm. James rubbed soap in his hair as the hot ran out. The others knew better and scrambled off. James had to rinse with a bucket of freezing rainwater. He sprinted back to Cathy's hut wearing wellies and a big towel.

Cathy was cooking bacon and eggs on a portable gas stove. It smelled good and there was plenty of it.

'Do you kids drink coffee?' Cathy asked. 'It's all I've got.'

James didn't care what it was as long as it was warm. He drank two cups and stuffed down four rashers of bacon and two runny fried eggs, mopping the yolk off his plate with white bread.

'I've got to go enrol Ross in school,' Cathy said. 'Then I'll go to Tesco. Anything you two want?'

'Mars bars,' James said. 'What about enrolling Courtney?'

'After you went to bed I met this guy Scargill,' Amy said. 'He said he'd try and fix me a job at Green Brooke.'

James was impressed Amy had made such a fast attachment to Scargill. He was also miffed that she'd got out of school.

'I guess you'll start school on Monday, Ross,' Cathy said. 'Friday night here is usually a laugh. Everyone turns up after dark. We build a bonfire and play music and stuff.'

*

Amy stayed in the hut making phone calls to Ewart Asker, telling him the change in her plans and getting him to sort out the paperwork she needed to get a job. James spent the morning exploring.

There were about fifty buildings at Fort Harmony. They varied – from the main hut, with space for thirty and its own supply of electricity, down to rat holes fit only for storing junk. Between huts were chicken coops, vegetable patches, strings of washing and a range of battered cars. There were rusty vans everywhere, though most had no wheels and rested on bricks.

Everyone James met had grubby clothes and long tangled hair. The older men had beards, most of the younger ones had daft goatees and piercings everywhere. They all acted friendly and everyone asked James the same questions about how he ended up here and how long he was staying. By the time he'd met five people James was sick of repeating himself.

Before long James realised he had a tail: three-year-old Gregory Evans. He was the son of Brian 'Bungle' Evans and his partner Eleanor. MI5 thought they might have links to Help Earth.

Gregory followed James at a distance. When James looked around Gregory would crouch down and cover his face with his hands. It turned into a game. James stopped walking and looked around every few steps. Gregory was giggling. After a bit Gregory got up his courage and start walking beside James. James remembered he had a couple of Maltesers in his pocket and gave them to the toddler. After stuffing them, Gregory ran off. He stopped, turned, and shouted at James.

'Come to my house.'

James felt odd being bossed around by a three-year-old. They ran about a hundred metres, Gregory leading James by the hand.

Gregory sat down on the doorstep of a smartly painted hut and pulled off his wellies.

'Come in,' Gregory said.

James put his head in the door. The hut had room for six to sleep. The floor was painted bright orange, with shocking green walls and a purple ceiling. Plastic dolls hung everywhere. James noticed they were mutants, with blood painted on their faces and freaky punk hairstyles.

'Who's that?' Bungle asked, with an American twang.

James was embarrassed, standing in a strange doorway on the orders of a three-year-old.

'Sorry, Gregory brought me here,' James explained.

'What you sorry for, boy?' Bungle said. 'We're a community. Come in, get your boots off. Gregory's always dragging kids in here. You want hot milk?'

James pulled his wellies off and stepped inside. It was wonderfully warm, but smelled like farts and sweat. Eleanor lay on a mattress. She had nothing on but knickers and a Nirvana T-shirt stretched over a pregnant belly.

Gregory gave his mum a cuddle. Bungle made introductions, asked James the same questions as everyone else, then handed him a mug of hot milk.

'Unzip your tracksuit top, Ross,' Bungle said.

James was mystified but did what he was asked.

'Reebok,' Bungle said triumphantly.

'What?' James asked, confused.

'He hates people who wear clothes with trademarks on,' Eleanor explained.

'What's wrong with what I'm wearing?' James asked.

'I don't hate the people,' Bungle said. 'I hate the clothes. Look at yourself, Ross. Puma jacket, Nike tracksuit, Reebok T-shirt, even his socks have got a logo on them.'

'Just ignore Bungle,' Eleanor said. 'He thinks people wearing labels on their clothes is a sign that they can't think for themselves.'

Bungle rushed over to a bookshelf and passed James a book called *No Logo*.

'Give your brain a bit of exercise,' Bungle said. 'Read it. If you want we can discuss it when you bring it back.'

James took the book.

'I'll look at it,' James said. 'All my stuff is Nike and that. At my old school you got your head stuck down the toilet if you wore unfashionable clothes.'

'For god's sake, Bungle,' Eleanor said. 'He's a kid. He's not interested in that stuff.'

James didn't care what some hippy thought about his clothes, but the book gave James an excuse to come back and hang around a prime suspect, so he put it in his pocket and said thanks.

'Ross, ask him about the dolls before he bores you to death talking about the evils of world capitalism,' Eleanor said.

Bungle sounded annoyed. 'You handed out leaflets with us, Eleanor.'

Eleanor laughed. 'Ross, in principle, I support fair wages for people in poor countries. I want to help save the environment. I want Bungle and his pals to save the world. But I'm eight months pregnant. The baby presses on my insides, so every half hour I waddle through two hundred metres of filth to go sit on a stinking portable toilet. Gregory is driving me crazy. My ankles are swollen like beach balls and I'm half terrified the car we borrowed is going to break down on the way to the hospital when I go into labour. I'd happily surrender all my principles for a comfy bed in a private hospital.'

James sat on the floor and sipped his hot milk.

'The dolls are excellent,' he said. 'Did you make them?'

'That's my living,' Bungle said.

Bungle pulled one of the dolls off the ceiling and dropped it in James' lap. It was the torso and head of an Action Man. but it wore a tutu and had skinny ballerina legs glued on. The hair was spiky purple. One hand was cut off and the stump was painted with fake blood.

'Cool,' James said.

'I buy the dolls at jumble sales and boot fairs. Then I mix all the bits up and make weird costumes and stuff out of scraps.'

'How much?' James asked.

'Depends where,' Bungle said. 'Cardiff market, they're all poor, nobody will pay more than ten pounds. If I get a stall at Camden in London you can sell them for eighteen a throw. When it's packed out in the summer you can shift sixty dolls a day. One time I sold eighty-four.'

'One thousand, five hundred and twelve quid in a day,' James said. 'You must be loaded.'

'You some sort of human adding machine?' Bungle asked.

James laughed. 'Kind of.'

'Takes over an hour to make each one. Painting all the fiddly bits does your eyes in. You want a doll, Ross?'

'They're cool,' James said. 'I haven't got any money though.'

'Take one,' Bungle said. 'Maybe you can do us a favour. Look after Gregory for a couple of hours one day or something.'

*

It was an unwritten Fort Harmony rule that there was a free evening meal in the main hut for anyone who wanted it. Gladys Dunn bought vegetables from local farmers with the money she earned from her book. Joshua spent his afternoons preparing the vegetables and making either stew or a curry. Everyone eating together was what made Fort Harmony a community rather than a bunch of separate families.

James ate with the kids when they got out of school. Michael Dunn collected a vanload of scrap from a local dump. All the kids helped pile up old doors and bits of furniture to make a bonfire for the evening festivities. James tried to make friends with Sebastian and Clark Dunn. They were ten and eleven-year-old brothers; cousins of Fire, World and Scargill. The Dunns were a close family, and Sebastian and Clark were James' best chance to pick up all the gossip.

31. NIGHT

James found Amy and Scargill sitting on Amy's bed smoking. Scargill looked like a geek: spindly arms and legs, greasy black hair tied back in a pony-tail. He wore a kitchen uniform from his job at Green Brooke.

'It stinks in here,' James said, stepping in through the hole between the old and new parts of Cathy's hut.

'This is my little brother, Ross,' Amy said. 'He's a whiny little shit.'

'You're *harsh*, Courtney,' Scargill said, laughing.

James was hurt. They had to act like brother and sister, but he didn't see why she had to be nasty. He was also jealous: Scargill was getting to spend all his time with Amy.

'Why are you here, Ross?' Amy asked.

'This *is* my room as well,' James said.

'Scargill and me want privacy, so get what you came in for and sod off.'

'Did you get a job?' James asked.

'I'm an attendant at Green Brooke spa,' Amy said. 'Four days a week.'

James started rummaging through his stuff.

'What do you want, Ross?' Amy asked.

'My mobile,' James said. 'I was gonna see how Mum is.'

'Take mine, it's charging up in the car.'

'Thanks, Courtney,' James said.

*

James sat in the front seat of the Land Cruiser and made a call to Ewart Asker.

'Hey, James, how's it going?' Ewart asked.

'Not bad, Amy's pissing me off.'

'She with Scargill?'

'Permanently,' James said.

'That's her job, James. She's got to get as close to him as she can.'

'She told him I was a whiny shit.'

Ewart cracked up. 'That gives Scargill a sign that she prefers him to her kid brother. She doesn't mean it.'

'Scargill must be in heaven,' James said. 'Scrawny little nerd and he's got Amy all over him.'

'You've got a bit of a soft spot for Amy, don't you?' Ewart asked.

James' instinct was to deny it.

'A bit,' he admitted. 'If I was older I'd ask her out. How did you know?'

Ewart laughed. 'You get this glazed look in your eyes when she's in the room.'

James panicked. 'What? Is it that obvious?'

'I'm joking, James,' Ewart said. 'So how's Cathy?'

'Seems OK now,' James said.

'How did you get on with Sebastian and Clark Dunn?'

'Bad,' James said. 'They're weird kids. Tough-looking and

smelly. They talk to each other as if you're not even there. None of the other kids hang out with them much either.'

'Keep trying, but don't force it. Any other news?'

'I got one good break,' James said. 'I made friends with Gregory Evans, Bungle's son. I spent nearly an hour with them. Bungle gave me a book called *No Logo* to read.'

'Good book,' Ewart said. 'Read it. Go and see him, pretend you don't understand something and use it as an excuse to hang around.'

'There's not much about Bungle on file, is there?' James said.

'No. He's been seen with all the bad guys, but he's never been arrested. There are over a thousand people called Brian Evans in Britain; we don't know which one he is. We don't even know exactly how old he is or where he comes from.'

'He sounds American,' James said. 'He's got that twangy sound in his voice. I think they call them rubbernecks.'

'What's a rubberneck?'

'Like in the movies. Cowboy types, kind of stupid, he sounds like one of those.'

Ewart laughed. 'You mean a redneck?'

'That's it,' James said. 'He sounds like a redneck.'

'That's useful to know. I'll get the Yanks to see if they have anything on him. What we need is for you to get in Bungle's hut, take some pictures and have a rummage through any paperwork you can find. But don't take any risks to make it happen. If you're seen taking pictures for no good reason it will blow your cover.'

'Bungle said they might ask me to keep an eye on their little boy when they go out.'

'That would be an ideal opportunity, specially if the kid falls asleep. Are you sure they'd trust someone your age to look after him?'

'Bungle suggested it,' James said.

'Don't sound too eager, they might think it's odd. Anything else?'

'That's all I can think of,' James said.

'Keep in touch, James,' Ewart said. 'It sounds like you're doing a grand job.'

'Thanks, bye Ewart.'

*

It was past eleven and people were still arriving. They came in groups of four and five, pulling booze, food and firewood out of cars. Portable CD players competed with didgeridoos, tom-toms and guitars. The crowd was mostly teenagers and twenty-somethings: students from Cardiff and kids from the local villages, with a few old hippies who had turned up every Friday since the year dot.

James wandered. He felt awkward. Younger kids rushed around chasing and fighting, older ones drank beer and snogged. James didn't fit well with either group. He moved away from the party into the forest. He could hear bangs from a clearing in the distance. As James got closer he worked out it was the sound of an air pistol. The kids were Sebastian and Clark Dunn. They were freaks. If James wasn't on a mission he would have steered clear, but it was his job to make friends. He decided to have another go.

Sebastian and Clark vanished before James reached the clearing. There was a bird on the ground, cooing loudly and struggling in the mud. It was hard to see what was wrong in the dark, but the bird was in a bad way. James crouched down. He wondered if he should bash the bird with a rock to put it out of its misery.

Sebastian bolted out from the trees. He landed on top of James and tried to pin him, but James was too strong. James elbowed Sebastian in the stomach. Clark came out to help with the ambush. He was almost as tall as James and probably heavier. Clark bashed James over the head with a heavy torch. The brothers managed to get James under control.

Clark pressed the torch head into James' eye and clicked the bulb on. Squeezing his eyelid tight didn't stop the light from burning his eye. James was worried. Hopefully they would just rough him up, but who knew how crazy these kids were? If James yelled nobody would hear over all the noise from the party.

'Why are you following us, scum?' Clark asked.

'I wasn't,' James said. 'I just came this way.'

Clark grabbed a chunk of James' hair and tugged his head out of the mud. James felt Sebastian, who was sitting on his legs, shift his weight slightly. James kicked up both legs, hitting Sebastian in his back. Sebastian yelled out and tumbled off. Now his legs were free, James thrashed about and tried to release his arms, which were pinned to his sides by Clark's thighs.

'I'll knock you out,' Clark said.

Clark punched James in the head. James put all his strength into lifting his stomach off the ground, making space under himself to slide out his hands. He scrambled from under Clark and stood up. Clark ran at James. James realised that months of getting hammered by black belts at CHERUB was about to pay off. Without the element of surprise, Sebastian and Clark didn't have a chance.

James waited until Clark got close. He sidestepped, kicked Clark full force in the stomach, punched him in the mouth and finished off stamping him behind the knee so he smacked into the ground. Sebastian looked angry but didn't fancy joining in. Clark looked pleadingly at James from his knees, hoping his beating was finished.

'I don't want to hurt you,' James said. 'Just say you quit.'

Clark scrambled up, gasping for air. He was hurt, but a smile came on to his face.

'I've battered kids heaps bigger than you,' Clark said. 'Where'd you learn to fight?'

James found a tissue in his pocket. He gave it to Clark to wipe the blood off his split lip.

'Self defence classes,' James said. 'Back in London.'

Clark turned to his brother.

'They were serious punches, Sebastian.'

'You have to put your whole body into it,' James said. 'Starts at the hips. If you get the technique right it's eight times harder than a normal punch.'

'Let him hit you in the guts, Sebastian,' Clark said. 'I bet you double over.'

'I don't want to hit him,' James said.

'We hit each other to keep tough,' Clark said. 'If I hit him in the guts he doesn't even flinch.'

Sebastian stood with his hands behind his back ready to take a hit.

'I'll hit his shoulder,' James said.

'You can hit my guts,' Sebastian said. 'I can take it.'

'In the arm first,' James said. 'Then I'll do it in your guts if you still want me to.'

Sebastian turned so his side was facing James. James didn't want to have to hit him in the stomach, he knew it could do serious damage, so he gave Sebastian his hardest shot in the arm. Sebastian stumbled sideways and screamed out in pain, clenching his upper arm with his hand. Clark was wetting himself laughing.

'I told you it was hard,' Clark said.

Sebastian tried not to show the pain. James felt bad for hitting him so hard.

All this time the pigeon was still thrashing about in the mud. James looked at it.

'What happened to it?'

'Shot it with the air pistol,' Clark said.

'Wasn't dead,' Sebastian said. 'So I cut one of its wings off with my pen knife.'

'You guys are lunatics,' James said, grimacing.

'Better hope the shot kills you,' Clark grinned. 'If it doesn't it's torture time.'

'Can't you put the poor thing out of its misery?' James said.

'If you want me to,' Sebastian said.

Sebastian walked towards the bird. It didn't have much life in it. Sebastian pressed his heel into the bird. It let out a final desperate noise as its bones were crushed. Sebastian had a big smile on his face.

James realised he'd made friends with a couple of seriously twisted kids.

32. GIRL

Sebastian, Clark and James went to the main hut to feed. Guests had brought meat to barbecue, as well as the cold dishes laid out on a long table. Joshua Dunn was serving vegetable curry. James wasn't mad on curry, but it was good stuff after being out in the cold. They took the food outside to the bonfire. A few dozen people sat on waterproof sheets around the fire. Sebastian and Clark found Fire and World and sat beside them.

'Hey, little psychos,' Fire said.

'Hey, jailbirds,' Clark said, referring to his cousins' spell in prison.

Fire and World were non-identical twins, with plaited hair and pierced eyebrows.

World looked at James. He sounded drunk. 'Care to tell me what your sexy sister sees in our baby brother?'

James shrugged. 'She's not fussy. Snogs anything with a pulse.'

'What was that?' Amy said.

James hadn't noticed her sitting a few metres away. All the Dunns laughed. Amy faced James off with her hands on her hips. James couldn't decide if she was angry or just messing.

'Nothing,' James squirmed. 'I was just saying what a nice couple you and Scargill make.'

Amy crushed James with a hug that took his feet off the ground.

'That's really sweet of you, Ross,' Amy said. 'Because after what I thought you said, I was going to kick all your teeth out.'

*

James finished his curry and wandered off on his own. He noticed a girl leaning against a tree smoking. Long hair, baggy jeans. She was about James' age, nice looking. He didn't remember her from any of the intelligence files.

'Hey, can I have a drag?' James said, trying to sound cool.

'Sure,' the girl said.

She passed James the cigarette. James had never tried one before and hoped he wasn't about to make an idiot of himself. He gave it a little suck. It burned his throat, but he managed not to cough.

'Not seen you here before,' the girl said.

'I'm Ross,' James said. 'Staying here with my aunt for a bit.'

'Joanna,' the girl said. 'I live in Craddogh.'

'Haven't been there yet,' James said.

'It's a dump, two shops and a Post Office. Where you from?'

'London.'

'I wish I was,' Joanna said. 'You like it here?'

'I'm always covered in mud. I want to go to bed, but there's a guy playing a guitar three metres from where I sleep. I wish I could go home, have a warm shower, and see my mates.'

Joanna smiled.

'So why are you staying with your aunt?'

'Long story: parents getting divorced. Mum freaking out. Got expelled from school.'

'So you're good looking *and* you're a rebel,' Joanna said.

James was glad it was quite dark because he felt himself blush.

'You want the last puff, Ross?'

'No, I'm cool,' James said.

Joanna flicked the cigarette butt into the night.

'So, I paid you a compliment,' Joanna said.

'Yeah.'

Joanna laughed. 'So do I get one back?' she asked.

'Oh, sure,' James said. 'You're really like … nice.'

'Can't I get any better than nice?'

'Beautiful,' James said. 'You're beautiful.'

'That's more like it,' Joanna said. 'Want to kiss me?'

'Um, OK,' James said.

James was nervous. He'd never had the courage to ask a girl out. Now he was about to kiss someone he'd known for three minutes. He pecked her on the cheek. Joanna shoved James against the tree and started kissing his face and neck. Her hand went in the back pocket of James' jeans, then she jumped backwards.

'What did I do?' James asked. He'd just started enjoying himself.

'Police car,' Joanna said. 'Hide me somewhere.'

James saw a flashing blue light and a couple of cops getting out of a car a few hundred metres down the hill.

'Are you a runaway or something?' James asked.

'Hide me first, questions later.'

James led Joanna up the hill. The policemen were heading in the same direction. They seemed friendly and stopped to chat with a couple of people. James undid the padlock on Cathy's hut and clambered inside. Joanna slammed the door behind her.

'What's going on?' James asked.

'Peek outside,' Joanna said. 'Tell me what the police are doing.'

James stepped up to the window. 'I can only see one of them,' he said. 'He's talking to some guy.'

'What's he saying?'

'He's standing twenty metres away and it's dark. You expect me to read his lips? ... Wait ... The guy he's talking to is pointing at this hut.'

Joanna sounded hysterical. 'I'm in so much trouble.'

'Why?'

'I'm supposed to be sleeping over at my friend's house, but we came up here instead.'

'Where's your friend?' James asked.

'She met up with her boyfriend and abandoned me.'

'But why are the police out searching for *you*?'

The door of the hut came open and a policeman shone his torch in Joanna's face.

'Hello, Daddy,' Joanna said.

'You'd better get out here, young lady. I'm driving you home. And as for you...'

The policeman moved the beam of his torch so James' face lit up.

'...I don't know what you and my daughter have been up

to, but you'll stay away from her if you know what's good for you.'

James watched Joanna's dad take her to the police car. He didn't feel like going back outside. He lit the gas lamp, found his packet of Mars bars and poured a glass of unrefrigerated milk.

*

'I hear you tried to jump Sergeant Ribble's daughter,' Cathy said.

She looked smashed.

'I met her five minutes before her dad turned up,' James said. 'We had one little kiss.'

'So you claim, stud,' Cathy said.

She pinched James' cheek and laughed. Nobody had done that to James since he was about five.

'It's nice having you kids here,' Cathy said. 'Livens the place up.'

'I thought you didn't want us,' James said.

'It was a shock. But it gets dull here after thirty years.'

'Why don't you move on?'

'I might after you two go,' Cathy said. 'Cash in that monster car, travel for a bit. Don't know what after that. Maybe I'll try getting a flat and a job. I'm getting too old to keep scratching for a living round here.'

'What kind of job?' James asked.

Cathy laughed. 'God knows. I don't suppose there's anyone queuing up to employ fifty-year-old women who last had a job in 1971.'

'What doing?' James asked.

'I worked in the Student Union shop at my university.

Met Michael Dunn there. Married him a few years later. Came here. Had a little boy. Got divorced.'

'You have a son?' James asked.

'Had a son,' Cathy said. 'He died when he was three months old.'

'I'm sorry,' James said.

Cathy looked upset. She dragged out a wicker hamper and found a photo album. She flicked to a picture of a newborn in a white crochet hat.

'Harmony Dunn,' Cathy said. 'That's my only picture of him. Michael took it the day he was born.'

Seeing Cathy upset about her baby made James think about his mum. He felt a tear well up. He wanted to tell Cathy about his mum dying, but it would be breaking the rules of the mission. Cathy noticed James looked upset and put her arm around him.

'There's no need to get upset, Ross. It happened a long time ago.'

'Your whole life might have been different if he'd lived,' James said.

'Maybe,' Cathy said. 'You're a nice boy, Ross, or whatever your real name is.'

'Thanks,' James said.

'I don't think it's right the government using kids. You two could get hurt.'

'It's our choice,' James said. 'Nobody forces us to do it.'

'Courtney is using Scargill to get to Fire and World, isn't she?'

James was impressed Cathy had worked it out. It seemed pointless to deny it.

'Yeah,' he said.

'All the Dunn family have been good to me, even after I divorced Michael,' Cathy said. 'But those two have always been different. They're definitely up to something.'

'What makes you sure?' James asked.

'I've known Fire and World since they were born. There's something not right about them. A shiver goes up me when they walk into a room.'

33. FREAK

7 a.m. Monday, James' travel alarm went off to wake him for school. Amy threw a pillow at him when he didn't turn it off. He stumbled out of bed, rubbing his face, and unpinned a corner of the sheet over the window to let in some light.

'Can't you leave it dark?' Amy moaned from under her covers.

'I've got to go to school.'

James started putting on a sweatshirt and tracksuit bottoms.

'It's freezing,' James said.

'It's warm under here,' Amy said smugly. 'I don't have to get up for three hours.'

'I can't believe you got out of school, it's not bloody fair.'

Amy giggled under her covers. 'It's toasty at Green Brooke. The water in the Jacuzzi is beautiful, and I get a hot shower before and after my shift.'

'I'm filthy,' James said. 'I'm gonna get so much stick from the other kids going to school looking like this.'

'Put clean clothes on and use some of my deodorant.'

'I'm wearing clean stuff. I'll still be covered in mud three steps out the door. Where's your deodorant?'

'Down the end of my bed.'

Amy's deodorant was in a pink can with pictures of butterflies on it. James figured it was better smelling girly than stinking of BO so he gave himself a good blast.

'I'm glad I don't have to get up,' Amy giggled. 'This bed is really comfortable.'

James noticed Amy's leg poking out and tickled the sole of her foot. She pulled her leg in and squealed.

'Serves you right for teasing,' James said.

Amy flew out of bed, grabbed James around the waist and started tickling under his ribs.

'No, please,' James giggled.

James' legs buckled from laughing. His face was red and spit dribbled down his chin.

'Beg for mercy, weakling,' Amy said.

'No way,' James spluttered.

James couldn't wriggle free. Amy unleashed another wave of tickles.

'Oh no. Please... OK mercy. Stop... Mercy. I SAID MERCY.'

Amy stopped. Cathy's head poked in from her part of the hut. Her hair was all tangled.

'What's going on?' Cathy asked.

'Tickling,' James said, gasping for air.

'I thought you were dying or something. I was trying to sleep.'

'I've got to go to school,' James said.

'Do it quietly, Ross,' Cathy said. 'I'm laying in all morning.'

'Nice life for some,' James said. 'Is there anything for my breakfast?'

Cathy thought for a second.

'There's cold curry, or you could have the last one of your Mars bars.'

'Great,' James said.

Amy had snuggled back into bed and was laughing under her sheets.

*

It was a two-kilometre walk to the school bus stop in Craddogh. A few older Fort Harmony kids showed James the way. Joanna was at the stop with some friends. James said hello but she ignored him. The village kids wore smart casual clothes. Fort Harmony kids were tramps in comparison.

It was a half-hour ride to school, stopping a few times to pick up more kids. James rested his face against the window and watched the sun rise over the passing countryside.

*

Gwen Morgan school looked better than James' old school in London. The modern classrooms were in single storey clusters with covered walkways between them. The areas between buildings had flower beds and neatly trimmed grass with *Keep Off* signs. When the bell rang kids walked to registration. No shoving or fights breaking out. Even the boys' toilets were clean. James washed as much filth as he could off his face and hands before finding his class. He handed a note to his form teacher and found a desk.

'This is Ross,' the teacher announced. 'Please make him feel welcome here at Gwen Morgan and help him find his way around.'

The kids all looked polite and well behaved. Nobody spoke to James.

First lesson was science. James asked a kid if it was OK to sit next to him. The kid shrugged.

The lesson was dull. They were halfway through a topic, but James was bright enough to pick up what had gone on before and was soon bored. It felt really different to CHERUB where all the kids were clever and the teachers kept you on your toes. He wrote neatly in his new exercise book and homework diary, but it seemed like a waste of time. He would only be here a few weeks.

Between first and second lesson a couple of kids in James' class called Stuart and Gareth gave him a shove.

'Wait till break time, hippy boy,' one of them said.

James wasn't worried. He'd be able to fight them off if they tried anything.

He got another shove and a punch in the back from Gareth at the start of morning break. James knew he'd become a target if he looked soft, but he didn't want to end up rolling around the floor fighting on his first day, so he punched Gareth in the face and ran off. He spent the rest of morning break wandering on his own, paranoid that everyone was staring at him like a freak.

Gareth had a tissue plugged up his nose to stop it bleeding for the whole of third period. After lunch James wanted to join the kids playing football on the all weather pitches, but Gareth, Stuart and a couple of their pals were playing. James thought it best to steer clear. He found a quiet spot at the back of the school, sat against the outside wall of a classroom and started doing his homework.

*

James noticed a shadow over his science book and looked up. Gareth and Stuart were standing over him with six friends for back-up. James was furious with himself for letting them get so close without noticing.

'You killed my nose, Harmony boy,' Gareth said.

'I didn't ask for trouble,' James said. 'Leave me alone.'

Gareth laughed. 'In your dreams.'

'We hate all you Fort Harmony filth,' Stuart said. 'They should send the police up there and set dogs on you.'

James reckoned he could have beaten any two of them, managed to get a few hits in and escape against three or four, but eight against one … No chance.

'Stand up, hippy,' Gareth said.

If he stayed on the ground he could roll in a ball to protect himself. Standing would only mean getting knocked back down.

'Get your arse *up*,' Gareth repeated.

'Piss off,' James said. 'Haven't got the guts to fight me on your own, have you?'

Gareth kicked James in the knee. A few of the others moved closer so there were ten legs circling. James braced himself for pain. Kicks came fast, luckily there were so many legs flying they used a lot of energy hitting each other. James tried to tuck his knees into his chest, but a trainer clamped his stomach to the floor. He kept his legs together to protect his balls and wrapped his arms over his face.

The main beating lasted about a minute. A couple of the kids who weren't in the surrounding group gave some brutal kicks in the side to finish off.

'Better learn some respect, hippy,' Gareth said.

The gang walked off, mocking the way James was groaning in pain on the floor. James couldn't stop the tears forming, but he was determined not to cry out. His arms and legs were dead from the beating.

James got his books into his backpack and stumbled a couple of metres holding on to the wall before his knee gave out. He sat there until a teacher came to unlock his classroom. He tried to pretend he'd slipped and twisted his ankle, but the teacher could see James was hurting all over. The teacher put his arm around James and helped him hobble to the first-aid room.

*

Mr Crow, the Deputy Headmaster, came into the first-aid room. James was sitting on the edge of a bed in his boxers, holding a cup of orange squash. He had plasters on his legs and arms.

'Who did this to you, Ross?' Crow asked.

He was a small, friendly-sounding man with a Welsh accent.

'I don't know,' James said.

'Were any of them in your class?'

'No,' James said.

James thought it was best not to grass. The school wouldn't expel eight kids. They would only get suspended for a few days. Then all their mates and older brothers would be after James for grassing. His life would be hell. If he didn't grass and managed to make a few friends to back him up, things might be OK.

'Ross, I understand it's your instinct not to tell on your

classmates. But this is your first day here and you've been seriously assaulted. That is not acceptable. We want to help you.'

'I'll be OK,' James said. 'It's no big deal.'

*

By home time, James could walk again, sort of. He was let out of the first-aid room before the bell, giving him a chance to get on the bus without being caught up with everyone else. Joanna climbed on and sat next to him. It was the first good thing that had happened to him all day.

'What happened to you?' Joanna asked.

'What does it look like?' James said angrily. 'I got the crap beaten out of me.'

'Gareth Granger and Stuart Parkwood,' Joanna said.

'How did you know?' James asked.

'It's always them. They're not even tough; it's just they hang out in a big group and stick up for each other.'

'I just hope they don't make it a regular thing,' James said.

'You need a bath,' Joanna said.

'No chance of that at Fort Harmony.'

'Have one at my house if you want.'

'What about your dad?'

'Working till six. Then he usually goes for a drink.'

'Your mum?'

'Lives in Cardiff with my big brothers.'

'Are they divorced?' James asked.

'A few months ago.'

'What happened after your dad caught you on Friday?'

'Lost my pocket money, grounded for a fortnight.'

'Rough,' James said.

Joanna smiled. 'It's so stupid. My dad grounds me, but he's never home to stop me going out.'

*

Joanna's house was a little cottage on the edge of Craddogh with frilly net curtains and ornaments everywhere. Joanna flicked on MTV. They ate cheese on toast and drank tea while James' bath ran.

The soap made his cuts sting, but the hot water soothed his pains and it was nice feeling clean again. Joanna opened the bathroom door and tossed in a clean T-shirt and an old set of her brother's boxers. She cracked up when she saw James in the huge pair of shorts and a Puma T-shirt almost down to his knees.

Joanna took him into her room.

'Lie on my bed.'

She peeled off all James' soggy plasters, wiped his cuts with disinfectant and stuck on new ones. James stared at Joanna's long hair and the curve of her back as she leant over him. She looked beautiful.

James wanted to kiss her again, but Joanna was a year older and she'd mentioned a couple of previous boyfriends. He felt like he was in way over his head.

34. SICKIE

It was cold, spitting with rain. Every step back to Fort Harmony was agony for James' battered legs. He was facing an evening sitting around in a cold hut with no TV. Then he had to spend the night on a crappy mattress listening to Amy snore. Tomorrow he'd probably get beaten up at school.

But James was in the best mood: ninety minutes lying on Joanna's bed kissing and moaning about their lives. She put on a Red Hot Chilli Peppers CD and they sang all the words out loud. Every time James thought about Joanna he got such a rush nothing else mattered. When he got back to the hut Cathy and Amy were out. He was too excited to eat. James crashed on to his bed and daydreamed about Joanna.

*

'Are you deaf?' Sebastian shouted, a few centimetres from the end of James' bed. 'I knocked four times. Fire's got our radio-controlled cars running. Want to try them?'

James turned over. He didn't want to get up, but it was part of his mission.

James had had a radio-controlled car before his mum died. It was good fun, but it wasn't safe using it around his flats. Someone would have stolen or smashed it in five minutes. Sebastian and Clark's cars were superb. They were beach buggies with big rear tyres that sprayed up mud. Instead of batteries there were tiny petrol engines between the rear wheels. Clark stopped his car in front of James and handed him the radio control.

'Gently,' Clark said.

'I've driven a car before,' James said, as if Clark was stupid.

James put the car full on forward. The engine buzzed noisily and a blue plume shot out the exhaust. It didn't move a millimetre. The wheels dug into the mud.

'Gently, dingus,' Clark said.

Sebastian lifted the car. James lightly nudged the stick and the car blasted off at about fifty kilometres an hour.

James laughed out, 'Cool.'

He drove a big circle, nearly crashing into some trees, running under the Land Cruiser and almost rolling the car on its side as he did a sharp turn to bring the car back near to his feet.

'That was excellent,' James said. 'So fast. Where did you get them?'

'Fire and World made them when they were teenagers.' Clark said. 'Only thing is they're always going wrong and Fire never wants to fix them for us. He's got about six more cars in his workshop.'

'Can I see them?'

'Won't let us in there any more.'

The workshop sounded interesting, but James didn't want to seem pushy about finding more out.

'What do they do there?' he asked.

'Dunno,' Sebastian said. 'Trying to take over the universe knowing those two.'

'Anyway, I heard you got battered at school today,' Clark said.

'Yeah,' James said.

'Didn't grass, did you?'

'No way.'

'Me and Sebastian used to get beaten up all the time because we're from Fort Harmony. It's not so bad now, we're two of the biggest in our school.'

'We're the kings,' Sebastian said. 'There's a guy in my class so scared of us we click our fingers and he licks our trainers. Don't have to hit him or nothing.'

'You start at Gwen Morgan in September?' James asked.

'Both of us do,' Clark said. 'There's only a ten-month age gap between us.'

'At least you can back each other up.'

'We've been suspended for fighting three times,' Clark said. 'Next time we get expelled, but I'd rather be expelled than let people dump on us.'

'What do your mum and dad say?'

'Never met our dad. Our mum knows the score. All the boys who live at Fort Harmony get bullied by the normal kids.'

'What did you think of us at first?' Sebastian asked.

James laughed. 'Not much. You weren't exactly friendly.'

'If you got treated like you were today, every single day since you were five years old, you wouldn't be friendly either.'

'What should I do?' James asked.

'You were right not to grass,' Clark said 'If you're a snitch the whole school will be against you. Never give in. Never grovel or beg, it only encourages them. For a tough kid like you, Ross, best thing to do is get one of the leaders on his own and massacre him.'

'They'll kill me if I do that,' James said.

'There's a big choice of targets,' Clark said. 'A gang will think twice before picking on a kid who can get them back when they're on their own.'

'I don't want to get in trouble,' James said. 'I got expelled from my last school.'

Sebastian laughed. 'Better get used to having someone standing on your nuts then.'

*

After eating in the main hut James lay on his bed again. Amy was furious when she got out of work and saw the state he was in.

'I'll go down that school and kick their butts myself,' Amy screamed. 'Nobody does that to my baby brother.'

'I can handle it,' James said.

'You can't handle it. Why didn't you tell the school who did it?'

'I'm not a grass,' James said. 'Grasses are lower than kids who wet their pants.'

'I think you should go to a hospital, you might have concussion,' Amy said.

'I can't have concussion, I didn't get kicked in the head,' James lied. 'Can we talk about something more important?'

'What's more important than you coming home looking like a bus ran over you?'

'Have you seen Fire and World's workshop?' James asked.

'I've seen their hut. You certainly couldn't call it a workshop.'

'Sebastian said they've got a workshop. Him and Clark aren't allowed in it any more. Sounds like the sort of place we should be checking out.'

'Did you ask where it was?'

'No, I'll try and find out.'

'I'll see if I can wangle something out of Scargill,' Amy said. 'I bet it's one of those huts that looks like it's been abandoned.'

*

James sat in the Land Cruiser and phoned his daily report to Ewart. He left out how much of a crush he had on Joanna.

'Does it matter if I get in trouble at school?' James asked.

'Like how?' Ewart asked.

'If I get suspended. I figured it might even be good for the mission because I'd get to spend more time snooping around here.'

Ewart laughed. 'And by lucky coincidence you get out of school for a few days.'

'That hadn't even crossed my mind,' James said, but gave himself away by laughing.

'I suppose it wouldn't be much of a problem. But you're not above the law just because you're on a mission, so don't go burning down the school or anything.'

*

7 a.m. Tuesday, James' travel alarm went off for school. He turned it off and pulled the covers over his head.

'You'll miss the bus if you don't get a move on,' Amy said.

'Not going,' James said. 'My back's stiff. I can hardly move.'

'You were shooting stuff with Sebastian and Clark until nearly midnight. You seemed all right then.'

'Must have tightened up in the night,' James said.

Amy laughed. 'Pull the other one. It's got bells on.'

James lay in until ten, deliberately staying under the covers until after Amy got up for work. Cathy was in a good mood. She sent James out to collect eggs from the chicken coop and made omelettes with mushrooms and bacon.

James read the first few chapters of *No Logo*, in case Bungle asked him any questions about it, then went for a walk. Joshua Dunn was in the main hut preparing a mountain of vegetables. Gladys Dunn was there as well, reading the morning paper.

'Can I look at the sports?' James asked.

She handed him the paper.

'Rough time at school, I hear,' Gladys said.

'Yeah.'

'Not a good place for young boys here,' Gladys said. 'All my grandsons are a funny lot. Get bullied at school. Take it out on the local wildlife or hide inside books.'

James smiled. 'They're not so bad.'

'You've brought it home to me, Ross. One day and you're beaten up. You don't even look or dress like the other kids here. Boys are so cruel.'

'What can you do?' James asked.

'We had a school here once. Parents took it in turns to teach the kids. All turned into squabbling about who taught the lessons.'

'Everyone here has been really nice to me,' James said. 'But I don't understand why people want to live here.'

Gladys wagged her finger, 'You put your finger on a question I've been asking myself lately. At first Fort Harmony was about freedom and some young people having fun. When the police tried to destroy us, we sent out a signal that a bunch of nobodies could stand up against the government and win. But what are we now? A trendy campsite for backpackers. Half the people who live here clean and cook for rich businessmen in that bloody conference centre.'

James was a bit stunned. 'So why stay?'

'Can you keep a secret, Ross?' Gladys asked.

'I guess.'

'My second book comes out in September. It should earn me enough to buy a house somewhere warm. I'll take Joshua. The others can fight over Fort Harmony.'

'I read your first book,' James said. 'It was interesting.'

Gladys looked surprised. 'I didn't have you pegged for a bookworm, Ross.'

James kicked himself for revealing that he'd read the book. Twenty-year-old memoirs of life on a commune aren't exactly standard reading for twelve-year-old boys.

'Cathy had a copy,' James stuttered, wondering if she actually did. 'And there's no TV here.'

'Thank goodness,' Gladys smiled.

'I liked the bit where you were all hiding from police in the tunnels and you were trying to keep the kids quiet. Must have been scary.'

'I should never have taken my boys underground. Joshua

was the brightest one, now he's happy spending four hours a day peeling vegetables.'

'I suppose the tunnels are all gone,' James said.

'There's bits and pieces left. I wouldn't try playing in them, Ross, not very safe.'

'Don't worry, I wouldn't go into them. It's just that I've not seen any sign of them.'

'That's because the camp has moved. We started off at the bottom of the hill down by the road. The main hut was under a metre of water sometimes, so we moved up here where the water drains away.'

*

James stuck his head round the door of Bungle's hut. He was sitting around drinking coffee with Fire, World and Scargill. Gregory was racing Matchbox cars over his parents' bed.

'I just came to say hello,' James said. 'I'll go away if you're busy.'

Bungle laughed. 'You're too polite, Ross. Sit down, you want coffee or tea?'

'Tea,' James said.

James sat on the floor. He assumed Bungle and the Dunns would be having some deep political conversation, but they were debating who was sexier out of Julia Roberts and Jennifer Lopez. Gregory got a picture book and sat on James' leg.

'Trains,' Gregory said.

James opened the book on Gregory's lap. Gregory told him what colour all the trains in the book were and James pretended to be impressed. Bungle passed out jam rings and Gregory thought it was great dipping his biscuit in James' mug, especially when the end dropped off into the tea.

'I'm taking these guys into town and picking Eleanor up from the village,' Bungle said. 'Can you keep an eye on Gregory for an hour?'

'No worries,' James said.

'If you have any probs there's a mobile phone on the table, and there are plenty of adults around. I'm on the speed dial.'

James was well pleased. Now he could get photos of Bungle's hut and have a rummage around. It made his decision not to go to school look like a masterstroke.

35. PAST

James left Fort Harmony after lunch. He ran a couple of kilometres, checked nobody was around, and waited for Ewart. Ewart drove up in a BMW. He'd taken all his earrings out and was dressed like a businessman in a pinstriped suit and tie.

'Nice threads,' James laughed.

'Got to blend in at Green Brooke.'

Ewart drove a few kilometres and parked in a farm access road.

'So, what did you get?' Ewart asked.

James handed over the memory card from his digital camera and some screwed-up pieces of notepaper.

'Plenty of pictures there,' James said. 'Everything in Bungle's room, on the bookshelves, close-ups of stuff like his address book. I've written a list of all the numbers stored in his mobile, plus there's his bank account and passport details.'

'Good job, James. Look at this.'

Ewart handed James a folder with an FBI crest on the front. James opened it and saw a black and white picture of Bungle, looking about ten years younger with long hair.

'That's him,' James said.

James flipped to the next page. It was a standard FBI record. James had seen a few when he was preparing for the mission. Bungle's rap sheet only had three typed lines.

Student at Stamford, MA. Room-mate of known felon Jake Gladwell.
Questioned. Released. 6.18.1994
Traffic violation Austin TX 12.23.1998

'Not very exciting,' James said.

'That's what I thought,' Ewart said. 'Then I had a little look into Jake Gladwell. He's doing eighty years in San Antonio prison, Texas.'

'What for?'

'Trying to blow up the governor at a charity fundraiser. The bomb was found before the event and defused. Police caught Gladwell on the night of the fundraiser. He was outside the hotel with a radio control under his jacket. Know what the former governor of Texas is up to these days?'

'What?' James asked.

'George Walker Bush. President. And you know what else? There were eight big cheeses from the Texas oil industry sitting around Bushy when that bomb was supposed to go off.'

'Bungle was hanging around with Fire and World today,' James said.

'I found the connection between Fire, World and Bungle.

Fire and World did two years at York University before they went to prison. York has a teacher exchange program with Stamford University in America. Bungle was a guest professor at York. He taught Fire and World microbiology for two terms before he quit his job and moved to Fort Harmony.'

'So we're sure they're part of Help Earth?' James asked.

'We can't prove squat. We always thought Bungle, Fire and World were involved. Now we've found out Bungle's background I'd bet my life savings, but there's still no hard evidence. All we can do is keep working and hope you or Amy get a lead before a bomb goes off.'

Ewart reached around to the back seat and handed James a small box of fancy chocolates.

'Give them to Joanna, they're her favourites.'

James was freaked out.

'What are you on about? I only went round to her house for a bath.'

Ewart laughed. 'That's not what I heard. What about all the smoochies?'

'Are you having me watched?' James asked.

'No.'

'So how do you know we kissed?'

'M15 is monitoring all the Internet use around here. They send me a briefing if anything interesting crops up. About eight o'clock last night Joanna logged into a chatroom. Spoke about a new boyfriend called Ross. Says he's a total hunk. Got really cute blond hair. Can't wait to see him at the bus stop in the morning.'

'I wish I'd gone to school now,' James said. 'What about the chocolates?'

'I hacked her user profile on the website. She likes Thornton's handmade chocolates, rock music, blond-haired boys and her ambition is to ride a Harley Davidson across America.'

'Can you drop me near the village so I can give them to her when she gets off the bus?'

*

Joanna hugged him when he gave her the chocolates. They went back to the cottage, drank cocoa, slagged off all the bands on MTV Hits and chased around tickling and throwing sofa cushions at each other. James stayed until her dad got in from work, then sneaked out the back door and walked to Fort Harmony with an ear-to-ear grin.

James was starting to understand all those terrible romantic films his mum used to watch where the leading man ends up in a state over some woman. He lay awake half the night thinking about Joanna. He realised when the mission ended he'd have to go back to CHERUB and never see her again.

He got up extra early and waited for her at the bus stop.

*

Everyone looked at James when he got to class. Stuart and Gareth dropped snide comments all morning.

'After school it's round two,' Stuart said, as James stood in the line to get lunch.

The last thing James wanted was to miss the bus and lose time with Joanna.

'What about right here, right now?' James said. 'Without all your pals backing you up?'

'If you want to start it, hippy boy, we'll finish it.'

The kids standing around them in the queue were excited

about a punch-up. Normally James wouldn't start a fight where everyone could see, but he was trying to get suspended so it didn't matter. James waited while the queue shuffled forward.

'Chickened out, did you?' Gareth asked.

James flicked Gareth off. He was waiting until they were level with the baked beans. When they got there, he hit Gareth in the stomach, grabbed him behind the neck and dipped his face in the beans. Gareth screamed, hot orange sauce burning his face. Stuart whacked James over the head with his lunch tray. James doubled Stuart up with an elbow and followed with some punches that took him down. Gareth was blind, screaming, and wiping his face with his sweatshirt. James battered Stuart until he got dragged off by a couple of teachers. Two hundred sets of eyes were on James as the teachers dragged him off, kicking and shouting.

*

Joanna thought James getting suspended was superb. James was lying face down on her bed after a bath. Joanna rubbed his wet hair with a towel.

'You're so bad,' Joanna purred. 'And you don't even care.'

She threw the towel on the floor and kissed the back of James' neck.

'We'll run away to Scotland and get married when we're sixteen,' Joanna said. 'Then we'll go all over the country robbing banks. We'll live big with all the money we steal. Flash restaurants, big sports cars.'

'You've put a lot of thought into this,' James said, grinning. 'I've only known you for a week.'

'Then you'll get shot by the police in a robbery.'

'You're so full of shit.' James giggled.

'Don't worry, Ross. You'll recover, but you'll have to do five hard years in prison. You'll kiss my photo every day. I'll go to America and ride a Harley Davidson across the country. When you get out, you'll be all beefy from lifting weights, and have tattoos all over you. When the prison gates open I'll be waiting on my Harley. We'll kiss. You'll climb on the back and we'll ride off into the sunset.'

'I'm not so sure about getting shot and going to prison,' James said. 'Why can't *you* get shot and I'll ride the Harley across America?'

'You want me to be all muscled and covered with tattoos?' Joanna asked.

James rolled over and kissed Joanna on the cheek.

36. MESS

'Ring Ewart,' Amy said when James got back to the hut. 'He's pissed at you.'

James went out to the Land Cruiser and made the call.

'Hello James, nice time with your girlfriend?' Ewart asked bitterly.

'What did I do?' James asked.

'Your headmistress blew her stack over your antics in the canteen. She rang one of your supposed old schools; luckily she got the number from the fake file and the call went through to CHERUB, but if she'd got the school's real number and they told her they'd never heard of you it would have made a right mess.'

'Is the headmistress really mad?' James asked.

'I called her back pretending to be one of your old teachers and I think I smoothed things over. I said you were mischievous but basically harmless.'

'You said I was allowed to get suspended.'

'Yes,' Ewart said. 'But I didn't expect you to dunk a kid's head in a vat of baked beans. He's apparently got a nasty burn on his nose.'

'Sorry,' James said, trying not to laugh.

'Sorry solves nothing,' Ewart shouted. 'What time did you get back to Fort Harmony?'

'Just now. About half seven.'

'Have you seen Clark and Sebastian today?'

'No.'

'Why not?'

'You know why, I was with Joanna.'

'The mission is about Sebastian and Clark, not your little girlfriend. I've told Cathy to ground you for getting suspended from school. You can't leave Fort Harmony for a week.'

'But what about Joanna?' James asked.

'Tough,' Ewart said. 'Focus on your mission. You mess up like this again and I'll have you back at CHERUB scrubbing toilets on your hands and knees.'

'I've got to see Joanna, please,' James begged.

'Don't wind me up, James, I'm in no mood. There's two things for you to keep an eye out for. In your photos of Bungle's shack there's a white folder with a RKM logo on the side. It's on the bottom of the bookshelf under the window. Try and get a look at it. It looks like a computer manual, but Bungle doesn't have a computer. It might give us a clue what they're up to. Second, look out for a red van. Amy spotted Fire and World getting out of it, but couldn't get the whole number plate. Got all that?'

'Yes, Ewart,' James said miserably.

'Start using your brain, James.'

James heard the line go dead. He punched the dashboard, ran back to his bed and yelled into his pillow.

'What happened?' Amy asked.

'Leave me alone,' James said.

'It can't be so bad, Ross. You got out of school.'

'He said I can't go down to the village and see Joanna.'

'You know we'll only be here for a few weeks,' Amy said. 'I wouldn't get too fond of her.'

James got off his bed, put his boots on and walked out into the dark.

He lay in the long grass down the bottom of the hill and didn't care that his clothes got soaked. He thought about sneaking down to the village to see Joanna, but he wasn't brave enough to mess with Ewart. If Ewart sent him back to campus in disgrace he'd never get another decent mission.

James wanted to go back to the hut, but Amy would be there with a lecture waiting. He thought about finding Sebastian and Clark, but he didn't want to spend all night shooting the local wildlife. So he stayed where he was, sulking.

*

James heard an animal or something running through the grass around him. He looked up and saw it was two radio-controlled cars. Electric ones. The only noise was rustling as they brushed the grass. He spotted the chromed radio control aerials reflecting moonlight. World and Scargill had them. After a couple of quick circuits they picked the cars up, pulled up their sweatshirt hoods and jogged away.

James decided it was too risky to follow. He crawled through the mud towards where Scargill and World had been standing and almost fell into a hole. It was one of the old tunnels. James grabbed his mobile and called Amy.

'Where are you?' Amy asked.

'Down near the road, something weird is going on.'

James explained everything.

'The tunnel has a door with a padlock on it,' James said. 'I don't have my lock gun.'

'I'll be five minutes,' Amy said. 'Do nothing. If they come back, say you were just exploring.'

Amy ran down to James, keeping herself low to the ground. She shone a torch into the hole and quickly shut it off again.

'They could be back any minute,' Amy said. 'You any good with the lock gun?'

'OK,' James said.

'Got your camera?'

'Yes.'

'Go have a look,' Amy said. 'Take as many pictures as you can and get out fast.'

'Will you keep look-out?' James asked.

'No. If they catch you, say the lock was left off and you just walked inside. Me sitting out here looks suspicious. I'll keep back unless something starts getting heavy.'

James took Amy's torch and lock gun and dropped into the hole. There was a deep puddle in the bottom. The padlock was easy. Inside was three metres of wood-lined tunnel with a low room at the end. James crawled down and started taking pictures. There wasn't much to see. Shelves of radio-controlled cars and spares, and a workbench with an orange plastic tub underneath. James opened every drawer and took pictures inside.

James turned to leave, half-convinced someone would be

behind him. Nobody was. He scrambled back down the tunnel, shut the padlock and ran uphill to Amy.

'Sweet,' Amy said. 'See anything?'

'Toy cars and junk. Hard to see with the torch.'

'The flash on the camera will pick up more than you saw in the dark,' Amy said. 'Maybe something will turn up on the photos.'

'There must be stuff worth hiding in there,' James said. 'Otherwise they wouldn't bother keeping it secret.'

'I'm gonna stick around and see if they come back,' Amy said. 'You go up to the hut and ring Ewart. Arrange to meet him somewhere. He'll want to look at the pictures straight away.'

*

After he'd met Ewart, James went back to the hut and fell asleep. He got the best sleep he'd had in ages, without Amy there snoring.

Amy shook James awake at 2 a.m. She looked happy.

'It's all going down, James. Fire came to the workshop. You were nearly caught, only missed him by about three minutes. He took a big backpack of stuff out and walked off. I followed him up the hill to Green Brooke. You'll never guess what the radio-controlled cars are for.'

'What?' James asked.

'They have a storage tray. They load them up with stuff and push them through a tiny gap in the security fence around Green Brooke. They drive the cars inside the fence and drop the cargo at the back of the conference hall. The cars are too small and fast to get detected by the security cameras and alarms.'

'Couldn't they book a room and bring the stuff into the hotel?' James asked.

'Every guest brings luggage into Green Brooke hotel,' Amy said. 'But the conference hall is under police guard until Petrocon starts. Everyone gets searched on the way in. There's X-ray machines. All your bags get turned out, they pat you down and go in your pockets.'

'So,' James said. 'They're smuggling a bomb into the conference hall, bit by bit, on the back of radio-controlled cars. There must be someone working on the inside screwing all the pieces together.'

'Must be. I spoke to Ewart. They're sending people down to look at the stuff the cars dropped, but they won't take it away. They want to see who comes and picks it up.'

James laughed. 'They're gonna lock those guys up and throw away the key.'

'Poor Scargill,' Amy said.

'You don't actually *like* that freak, do you?' James asked.

Amy shrugged. 'I feel sorry for him. He's just a lonely kid trying to impress his big brothers. The tough guys in prison will eat him for breakfast.'

'You *do* like him,' James laughed. 'He's the world's biggest nerd.'

'You're such a twelve-year-old sometimes, James,' Amy said. 'You've never even had a conversation with Scargill. There's more to a guy than looking good and having big muscles.'

'Marry him and get it over with,' James said. 'So what happens next?'

'Nothing changes. We keep our ears to the ground and

see what comes up. Ewart wants you to concentrate on Bungle and Eleanor. We know they're involved, but there's still no proof.'

37. BUG

Amy shook James awake. It was still dark.

'Get dressed now,' Amy snapped. 'I just had Ewart on the phone. He's coming to get us.'

James rubbed his eyes. Amy was on one leg, stepping into a pair of ripped jeans.

'What's going on?'

'I have no idea,' Amy said. 'Ewart said our lives are in danger if we don't get out fast.'

James put on jeans and trainers. He grabbed his jacket and dashed after Amy. Cathy woke up and asked what was going on. She didn't get an answer. They ran to the bottom of the hill where the BMW was waiting.

'Both of you in the back,' Ewart said.

The tyres squealed. Ewart was in a major hurry about something. He threw some medical supplies at Amy.

'Give James four tablets and two shots in the arm. You OK with injections, Amy?'

'In theory,' Amy said.

Branches thrashed the side of the car as it sped down an unlit country lane.

'What's wrong with me?' James asked nervously.

'Get your coat off,' Amy said.

She squeezed four pills out of their blisters and handed them to James. James looked at the box. It was an antibiotic called Ciprofloxacin.

'I need water to swallow them,' James said.

'None here,' Ewart said. 'Forgot. Ball up some spit. The faster they're in your system the better.'

James' mouth was dry from running. It took a while to get the tablets down.

'I can't hold the needle still while the car's moving,' Amy said.

Ewart stamped the brakes and pulled into the side of the lane. Amy roughly stabbed James with the first needle. It hurt like hell.

'Have you ever done that before?' James asked.

Amy didn't answer and punched him with the second jab. Ewart hit the accelerator.

'Will you tell me what the hell is going on?' James shouted.

'It wasn't a bomb they were building,' Ewart said. 'It was a bio-weapon. The radio-controlled cars were carrying cylinders of bacteria.'

'Oh, god,' Amy said. 'It's obvious now you say it. Bungle was a microbiology professor. Fire and World studied biology at university. They'd know all about that stuff.'

'It all fell into place at once,' Ewart said. 'The best way to spread a disease through a large building is the air-conditioning. I checked out the van Amy saw. It belongs to a man who services the air-conditioning at Green Brooke. Then there was the folder with the RKM logo in Bungle's hut. I thought it was a computer manual, but RKM also make air conditioners.'

'What is it?' Amy asked.

'The police haven't analysed the cylinders,' Ewart said. 'But anthrax is most likely.'

'Jesus,' Amy said.

'I don't understand half what you two are on about,' James said. 'Can one of you speak to me in English?'

'Do you know what anthrax is, James?' Ewart asked.

'No idea, but I'm guessing it's not good and you think I've got it.'

'Anthrax is a unique disease. Most diseases can only survive outside your body for about eight minutes,' Ewart explained. 'Anthrax can survive in almost any temperature for up to sixty years. That makes it easy to store and use as a weapon. A cupful of anthrax spores in the air could kill hundreds of people.'

'How did I get it?' James asked.

'You might not have it,' Ewart said. 'The antibiotics are a precaution. Remember the bright orange box under the bench in the underground workshop?'

'Yeah,' James said.

'It's a sealed disposal unit for toxic waste. You're supposed to incinerate it in a two-thousand-degree furnace.'

'I pulled the lid off and stuck my hand inside,' James said.

'Unfortunately you did,' Ewart said. 'I've got a picture you took of the contents. Gave me a heart attack when I saw it. Looks like the gloves and face masks they used when they were handling the anthrax bacteria ended up in there.'

'Could I die?' James asked.

'I've got to be honest, James. If you breathed the bacteria you're in trouble. Even with the antibiotics we've given you there's a fifty per cent death rate.'

'Could I have given it to Amy or anyone?' James asked.

'It's possible some bacteria stuck on your fingers, but the disease is only serious if you breathe thousands of spores. They'll check out Amy at the hospital to be safe.'

'If I die,' James asked, 'how long will it take?'

'It starts off like the flu about a day after infection. Most people die within nine days.'

'What hospital are we driving to?' Amy asked.

'There's a military hospital near Bristol, about seventy kilometres away,' Ewart said. 'They've got a doctor flying in from Manchester. He knows as much about anthrax as anyone on the planet.'

*

Four nurses in army uniform grabbed James out of the car and stuck him on a trolley, even though he could walk. They burst through doors. Lights on the ceiling whizzed by. James spotted Meryl Spencer and Mac running behind the trolley. They had flown from CHERUB by helicopter.

The nurses wheeled James into a huge ward. There were thirty beds in three rows, all empty. A male nurse pulled James' trainers and socks off, then grabbed his jeans and boxers down in one. James was embarrassed because Amy, Ewart, Meryl and everyone were standing around watching. Once James was naked they lifted him on to a bed.

'Hello, James. I'm Doctor Coen.'

The doctor looked like he'd been dragged out of bed. He

wore Nikes, jogging bottoms and a shirt with the buttons done up in the wrong holes.

'Has the disease been explained to you?' the doctor asked.

'Mostly,' James said. 'Do I need thirty people standing around looking at me naked?'

Dr Coen smiled. 'You heard the patient.'

Everyone but three nurses and a couple of doctors headed out. Dr Coen continued:

'First we need to take blood samples and see if you've been infected with anthrax. However, if you have the disease your chances of survival decrease with every minute treatment is delayed, so we're going to assume the worst and begin treatment now. A nurse will fix a tube into your arm. We're going to pump you with a mixture of antibiotics and other drugs. Some of the drugs are toxic. Your body will react violently. You can expect vomiting and fever.'

*

Amy and Meryl stayed by James' bed. He started feeling weak and shaky a couple of hours after treatment started. His face went pale and he asked for something to throw up in.

Amy went outside looking upset. Meryl gripped his hand.

It got worse in the hours that followed. James' stomach and ribcage felt like they were tearing apart. The tiniest movement, even a deep breath or a cough, made his vision blur and a wave of nausea shoot up from his stomach. The two Army nurses wiped up every time he got sick. When he got really bad they injected him with anti-vomiting drugs.

The wait for test results was unbearable. James wanted to pass out or fall asleep. He watched the door, silently praying for Dr Coen to come back with good news. James wondered if this room might be the last thing he ever saw.

*

Doctor Coen didn't come back until 8 a.m. on Thursday.

'It's bad,' Dr Coen said. 'We just got the results from your tests. We'll keep giving you the drugs.'

38. DEATH

James woke up. He'd been in the hospital thirty hours. A drip ran up his nose and down into his stomach. Meryl had stayed the whole time.

'How do you feel?' Meryl asked.

'Weak,' James croaked; the tube down his throat made it hard to speak.

'The doctor says the level of bacteria in your system is going down. The antibiotics are working.'

'What are my chances?' James asked.

'Dr Coen said over eighty per cent because the treatment started so early.'

'I feel so rough I wish I was dead.'

'Lauren's here,' Meryl said.

'Is she OK?'

Meryl shrugged. 'Pretty shook up. She waited all day for you to come around. She's sleeping upstairs.'

'Me dying, after Mum and that,' James said. 'She'll be in a right state.'

Meryl stroked the back of James' hand.

'You won't die,' she said. 'Fort Harmony has been in all

the papers. Headline news.'

Meryl handed James a *Daily Mirror*. He could see the giant headline, but his vision was too blurry to read the text.

'Read it to me,' James said.

FORT TERROR

Britain's oldest hippy commune, Fort Harmony near Cardiff, was rocked in a stunning raid by anti-terrorist police yesterday.

Three grandsons of the cult writer Gladys Dunn were arrested after anthrax bacteria was found at the nearby Green Brooke Conference Centre.

Twins, Fire and World Dunn, 22, and their brother, Scargill Dunn, 17, were arrested early yesterday morning.

Also in custody are Kieran Pym, an air conditioning engineer, and Eleanor Evans.

Police are seeking a sixth suspect, Brian 'Bungle' Evans. Police believe he is the ringleader and a founder member of the terrorist group Help Earth.

Police also discovered an underground bunker where the deadly cargo was stored before being smuggled into a secure area at Green Brooke. The bunker was not equipped to manufacture the bacteria.

A nationwide search has been launched for the hi-tech laboratory where the killer bug was bred.

It is believed the terrorists were targeting the upcoming Petrocon conference at Green Brooke. If anthrax had been successfully used during the conference, most of the 200 oil industry delegates would have been killed, alongside more than fifty Green Brooke staff and bodyguards.

MORE ON PAGES 2,3,4 & 11
LOTTERY PAGE 6

'It's the main story on TV,' Meryl said. 'Bungle's picture was on the cover of every paper. There's all kinds of rumours about where he's gone.'

'I feel sorry for their little boy,' James said, 'He's only three.'

*

Mac came into the ward an hour later. Lauren was with him, dressed in pyjamas. She jumped on the bed and gave James a hug. She looked like she'd just heard the funniest joke ever.

'There's nothing wrong with you,' Lauren squealed. 'Thanks for scaring me.'

'What are you on about?' James asked.

'James,' Mac said. 'Have you spoken to Doctor Coen yet?'

James shook his head. 'No.'

'We just found out that the bacteria in your system is harmless,' Mac said. 'Scargill Dunn claimed they were using a weak strain of anthrax. They were only going to use the bad stuff on the day of the conference. A laboratory in London rechecked your blood sample and the anthrax inside you couldn't kill a flea.'

James let out a big smile.

'I don't understand,' he said. 'What's the point of harmless anthrax?'

'Bungle only wanted to kill the Petrocon delegates,' Mac said. 'He made the first batch of anthrax with what's called an *attenuated strain*. It's used in the anthrax vaccine. It makes you immune to the nasty variety. It's been in the air-conditioning at Green Brooke conference hall for weeks.

'Security guards, cleaners, catering staff and anyone else who works regularly in the conference hall would be vaccinated by the time Petrocon started. On the first day of the conference a lethal strain of anthrax was going to be put in the air-conditioning, but only the conference guests would get the disease.'

*

Dr Coen stopped James' antibiotics. By Friday evening he felt much better. The drip was taken out and James managed to eat without feeling sick. By Saturday morning he was almost back to normal. Ewart drove up from Wales.

'Is Amy with you?' James asked.

'No, she's back at Fort Harmony, keeping her ear to the ground to see if any information comes through about Bungle. It's not very likely with all that's going on: there are about fifty cops camped out at the bottom of the hill and loads of huts have got police on the doorstep guarding evidence.'

'How did Amy explain me disappearing?'

'You got into a fight with Amy in the night. Ran off. Stormed down the road and got run over by some lunatic driving a BMW. Amy lifted you into the car and the driver rushed you to hospital. You lost some blood and you've got a broken arm, but otherwise you're OK. They're keeping you in for observation.'

'Good story,' James said. 'I should be allowed out of here today.'

'After all you've been through this week I'll understand if you want to go back to CHERUB and rest,' Ewart said. 'But I'd appreciate it if you could show your face at Fort Harmony for a few days. A week at most.'

'Will I be allowed to see Joanna?' James asked.

'Why not?' Ewart grinned. 'Keep hanging out with Sebastian and Clark. Some little titbit of information might pop out, but mostly it's to cover Cathy. It would look suspicious if you disappeared on the morning before the arrests never to be seen again.'

*

A nurse fitted James with a plaster cast on his fake broken arm. On the drive back to Wales James read all the latest stuff in the papers about the anthrax terrorists and the continuing hunt for the laboratory and Bungle. It was odd seeing the newspapers filled with stuff he knew about.

The stories made Bungle sound like a supervillain, but James could only remember a big friendly American who cared about workers' rights and the environment.

*

Cathy was waiting in the Land Cruiser fifteen kilometres outside Craddogh. James ran between the two cars and waved to Ewart as he drove off.

'Hello, Ross,' Cathy said. 'Fake broken arm?'

James nodded. 'It itches exactly like a real broken arm.'

As they got near the camp a policewoman pulled the Land Cruiser over and asked Cathy where she was going. Cathy got waved on. She had to drive across country because the bottom of the hill near the underground workshop was sealed off by police.

The main hut was packed when James and Cathy arrived. The residents seemed edgy about all the police and media people hanging around. A few journalists and photographers were scrounging free stew. Amy hugged James when she saw him. James wanted to go down the village and see Joanna, but it was already late and he didn't know if her dad was home.

Sebastian tapped James on the back.

'Hey, cripple,' Clark said. 'Feeling OK?'

'Not bad, a bit weak.'

'You're lucky that driver didn't splatter you,' Clark said.

'Would have been wicked getting up and seeing you mashed into the road,' Sebastian laughed. 'Got any scars?'

James pulled up the sleeve of his T-shirt and showed the mass of bruises and cuts where the antibiotics had been injected.

'Is that where the car hit you?' Clark asked.

James nodded.

'We were gonna ask you something the night you got run over,' Clark said. 'But we couldn't find you.'

'Ask what?'

'If you wanted to sleep over in our hut.'

'Cool,' James said.

39. FUNERAL

James couldn't decide if he liked Sebastian and Clark. They had a dark side, but that made them interesting to be around. They slept in a rusty panel van next to their mum's hut.

James thumped the metal. Clark slid the side door open.

'Get your butt in here,' Clark yelled.

James bent over to slip off his boots. It had become habit after a few days at Fort Harmony.

'Leave them on,' Clark said. 'The filth is what gives our van character.'

James stepped inside. Two gas lamps pushed out gloomy orange light. His hair brushed the roof. Clark's mattress was below the cracked windscreen where the seats used to be. Sebastian lay at the other end, toying with a big hunting knife. The metal floor was wet and had grass poking up through rust holes. Everything was thrown about: dirty clothes, air guns, knives, shredded school books.

'Duck,' Sebastian shouted.

Sebastian flung his boot across the van. It skimmed past Clark and clanged into the side, leaving a muddy splat on the wall. The second boot hit James in the back.

James looked at the muck on his sweatshirt and smiled.

'You're so dead,' he said.

He hurled the boot back, then dived on to Sebastian and squashed him under the cast on his arm.

'Bundle,' Clark shouted and jumped on the pair of them.

The three boys rumbled until they were all red-faced and out of breath. James was almost as dirty as Sebastian and Clark by the time they'd finished. Clark passed a bottle of water. James took a few gulps and tipped some over his head to cool off.

'Want to go out and do something?' Clark asked.

James shrugged. 'Long as it doesn't involve killing stuff.'

You're such a girl,' Clark said. 'I want to go down the hill and shoot one of the cops up the arse with my air pistol.'

Sebastian laughed. 'That would be so cool. You haven't got the guts.'

Clark picked his air pistol off the floor, pumped it and loaded a pellet.

'Want a bet?'

'Five quid,' Sebastian said, holding out his hand for Clark to shake.

Clark thought about taking the bet, then started laughing.

'I knew you wouldn't,' Sebastian said.

'I hate the cops,' Clark said. 'Fire and World were the best guys around here.'

'I hope Mum lets us see them in prison this time,' Sebastian said.

'It would have been superb if they'd pulled it off,' Clark said. 'We would have been related to two of the biggest murderers in British history, and by the time people started getting sick Fire and World would have been gone. Nobody could have touched them.'

'Two hundred dead though,' James said. 'They all would have had families and stuff.'

'They were rich scum,' Clark said. 'With fat, ugly wives and spoilt kids. The world would have done fine without them.'

'Ross, you should have heard some of the stuff Fire told us about all the evil shit the big oil companies do,' Sebastian said. 'This farmer in South America had an oil pipe burst over his land. His whole farm was trashed. So he goes to the oil company and asks them to clean up the mess. They beat him up. He complained to the police, but the police were getting bribes from the oil company. They stuck the farmer in a cell and didn't give him anything to drink until he signed a confession saying he blew up the pipe himself. Once he'd signed the confession he got fifty years in prison. They only let him out when loads of environmentalists complained.'

'That sounds fake,' James said.

'Next time you go on the Internet look it up for yourself,' Clark said. 'There are tons of stories like that on there.'

'Fire told us loads of babies in poor countries die because their drinking water gets poisoned by spilled oil,' Sebastian said.

'Still, you can't go round killing people,' James said.

'You say we're sick,' Clark said. 'So how sick are those guys going to Petrocon? They've all got millions, but they won't spend any of it to stop babies getting poisoned.'

*

They decided it wasn't worth going out; you couldn't do

much with all the police and journalists around. Clark rigged up a target box at one end of the van and they had a shooting competition with air guns. James had shot real guns in basic training and wasn't bad, even though he could only hold the gun with one hand. Sebastian and Clark were brilliant. Every pellet passed through the centre of their paper targets. Afterwards the brothers showed off tricks. Clark managed to shoot between the eyes of the grinning kids on the cover of his maths textbook while holding the gun behind his back.

At midnight Clark and Sebastian's mum stuck her head in and told them to go to sleep. They rearranged the mess so there was room for James to lay out his sleeping bag and turned out the gas lamps. The boys talked in the dark, mostly about Fire and World. Sebastian and Clark knew tons of funny stories about things Fire and World did at school and in prison. They sounded cool. James almost felt bad about being one of the people who'd got them caught.

*

Somehow they ended up fighting again. Battering each other with pillows and throwing stuff around. The darkness made it more exciting because everyone could launch sneak attacks. James' sleeping bag got ripped open in a tug of war and the stuffing flew everywhere.

Clark fired his air pistol. Sebastian and James dived for cover. They couldn't tell if they were being shot at, or if Clark was only trying to scare them. Sebastian and Clark's mum came back. All three boys dived under their covers, giggling.

'It's one in the morning,' she shouted. 'If I hear any more noise I'm coming in there and you'll be sorry.'

Their mum must have been tough because after she threatened them Sebastian and Clark straightened up their beds and said goodnight. James was sweaty, filthy, and his burst sleeping bag was on a metal floor, but he was so knackered after the last few days that he closed his eyes and was instantly asleep.

*

James first thought the banging was some prank by Sebastian and Clark. Clark lit his torch.

'What is that?' James asked.

Someone was thumping on the outside of the van.

'Open up in there. Police.'

Clark shone the torch on the back of Sebastian's head.

Clark laughed. 'Nothing wakes him up. I set a firework off next to his ear once and he didn't even budge.'

Clark got out of bed wearing shorts and a T-shirt and unlocked the door. Two powerful torches pointed in his face. A policeman grabbed Clark out of the van and turned his torch on James.

'Boy,' the policeman shouted to James, 'get out of there now.'

James put his bottoms and boots on with his free arm and stepped out. Fort Harmony was ablaze with flashing blue lights and torch beams. Police in riot gear were dragging everyone out of their huts. Kids were crying. Residents and police shouted at each other.

The policemen knocked James against the van beside Clark.

'Anyone else in there?' one policeman shouted.

'My little brother,' Clark said. 'I'll go and wake him up.'

'No you don't, I'll do it,' the policeman said.

One policeman stepped into the van. James spoke to the other one.

'What's going on?'

'Court order,' the policeman said. He pulled a piece of paper out of his pocket and read from it. 'By order of the High Court all residents of the community known as Fort Harmony shall leave within seven days. Dated 16th September 1972.'

'That's over thirty years ago,' James said.

The policeman shrugged. 'It took us a bit longer than expected.'

The policeman inside the van screamed. He staggered out, holding his thigh. James spotted the glint of Sebastian's hunting knife sticking out of his leg. The other policeman shouted into his radio.

'Code one. Code one. Officer down. Serious injury.'

About ten cops came swarming over. Two grabbed the cop with the knife in his leg and carried him off. Two slammed James and Clark hard into the side of the van and started searching them for weapons.

'Not those two, there's a kid in the van,' a policeman said.

Clark shouted out, 'I said I'd wake him up for you. He's scared of the dark so he sleeps with the knife beside him.'

'Shut your hole before I shut it for you,' a policeman said.

Six policemen surrounded the door of the van. Three of them had guns drawn.

'Get out here, now,' a sergeant shouted.

Sebastian shouted from inside, 'Don't shoot me. Put the guns away.'

'Put them down, he's only a kid,' the sergeant said. 'What's your name, son?'

'Sebastian.'

'Sebastian, I want you to come slowly out of the van with your hands in the air. We know it was an accident. We won't hurt you.'

Sebastian stepped into the torchlight. When he got near the door the police grabbed him and slammed him into the mud. One cop put his boot on Sebastian's back and locked on handcuffs. He looked tiny compared to the policemen all bulked out by riot gear. They dragged Sebastian off to a police car.

'Let me go with him,' Clark said.

A policeman slammed Clark against the van again.

'You don't learn, do you?' the policeman said.

Sebastian's mum was dragged out of her hut and put in the police car with her son.

'What about us?' James asked.

'We're taking everyone to the church hall in the village. There's a coach at the bottom of the hill,' the sergeant said.

'I need to get my tracksuit and boots,' Clark said.

'You can't go in there, it's a crime scene.'

'I'm barefoot,' Clark said. 'It's freezing.'

'I don't care if you've got to walk across broken glass,' the policeman shouted. 'Get down to that coach or you'll have more than cold feet to worry about.'

James and Clark walked off.

'I've got to find my sister and Auntie Cathy,' James said.

Police were everywhere, over a hundred. A chain of residents was heading down the hill. Anyone who put up a fight found the riot cops weren't shy about pulling batons. James and Clark dodged into some trees and re-emerged beside Cathy's hut. There was no sign of Amy, Cathy or the Land Cruiser. They went in the hut. Amy and Cathy had taken most stuff with them.

'What you looking for?' Clark asked.

'My mobile,' James said. 'Looks like my sister took it with her. What shoe size are you?'

'Two.'

James kicked a pair of his Nikes into the middle of the floor.

'Those are a three, you'll grow into them. Take whatever clothes you want.'

'Cheers,' Clark said.

Clark put on tracksuit bottoms and trainers. James found him a warm top with a hood.

'My sister's probably down at the village,' James said. 'Might as well get on the coach.'

*

James and Clark sat next to each other on the coach. It gradually filled up with residents, all of them carrying what they could. Clark was trying to hide how upset he was from James, but couldn't hold himself together.

'He's only ten, they'll realise it was an accident,' James said.

'Don't bet on it, Ross. The cops will switch their stories around so he gets done. Whose story are they going to believe? A couple of kids who are always in trouble, or the police?'

'I'll be a witness,' James said.

'If Sebastian gets sent away I'll stab a cop myself so I can stay with him.'

40. HALL

Craddogh Church Hall was a madhouse. Eighty people with no air to breathe. Kids ran around screaming. Journalists kept asking Gladys Dunn for quotes and pictures, but the old lady needed rest. Michael Dunn threw a punch and got dragged away by police in a blaze of camera flashes.

The residents wanted to go back to Fort Harmony to get their stuff, but police cars blocked the road and nobody got through. The police said everything was being collected and would arrive in a few hours.

Clark had turned into a basket case. Sobbing for his brother and mum and screaming to any nearby cop that he was going to kill him first chance he got. James tried to calm him down, without much success.

'You're the first kid who's ever been nice to us,' Clark said to James.

James felt bad. Clark wasn't his real friend. He'd used him to help with the mission.

*

On TV you knew who the baddies were and they got what they deserved at the end of the show. Now James realised baddies were ordinary people. They told jokes, made you cups of coffee, went to the toilet and had families who loved them.

James totted everyone up: Fire, World and Bungle were obviously bad guys for trying to kill everyone with anthrax. The oil company people were also bad for trashing the environment and abusing people in poor countries. The police were bad guys; they had a tricky job to do, but they seemed to enjoy throwing their weight around more than they should. The only good guys were the Fort Harmony residents and they'd all got chucked out of their homes.

James couldn't figure what he was himself. As far as he could tell, he'd stopped one small bunch of bad guys killing a big bunch of bad guys and as a result the good guys got chucked out of their homes by another bunch of bad guys. Did that make him good or bad? James only knew that thinking about it gave him a headache.

*

James left Clark with his family and went outside. There was no sign of Amy or Cathy. James didn't have his mobile and the village phone box had about twenty people queuing up, trying to find somewhere to stay now Fort Harmony was shut off. James realised he might be able to phone Amy or Ewart from Joanna's house. He was sure Joanna's dad would be on duty with all that was going on.

Joanna and her dad stood by their garden gate in night clothes, watching the arguments and blue lights in the centre of the village.

'Hey,' James said.

Joanna gave James a smile that made him feel better. James was still wary of Sergeant Ribble after he'd caught them in Cathy's hut, but he sounded OK.

'What's going on up there?' Sergeant Ribble asked.

'Everyone's been chucked out of Fort Harmony,' James said. 'How come you're not involved? You're a policeman.'

'That lot don't give me the time of day. I'm just the local bobby,' Sergeant Ribble said. 'As soon as they found the anthrax, the terrorist squad turned up and took everything off my hands.'

'Can I use your phone?' James asked. 'I've lost my aunt and my sister.'

'Of course you can, son. Jojo will show you where the phone is.'

James took off his boots and stepped into the house with Joanna. She was wearing slippers and a Daffy Duck nightie.

'Hi Jojo,' James said, laughing.

'Shut up, Ross. Only my dad and big brothers call me that.'

'I'll probably have to go back to London now,' James said.

'Oh,' Joanna said.

James was glad she sounded upset. It meant Joanna liked him as much as he liked Joanna. She showed him the phone. It took a minute to remember Amy's mobile number.

'Courtney,' James said. 'Where are you?'

'Cathy went nuts,' Amy said. 'She thinks what happened tonight is her fault for letting us into Fort Harmony. She dumped me a few kilometres outside Craddogh with most of our stuff. Ewart's coming to fetch me. He should be here any minute.'

'I'm at Joanna's house in the village,' James said. 'What should I do?'

'Stay where you are,' Amy said. 'I'll get Ewart to pick you up after me. If anyone asks questions, say Ewart's a mini-cab driver and Cathy has arranged for us to get the first train to London from Cardiff in the morning. We should be with you in about half an hour.'

'Are we going home?' James asked.

'Mission's over, James. With no Fort Harmony, there's no reason to stay.'

James put the phone down and looked at Joanna.

'Mini-cab is on its way. I'm going back to my mum in London.'

'Let's go to my room,' Joanna said. 'Goodbye kiss.'

Joanna's dad was too busy watching outside to notice his daughter sneaking James into her bedroom. She didn't care that James was all muddy. She leant against her bedroom door to stop her dad bursting in and they started kissing. Joanna was soft and hot to touch, her hair smelled like shampoo and her breath like toothpaste. It felt great, but James ached knowing they only had a few minutes and then he'd never see her again.

The door hit Joanna in the back.

'What are you two doing in there?' Sergeant Ribble said.

James and Joanna moved away from the door. Her dad came in. They probably could have made some excuse, if Joanna's nightdress hadn't been covered in James' muddy handprints.

'Joanna, you're thirteen years old,' her dad yelled.

'But Daddy we were just…'

'Put something clean on and go to bed. And you…'

Joanna's dad grabbed James by the back of his neck.

'Did you make your phone call?'

'Yes,' James said. 'There's a mini-cab coming for me.'

'You can wait for it outside.'

Joanna's dad shoved James out of the house and made him sit on the garden wall facing the road. James felt totally miserable. He was worried what would happen to Sebastian, he felt guilty that he and Amy finding out about the anthrax had led to Fort Harmony being destroyed, and worst of all the best girl he'd ever met was trapped in a house a few metres away and he'd never see her again.

James heard a window open behind him. He watched Joanna throw out a paper aeroplane. Her dad charged back into the house.

'I ordered you to bed, young lady.'

James jumped into the garden and picked up the aeroplane. He realised there was something written on the paper and unravelled it.

Ross,
Please phone me. You're so cute.
Joanna.
XXX

James folded up the paper, put it in his pocket and felt even sadder.

*

Ewart drove Amy and James back to Fort Harmony in the BMW.

'Why are they smashing it up?' James asked.

'I spoke to someone at the anti-terrorist squad,' Ewart said. 'They say Fort Harmony is a security risk. They wanted it wiped before Petrocon started, and the law was on their side.'

'I wish I'd never come here,' James said. 'It's our fault this has happened.'

'I thought you hated Fort Harmony,' Amy said,

'I didn't say I wanted to live there,' James said. 'Just, it's not fair kicking everyone out.'

'Fort Harmony was doomed either way,' Ewart said. 'If Fire, World and Bungle had killed all those people, they would have wiped the camp out after the conference instead of before. All you would have done is delayed the end by a month.'

'Did you know it was going to happen, Ewart?' James asked.

'I wouldn't have sent you back for one night if I had.'

'Where's Cathy gone?' James asked.

'She was upset,' Amy said. 'She said something about staying with friends in London.'

'Cathy broke the deal,' Ewart said. 'She wasn't supposed to abandon Amy in the middle of nowhere. I want that money back when I catch up with her.'

'Leave her alone,' Amy said. 'She's lived at Fort Harmony for thirty years and got in a bit of a state when all those cops showed up. She did a perfect job looking after us until tonight.'

'A sixteen-year-old girl dumped in the middle of the countryside at night, with four bags of luggage,' Ewart said.

'Lucky your mobile had reception. You could have been picked up by some nutter and murdered.'

'But I *wasn't*,' Amy said sharply. 'So leave Cathy alone. We got everything we wanted from her.'

Ewart banged the steering wheel. 'OK Amy, if you say so. Cathy's come out of this with eight thousand quid and a car. It's better than she deserves after treating you like that.'

Ewart slowed down at a police checkpoint. He showed an ID and they waved him through. The sun was coming up. Riot police were working their way across Fort Harmony. One crew emptied out the shelters, bagging up the contents and loading them into a truck. A follow-up team worked with chainsaws and sledgehammers, knocking the huts down and smashing the timber into small pieces so there was no way anything could be rebuilt.

Ewart, James and Amy got out of the BMW. Ewart was wearing scruffy jeans and looked too young to be anyone important. A couple of policemen walked towards them.

'Get back in the car and drive on,' a policeman shouted.

Ewart ignored him and headed for Cathy's hut. James and Amy followed.

'You're asking for a day in the cells,' the policeman said cockily.

The cop made a grab for Ewart. Ewart dodged him and pulled out his ID. The policeman looked a bit stunned.

'Um, what are you here for?'

'Sir,' Ewart said.

'What?' the policeman said.

'Don't you call a senior officer sir?'

'What can I do for you, *sir*?'

'Get me some plastic bags,' Ewart said.

They walked across to Cathy's hut and started packing up. A chief inspector rushed over. She sounded apologetic.

'Sorry about the mix-up. We got a message not to touch this hut. Can I double-check your ID?'

Ewart handed it to her.

'I've never seen one of these before,' she gushed. 'Level one clearance. The Commissioner of the anti-terrorist unit only has level two. What are you doing here?'

Ewart snatched it back out of her hand.

'You should know better than to ask questions,' Ewart said. 'Take this down to my car.'

Ewart dumped a bin-liner stuffed with clothes in the chief inspector's arms. James thought it was funny watching a senior policewoman carrying a bag of his dirty clothes down a muddy hill.

'I thought only Mac had level one security clearance,' Amy said.

Ewart shrugged. 'That's right.'

'So what did you show her?' Amy asked.

'A very good fake.'

James laughed. 'That's so cool.'

They loaded all their stuff in the back of the car. James turned back for a last glance at Fort Harmony and took a couple of pictures of a tree with his digital camera.

'What's with the tree?' Amy asked, after they'd driven off.

'Not telling,' James said. 'You'll take the piss.'

Amy wriggled her fingers in the air. 'I'll tickle it out of you.'

'OK,' James said. 'But promise not to laugh.'

'I promise,' Amy said.

'It's where I first kissed Joanna.'

Amy smiled. 'That is *so* sweet.'

Ewart put his fingers in his mouth and pretended he was being sick.

'You promised,' James said.

Ewart laughed. 'Amy promised. I never said a word.'

'I can't wait to tell Kerry all about your smooching with Joanna,' Amy said.

'Oh god, don't ... Please,' James said.

'Why would you care what I told Kerry about you, unless you like her more than you're willing to admit?' Amy teased.

James wanted to storm off, but that was difficult in a car doing eighty kilometres an hour. He folded his arms and stared out the window, trying to hide how upset he was about not being able to see Joanna again.

41. DARK

When they got back to CHERUB Amy took James to the woodwork shop. She found an electric drill and fixed on a circular cutter. James gave the silver teeth a grim look.

'You're not cutting it off with that,' James said. 'You'll kill me.'

'Stop being such a pansy. Put these on.'

Amy threw James a set of protective goggles and fixed a pair on herself.

'Put your arm on the bench,' Amy said.

'Have you ever done this before?'

Amy smiled. 'No.'

James rested his cast on the workbench. Amy gave the drill a couple of test spins then set to work. Plaster shards pelted James' face and the white dust dried his mouth. James thought he felt the blade tickling the hairs on his arm, but hoped he was just imagining it.

Amy stopped the drill and cracked off most of the cast, leaving the part around the elbow.

'OK, last bit,' Amy said.

Amy cut in at a different angle. When she was done James pulled the last bit of plaster down his arm and went into a scratching frenzy.

'That feels so much better,' James said. 'OHHHHHH.'

'Leave it alone, you'll tear all your skin off,' Amy said.

'Don't care.'

James took off the goggles and flicked white dust out of his hair.

'Go have a shower and take your clothes to the laundry,' Amy said. 'Mac will want to see you in his office when you're ready.'

'Just me?' James asked.

'It's a standard thing,' Amy said. 'He does it with everyone after their first mission.'

*

Mac was dressed in shorts and a T-shirt when James got to his office.

'Come in, James. How you feeling?'

'Fine now,' James said. 'Bit tired.'

'Ewart seemed to think you had some doubts about the value of your mission.'

'It's confusing,' James said.

'He said you didn't seem sure that we'd done the right thing,' Mac said.

'I heard some stuff about the people going to Petrocon,' James said. 'They poison people and beat people up and stuff. I'm not even sure it's true.'

'It's mostly true,' Mac said. 'Oil companies have a terrible environmental and human rights record. Without oil and gas the world stops working. No aeroplanes, no ships, no cars, very little electricity. Because oil is so important, companies and governments bend rules to get it. Help Earth and a lot of other people, including me, think they go too far.'

'So you support Help Earth?' James said.

'I want to stop people getting exploited and poisoned by oil companies. I don't agree that terrorism is the way to do it.'

'I understand,' James said. 'Killing people never solves anything.'

'Think about what would have happened if all those people got killed at Petrocon,' Mac said. 'Would Help Earth have attacked somewhere else? What if the anthrax got into the hands of another terrorist group? You'll never know for certain what would have happened if Fire and World Dunn weren't caught. The next attack could have been in the middle of a city. Stick some anthrax in a London Underground station and you'd be looking at five thousand dead people. That's how many lives you and Amy might have saved.'

'Bungle's still on the loose though,' James said.

'Can I trust you with some information?' Mac asked.

'What?' James said.

'You're the only person who knows besides Ewart and myself, so if this gets out I'll know you leaked it.'

'I swear,' James said.

'MI5 knows where Bungle is,' Mac said.

'So why don't you get him?'

'They're tracking him,' Mac said. 'Bungle won't tell us anything if we arrest him, but by letting him wander he might lead us to other members of Help Earth.'

'What if you lose him?' James asked.

Mac laughed, 'You always ask me the question I don't want to answer.'

'Have they lost anyone before?' James asked.

'Yes,' Mac said. 'It won't happen this time. Bungle can't stick a finger up his nose without ten people knowing about it.'

'It makes more sense now you've explained it,' James said. 'I still feel sorry for all the people who got chucked out of Fort Harmony. They're a weird lot, but basically they're OK.'

'It's a shame,' Mac said. 'But a few families losing their homes is better than thousands of people getting killed.

'So I want to thank you for doing a brilliant job, James. You made friends with the right people, didn't break your cover and polished off the mission in half the time we expected.'

'Thanks,' James said.

'I also owe you a massive apology,' Mac said. 'You nearly died. We had no idea Help Earth was planning an anthrax attack. If we'd known, we never would have sent someone as inexperienced as you on this mission.'

'It's not your fault.'

'You must have been frightened, but you handled yourself tremendously. You kept a level head and even agreed to return to the mission. I've decided to classify your overall performance as outstanding.'

Mac pulled a navy CHERUB T-shirt out of his desk and threw it to James.

'Wow,' James said, grinning. 'When Kerry sees this she's gonna be so pissed off.'

'I'll pretend I didn't hear that,' Mac said. 'But if you use that sort of language in my office again I'll make you a very unhappy boy.'

'Sorry,' James said. 'Can I put it on?'

'Don't be modest on my account,' Mac said.

James ripped off his Arsenal shirt and pulled the navy CHERUB T-shirt over his head.

*

The kids at CHERUB were allowed to sleep late and wear normal clothes on Sundays. It was still early and nobody was around. James ate breakfast alone in the dining room, with one eye on the television. There was a story about Fort Harmony being destroyed on News 24. They cut to a clip of Michael Dunn waving his fists in the air and vowing he would spend the rest of his life rebuilding Fort Harmony if that was what it took.

Kerry came down in shorts and a denim jacket. She gave James a hug.

'I was so happy you *finally* got a mission,' Kerry said. 'I got back from my third mission on Thursday.'

James loved the way she couldn't resist mentioning it was her third mission. He wondered how long it would be before she noticed his navy shirt. Bruce came down and joined Kerry at the breakfast buffet.

'Good mission?' Bruce asked, as he put his tray on the table next to James.

James acted casual. 'Mac seemed to think I did OK.'

Kerry sat opposite James. She only had a bran muffin and a couple of bits of fruit.

'On a diet?' James asked.

'I'm trying to eat less greasy stuff,' Kerry said.

'Good,' James said. 'You're starting to look a bit fat.'

Bruce burst out laughing and spat half his bacon across the table. Kerry kicked James in the shin.

'Pig,' Kerry said.

'That kick hurt,' James said. 'I was only joking.'

'Did you see me laughing?' Kerry asked.

James got a punch in the back. 'Stop being rude to Kerry,' Lauren said. 'You should ask her out now you're back. It's *so* obvious you two fancy each other.'

James and Kerry blushed. Lauren got her breakfast and sat next to Kerry.

Callum and Connor sat at the next table a few minutes later. James hadn't seen them together since Callum restarted basic training.

'Which one of you is Callum?' James asked.

Callum raised a finger.

'You passed basic training now?' James asked.

'Got back from Malaysia on Tuesday,' Callum said. 'Slept for twenty hours solid.'

'Bet you're glad that's out the way,' James said.

'You know that navy T-shirt you're wearing is a CHERUB shirt?' Callum said.

James was pleased someone had finally noticed.

'Yes,' he said casually.

'You'd better take it off, James,' Bruce said. 'Kids work really hard to earn them. They'll kill you if they catch you wearing it.'

'It's my shirt,' James said. 'I did earn it.'

Kerry laughed. 'Yeah, James, and I'm the Queen of China.'

'Don't believe me then,' James said.

Bruce sounded a bit desperate. 'I'm serious, James. People get angry when you wear a shirt without earning it. Take it off. They'll stuff your head down the toilet or something.'

'I'd pay money to see him bog-washed,' Lauren giggled. 'Leave it on.'

'I'm not taking it off,' James said. 'It's mine.'

'You're such an idiot,' Kerry said. 'Don't say we didn't warn you when we're scraping you off the floor.'

Amy came in. She had Arif and Paul with her. The three of them rushed over to James.

'Too late now,' Bruce said. 'You're dead.'

James was worried. He wasn't sure if Amy knew Mac had awarded him the navy shirt. He stood up from the table and turned to face Amy. Paul and Arif looked intimidating, muscles everywhere.

Amy wrapped James in her arms.

'Congratulations,' Amy said. 'You really deserve that shirt. You were brilliant.'

Amy let go. Paul and Arif shook James' hand.

'I can't believe you're that wimp we had to keep throwing in the diving pool,' Arif said.

James looked back at his friends sitting around the table. They all looked amazed. Lauren jumped up and hugged her brother. Kerry's mouth was open so wide you could have shoved a tennis ball in it without touching a tooth. James couldn't help smiling.

It was beautiful.

EPILOGUE

RONALD ONIONS (UNCLE RON) has had difficulty adjusting to life behind bars. He received two broken arms during a fight with a fellow inmate. He is scheduled to be released in 2012.

GLADYS DUNN used the money from her second book to buy a farm in Spain. She lives on the land with her son JOSHUA DUNN, who makes curry, stew or paella every day for the thirty former Fort Harmony residents who joined them. Gladys jokingly refers to her farm as '*Fort Harmony 2, but warmer and without the mud.*'

CATHY DUNN sold the Land Cruiser, purchased a round-the-world air ticket and went backpacking in Australia.

SEBASTIAN DUNN was released from police custody without charge. The stabbing of the policeman was classified as an accident. The policeman returned to duty a few months later.

Sebastian now lives in a cottage in Craddogh with his

mother and brother CLARK DUNN. Sebastian and Clark have denied links to a number of cats that have disappeared since their arrival in the village.

FIRE & WORLD DUNN were tried and convicted at the Old Bailey in London. They were each sentenced to life in prison. The Judge recommended they serve a minimum of twenty-five years.

As SCARGILL DUNN was only seventeen and had no previous criminal convictions, he was sentenced to only four years in a young offenders' prison. With early release for good behaviour he could be out within two years. He has begun studying for A-level exams and hopes to go to university after he is released.

Police suspect ELEANOR EVANS is a member of Help Earth who helped to plan the anthrax attacks on Petrocon 2004. No evidence was found and she was released from custody without charge. She now lives in Brighton with her mother, her son GREGORY EVANS and her newly born daughter Tiffany.

BRIAN 'BUNGLE' EVANS slipped M15 surveillance after a few weeks. He is now one of the world's most wanted men. Police in Britain, the United States, France and Venezuela all wish to question him about terrorist activity.

JOANNA RIBBLE was disappointed that Ross Leigh didn't write or call. She now has a new boyfriend. James kept her paper aeroplane and the photograph of the tree where they first kissed.

KYLE BLUEMAN returned from his eighteenth mission and finally got his navy CHERUB shirt. He was reportedly '*upset*' that James got his navy shirt before him. Kyle reckons James only got the navy shirt because Mac felt sorry for him when he got anthrax.

BRUCE NORRIS & KERRY CHANG frequently remind James that although he earned a navy shirt, they have both done more missions than him and can easily kick his butt any time he starts to get cocky.

AMY COLLINS hopes to complete a couple more missions before she leaves CHERUB and goes to university.

LAUREN ADAMS (formerly LAUREN ONIONS) is enjoying life at CHERUB. She starts basic training shortly after her tenth birthday in September 2004.

JAMES ADAMS (formerly JAMES CHOKE) got his Karate black belt shortly after returning from his mission. His exuberant celebrations ended badly and his punishment was one month cleaning up in the CHERUB kitchen every night after dinner.

He is currently preparing for his second mission.

CHERUB: A HISTORY (1941-1996)

1941 In the middle of the Second World War, Charles Henderson, a British agent working in occupied France, sent a report to his headquarters in London. It was full of praise for the way the French Resistance used children to sneak past Nazi checkpoints and wangle information out of German soldiers.

1942 Henderson formed a small undercover detachment of children, under the command of British Military Intelligence. Henderson's Boys were all thirteen or fourteen years old, mostly French refugees. They were given basic espionage training before being parachuted into occupied France. The boys gathered vital intelligence in the run-up to the D-Day invasions of 1944.

1946 Henderson's Boys disbanded at the end of the war. Most of them returned to France. Their existence has never been officially acknowledged.

Charles Henderson believed that children would make effective intelligence agents during peacetime. In May 1946, he was given permission to create CHERUB in a disused village school. The first twenty

CHERUB recruits, all boys, lived in wooden huts at the back of the playground.

1951 For its first five years, CHERUB struggled along with limited resources. Its fortunes changed following its first major success: two agents uncovered a ring of Russian spies who were stealing information on the British nuclear weapons programme.

The government of the day was delighted. CHERUB was given funding to expand. Better facilities were built and the number of agents was increased from twenty to sixty.

1954 Two CHERUB agents, Jason Lennox and Johan Urminski, were killed while operating undercover in East Germany. Nobody knows how the boys died. The government considered shutting CHERUB down, but there were now over seventy active CHERUB agents performing vital missions around the world.

An inquiry into the boys' deaths led to the introduction of new safeguards:

(1) The creation of the ethics panel. From now on, every mission had to be approved by a three-person committee.

(2) Jason Lennox was only nine years old. A minimum mission age of ten years and four months was introduced.

(3) A more rigorous approach to training was brought in. A version of the 100-day basic training programme began.

1956 Although many believed that girls would be unsuitable for intelligence work, CHERUB admitted five girls as an experiment. They were a huge success. The number of girls in CHERUB was upped to twenty the following year. Within ten years, the number of girls and boys was equal.

1957 CHERUB introduced its system of coloured T-shirts.

1960 Following several successes, CHERUB was allowed to expand again, this time to 130 students. The farmland surrounding headquarters was purchased and fenced off, about a third of the area that is now known as CHERUB Campus.

1967 Katherine Field became the third CHERUB agent to die on an operation. She was bitten by a snake on a mission in India. She reached hospital within half an hour, but tragically the snake species was wrongly identified and Katherine was given the wrong anti-venom.

1973 Over the years, CHERUB had become a hotchpotch of small buildings. Construction began on a new nine-storey headquarters.

1977 All cherubs are either orphans, or children who have been abandoned by their family. Max Weaver was one of the first CHERUB agents. He made a fortune building office blocks in London and New York. When he died in 1977, aged just forty-one, without a wife or children, Max Weaver left his fortune for the benefit of the children at CHERUB.

The Max Weaver Trust Fund has paid for many of the buildings on CHERUB campus. These include the indoor athletics facilities and library. The trust fund now holds assets worth over £1 billion.

1982 Thomas Webb was killed by a landmine on the Falkland Islands, becoming the fourth CHERUB agent to die on a mission. He was one of nine agents used in various roles during the Falklands conflict.

1986 The government gave CHERUB permission to expand up to four hundred pupils. Despite this, numbers have stalled some way below this. CHERUB requires intelligent, physically robust agents, who have no family ties. Children who meet all these admission criteria are extremely hard to find.

1990 CHERUB purchased additional land, expanding both the size and security of campus. Campus is marked on all British maps as an army firing range. Surrounding roads are routed so that there is only one road on to campus. The perimeter walls cannot be seen from nearby roads. Helicopters are banned from the area and aeroplanes must stay above ten thousand metres. Anyone breaching the CHERUB perimeter faces life imprisonment under the State Secrets Act.

1996 CHERUB celebrated its fiftieth anniversary with the opening of a diving pool and indoor shooting range.

Every retired member of CHERUB was invited to the celebration. No guests were allowed. Over nine hundred people made it, flying from all over the world. Among the retired agents were a former Prime Minister and a rock guitarist who had sold 80 million albums.

After a firework display, the guests pitched tents and slept on campus. Before leaving the following morning, everyone gathered outside the chapel and remembered the four children who had given CHERUB their lives.

READ ON FOR A TASTE OF *ROCK WAR*, THE FIRST IN ROBERT MUCHAMORE'S EXPLOSIVE NEW SERIES!

Prologue

The stage is a vast altar, glowing under Texas moonlight. Video walls the size of apartment blocks advertise Rage Cola. Close to the stadium's fifty-yard line, a long-legged thirteen-year-old is precariously balanced on her big brother's shoulders. She's way too excited.

'JAY!' she screams, as her body sways. 'JAAAAAAAY I LOVE YOU!'

Nobody hears, because seventy thousand people are at it. It's noise so loud your ears tickle inside. Boys and girls, teens, students. There's a ripple of anticipation as a silhouette comes on stage, but it's a roadie with a cymbal stand. He bows grandly before stepping off.

'JET!' they chant. 'JET . . . JET . . . JET.'

Backstage the sound is muffled, like waves crashing against a sea wall. The only light is a green glow from emergency exit signs.

Jay is holding his queasy stomach. He's slim and easy on the eye. He wears Converse All Stars, ripped jeans and a dash of black eyeliner.

An immense roar comes out of the crowd as the video walls begin a thirty-second countdown film, sponsored by a cellphone maker. As Jay's eyes adjust to the light, he can see a twenty-metre-tall version of himself skateboarding downhill, chased by screaming Korean schoolgirls.

'THIRTEEN,' the crowd scream, as their feet stamp down the seconds. 'TWELVE, ELEVEN . . .'

On screen, the girls knock Jay off his skateboard. As he tumbles a smartphone flies out of his pocket and when the girls see it they lose all interest in Jay and stand in a semicircle admiring the phone instead.

'THREE . . . TWO . . . ONE . . .'

The four members of Jet emerge on stage, punching the air to screams and camera flashes.

Somehow, the cheering crowd always kills Jay's nerves. Thousands of bodies sway in the moonlight. Cheers and shouts blend into a low roar. He places his fingers on the fret board and loves the knowledge that moving one finger will send half a million watts of power out of speaker stacks the size of trucks.

And the crowd goes wild as the biggest band in the world starts to play.

1. Cheesy Crumbs

Camden, North London

There's that weird moment when you first wake up. The uneasy quarter second where a dream ends and you're not sure where you are. All being well, you work out you're in bed and you get to snuggle up and sleep another hour.

But Jay Thomas wasn't in bed. The thirteen-year-old had woken on a plastic chair in a school hall that reeked of burgers and hot dogs. There were chairs set out in rows, but bums in less than a quarter of them. A grumpy dinner lady squirted pink cleaning fluid on a metal serving counter at the side of the room, while a banner hung over the stage up front:

Camden Schools Contemporary Music Competition 2014

Debris pelted the floor the instant Jay moved: puffed wheat snacks, speckled with cheesy orange flavouring. Crumbs fell off his clothes when he stood and another half bag had been crushed up and sprinkled in his spiky brown hair.

Jay played lead guitar in a group named Brontobyte. His three band mates cracked up as he flicked orange dust out of his hair, then bent over to de-crumb a Ramones T-shirt and ripped black jeans.

'You guys are *so* immature.'

But Jay didn't really mind. These guys had been his mates since forever and he'd have joined the fun if one of them had dozed off.

'Sweet dreams?' Brontobyte's chubby-cheeked vocalist, Salman, asked.

Jay yawned and picked orange gunk out of his earhole as he replied. 'I barely slept last night. Kai had his Xbox on until about one, and when I *finally* got to sleep the little knob head climbed up to my bunk and farted in my face.'

Salman took pity, but Tristan and Alfie both laughed.

Tristan was Brontobyte's drummer, and a big lad who fancied himself a bit of a stud. Tristan's younger brother Alfie wouldn't turn twelve for another three months. He was Brontobyte's bass player and the band's most talented musician, but the other three gave him a hard time because his voice was unbroken and there were no signs of puberty kicking in.

'I can't believe Jay gets owned by his younger brother,' Tristan snorted.

'Kai's the hardest kid in my year,' Alfie agreed. 'But Jay's, like, Mr Twig Arms, or something.'

Jay tutted and sounded stressed. 'Can we *please* change the subject?'

Tristan ignored the request. 'How many kids has your mum got now anyway, Jay?' he asked. 'It's about forty-seven, isn't it?'

Salman and Alfie laughed, but stifled their grins when they saw Jay looking upset.

'Tristan, cut it out,' Salman said.

'We all take the piss out of each other,' Tristan said. 'Jay's acting like a baby.'

'No, Tristan, *you* never know when to stop,' Salman said angrily.

Alfie tried to break the tension. 'I'm going for a drink,' he said. 'Anyone else want one?'

'Scotch on the rocks,' Salman said.

Jay sounded more cheerful as he joined the joke. 'Bottle of Bud and some heroin.'

'I'll see what I can do,' Alfie said, before heading off towards a table with jugs of orange squash and platters of cheapo biscuits.

The next act was taking the stage. In front of them three judges sat at school desks. There was a baldy with a mysterious scab on his head, a long-limbed Nigerian in a gele headdress and a man with a wispy grey beard and leather trousers. He sat with his legs astride the back of his chair to show that he was down with the kids.

By the time Alfie came back with four beakers of orange squash and jam rings tucked into his cheeks there were five boys lining up on stage. They were all fifteen or sixteen. Nice-looking lads, four black, one Asian, and all dressed in stripy T-shirts, chinos and slip-on shoes.

Salman was smirking. 'It's like they walked into Gap and bought *everything*.'

Jay snorted. 'Losers.'

'Yo, people!' a big lad in the middle of the line-up yelled. He was trying to act cool, but his eyes betrayed nerves. 'We're contestant seven. We're from George Orwell Academy and we're called Womb 101.'

There were a few claps from members of the audience, followed by a few awkward seconds as a fat-assed music teacher bent over fiddling with the CD player that had their backing track on it.

'You might know this song,' the big lad said. 'The original's by One Direction. It's called "What Makes You Beautiful".'

The four members of Brontobyte all looked at each other and groaned. Alfie summed up the mood.

'Frankly, I'd rather be kicked in the balls.'

As the backing track kicked in, Womb 101 sprang into an athletic dance routine, with four members moving back, and the big guy in the middle stepping up to a microphone. The dancing looked sharp, but everyone in the room really snapped to attention when a powerful lead vocal started.

The voice was higher than you'd expect from a big black guy, but he really nailed the sense of longing for the girl he was singing about. When the rest of Womb 101 joined in for the chorus the sound swamped the backing track, but they were all decent singers and their routine was tight.

As Womb 101 hit their stride, Jay's music teacher Mr Currie approached Brontobyte from behind. He'd only been teaching for a couple of years. Half the girls at Carleton Road School had a thing for his square jaw and gym-pumped bod.

He tapped in time as the singing and finger clicking continued. 'They're really uplifting, aren't they?'

The four boys looked back at their teacher with distaste.

'Boy bands should be machine-gunned,' Alfie said. 'They're singing to a backing track. How's that even music?'

'I bet they win as well,' Tristan said contemptuously. 'I saw their teacher nattering to the judges all through lunch.'

Mr Currie spoke firmly. 'Tristan, if Womb 101 win it will be because they're really talented. Have you any idea how much practice it takes to sing and dance like that?'

Up on stage, Womb 101 were doing the *nana-nana* chorus at the end of 'What Makes You Beautiful'. As the song closed, the lead singer moved to the back of the stage and did a full somersault, climaxing with his arms spread wide and two band mates kneeling on either side.

'Thank you,' the big guy shouted, as the stage lights caught beads of sweat trickling down his forehead.

There weren't enough people in the hall to call it an eruption, but there was loads of clapping and a bunch of parents stood up and cheered.

'Nice footwork, Andre!' a woman shouted.

Alfie and Tristan made retching sounds as Mr Currie walked off.

'Currie's got a point though,' Jay said. 'Boy bands are dreck, but they've all got good voices and they must have rehearsed that dance routine for weeks.'

Tristan shook his head and tutted. 'Jay, you *always* agree with what Mr Currie says. I know half the girls in our class fancy him, but I'm starting to think you do as well.'

Alfie stood up and shouted as Womb 101 jumped off the stage and began walking towards the back of the room to grab drinks. 'You suck!'

Jay backed up as two of Womb 101's backing singers steamed over, knocking empty plastic chairs out of the way. They didn't look hard on stage, prancing around singing about how great some girl's hair was, but the physical reality was two burly sixteen-year-olds from one of London's toughest schools.

The one who stared down Alfie was the Asian guy with a tear-you-in-half torso.

'What you say?' he demanded, as his chest muscles swelled. 'If I see *any* of you boys on my manor, you'd better run!'

The boy slammed his fist into his palm as the other one pointed at Alfie before drawing the finger across his throat and stepping backwards. Alfie looked like he'd filled his BHS briefs and didn't breathe until the big dudes were well clear.

'Are you mental?' Tristan hissed, as he gave Alfie a hard shoulder punch. 'Those guys are from Melon Lane estate. Everyone's psycho up there.'

Mr Currie had missed Alfie shouting *You suck*, but did see Tristan hitting his brother as he got back holding a polystyrene coffee cup.

'Hitting is *not* cool,' Mr Currie said. 'And I'm tired of the negativity from you guys. You're playing after this next lot, so you'd better go backstage and get your gear ready.'

The next group was an all-girl trio. They dressed punk, but managed to murder a Paramore track by making it sound like bad Madonna. Setting up Tristan's drum kit on stage took ages and the woman judge made Jay even more nervous when she looked at her watch and shook her elaborately hatted head.

After wasting another minute faffing around with a broken strap on Alfie's bass guitar the four members of Brontobyte nodded to each other, ready to play. When the boys rehearsed, Salman usually sang and played, but Alfie was a better musician, so for the competition he was on bass and Salman would just do vocals.

'Hi, everyone,' Salman said. 'We're contestant nine, from Carleton Road School. Our group is called Brontobyte and this is a song we wrote ourselves. It's called "Christine".'

A *song* I *wrote*, Jay thought, as he took a deep breath and positioned his fingers on the guitar.

They'd been in the school hall since ten that morning. Now it all came down to the next three minutes.